THE FINDER'S TALES: MARCO

Tiffany Jo Howell

Thank you!
Tiffany Jo Howell

CONTENTS

CHAPTER 1

~~~

My name is Jordie, and I am a Finder.

I'm sure you have never heard of me. You may have seen me around but quickly forgotten me. I do my best to blend in and go unnoticed. I look like an average male human of medium height, medium build, brown hair, and brown eyes. Being inconspicuous is important in my line of work. For you see, we have found that humans make exceptional pets on other planets - and I am the one who chooses the best possible human pet for my client.

~~~

Jordie

My clock buzzes at precisely 5:30 am. I rise and start the day with a shower, the water set at precisely 107 degrees Fahrenheit. I shampoo, rinse, and repeat as the bottle recommends. After a thorough body cleaning, I step out of the shower at 5:41 am.

Schedules make life on the road more manageable.

I inspect the suit I laid out the night before and remove any lint that may have accumulated overnight. I have five of the same custom-made black suits, five white shirts, five different ties, and three pairs of shoes that are similar to each other.

My breakfast varies depending on where I am on Earth. In the United States, I enjoy an egg over easy and one piece of wheat toast with a pat of butter. In Japan, I prefer a small piece of grilled fish, rice, and miso soup. While in Indonesia, I eat warm rice porridge mixed with soy sauce, fried shallots, shredded chicken, all topped with peanuts.

My work has me traveling throughout all countries on Earth to obtain the best human to fit the lifestyle of my clients. In studying humans, I have come to understand you better than most other Finders in my field. I am highly sought after for my ability to match the perfect pet with my client.

I've spent a good deal of time on your planet and have grown quite fond of humans. You are an odd little species oblivious to all other forms of life outside your planet. But then again, you are a relatively new life form, and it will take time for you to completely understand your planet, much less planets beyond your galaxy. It's comical that you don't believe there is life on any other planet.... If you only knew.

My clients are not allowed to request details of what they want their pets to look like. They do not get to choose skin color, hair color, eye color, or other physical traits. They also don't choose what part of Earth they originate. The only choice I allow is whether the owner would like a male or female human.

These strict rules are what puts me above the other Finders.

The new batch of Finders is too eager to sell as many humans as possible and don't care to learn the nuances of the pets. Recently, an inexperienced Finder placed a human from the hot climate of Australia with an owner on a planet which is known to be bitter cold and to have very little natural sunlight. The pet was without a proper orientation and subsequently stayed fearful of his owner. The poor creature soon escaped and was found frozen to death a few hours later.

The new owner was, understandably, upset and demanded a full refund from the Finder. This entire situation could have been avoided if the Finder had researched his human pet and given him proper training. Sadly, these new Finders feel that an occasional loss of a pet is a normal part of business, and they don't worry about the individual humans.

Clients hire me based on my knowledge and understanding

of human behavior, as well as my willingness to take the time to match just the right pet to each owner. All my potential clients are subjected to an extensive interview process to establish who will make good pet owners. The better I know the personality, attitude, needs, and expectations of the owner, the better I can match them with the correct pet. I will not, under any circumstance, work with a client who is mentally unprepared to have a human pet. I test anger levels as well as compassion. I want my pets placed in the best homes possible.

I have found that there is no perfect age for a human to become a pet. Some humans tend to become independent sooner than others. Of course, they must be old enough to perform basic self-care responsibilities. Few pet owners want to bother with hand-feeding, potty training, bathing, and dressing their pet every day.

You humans like to think you are independent creatures, but your bodies are susceptible to the immediate environment and cannot withstand extreme temperatures without protection. You have no fur to protect you from the cold, and no covering to protect your skin from the sun. Humans cannot see at night – heck, some of you can't even see well during the day. Your bones break but usually do not repair themselves, and a lost limb will not regenerate. Other animals of Earth have these sustaining abilities, but not humans. Yet you do manage to work around these impediments.

Your personalities vary widely in that some of you are affectionate, others aloof, some humans chatter all the time, others are quiet. Some humans always appear happy no matter what their circumstances, while others are downright grim even in a peaceful environment. Quite a few of you are lively and make good pets for my more active clients. And even humans who are naturally lazy can still be ideal for my older clients who want a more docile pet.

But most important, the human I take must eventually be able to adapt to their new living situation.

I quarantine each human for approximately two Earth weeks

while I verify their health, fix physical anomalies such as poor eyesight or partial hearing, and clean and straighten teeth if needed. I also give each pet an orientation course. Humans do best if you understand what is happening and what can be expected in your new life.

Humans are still considered exotic pets and reserved for owners who crave, and can afford, the finer things in life. Yesterday I met with my current client. Jutte is a Mari from the planet Oonala. I completed a full inspection of his home, ensuring he has a suitable living space and sufficient food and water. Jutte is single, as most of his species are, and is eagerly anticipating the arrival of his new pet.

I matched Jutte with a human pet from a small Caribbean island. The name of the human is Marco (although Jutte is permitted to change that if he wishes). This human attends schooling and spends his off-days fishing. He is quick thinking and quite intelligent; plus, he has a pleasant personality.

Marco prefers to live with bare feet and comfortable clothing; he does not need a fancy lifestyle. He is self-assured while also humble and happy. It was this attitude and his swimming abilities that made him my choice. Having him comfortable in the ocean mattered because the Mari species have established cities above and below the water. The transition from above water to below is almost seamless.

I believe that I have chosen well for Jutte. Still, the orientation period will allow me to fully assess Marco's personality and determine whether he will make the ideal pet for his owner. If not, I will bring him back to Earth; but this return must be done within a very short period.

I shake my head when I hear humans talk about abduction by aliens and having tests run on them. We Finders don't run tests on you. Instead, these abductees were probably humans who would make lousy pets, and thus sent back to Earth. It's actually quite comical that you think you are advanced enough that we need to study you – we know your bodies better than you know yourselves.

I've watched Marco three times and soon learned his schedule. I like humans who keep a schedule; it lets me know they are organized and committed to a plan. Marco rises early for a run before he begins his day on the water.

I arrived on his island last night. Waiting for him, I check my notes against my watch. He should be running past here shortly.

Then I see him jog by, although he doesn't notice me. That's all right, I know he will come this way again.

About ten minutes later he walks past me on his way home. I don't respond when he raises his hand in a greeting. Idle chit chat is unnecessary.

Marco currently lives with his friend's family, but spends much of his time alone on the water. Taking him will be relatively easy. But I'm not without feelings. I know he will be upset to leave his home so I will try to make the transition as pleasant as possible. This allows him to live as a happy pet on the planet of Oonala.

Owners want happy pets.

~~~
Marco

Crap, it happened again. I wake up gasping for air and drenched in sweat that reminds me of saltwater. The horrifying dream comes at least once a month now. I pull myself out of bed, trying to shake the realness of it.

> *I can't breathe. Water is everywhere, and I fight to figure out which way is up. I look for light; I try to spot bubbles rising. My lungs are ready to burst, but the net will not release its death grip on me. I fling the net around, looking for an end, a hole, anything that will allow me to swim to the surface. Blackness is creeping in from the sides, and my vision fades. This is it; this is how I die, caught in my own fishing net.*

I change out of my damp shirt and check the time: 5:53am. I run a brush though my hair and realize it's about time for a trim, but then again maybe not. There's nothing wrong with full floppy hair.

I need to clear my mind and go for a run. First though, I check the latest carvings. I have two figures that are works in progress: an eagle ray and a dolphin. I set them down and tiptoe quietly through the living area so as not to wake Arturo or his family. After Grandfather passed away last month, Arturo's family wanted me to live here until we can figure out a more permanent plan.

Grandfather taught me how to carve animals and fish out of Gumbo Limbo wood from trees that grew near our house. His were good enough that he sold his carvings to tourists. Some evenings we would just sit and work on our carvings.

I miss everything about Grandfather. Just the two of us lived a quiet life in our home.

I still take a run each morning before I go out fishing. When I was young, father told me that I learned to run and swim without even bothering to walk first. I like that story. My father named me Marco, after the famous explorer Marco Polo. Dad had dreams that one day I would leave this island and explore the world; but I'm happy here and don't want to move away. Mom and Dad moved last year and now send money to Arturo's family.

The sun wakes up and stretches its way above the horizon. Low tide and calm waters mean a good fishing day ahead.

A good run wakes up my body and banishes the nightmare. I run along the beach for a couple of miles until I reach the fence of the school. I don't want to make a circle around the island and run past Grandfather's house. So, I turn around and walk home.

On the way I pass a new tourist, a guy sitting on a falling palm tree and looking out over the water. He obviously hasn't adapted to vacation mode yet because he's wearing a black suit – in the hot morning sun - on the beach. I suppress a laugh and give him a small wave. He simply watches me. I get it, I'm not the most pleasant person first thing in the morning either.

Arturo's parents own one of the restaurants and hotels on the island. His mom is usually awake when I get back. "Marco!" she calls out to me. Every morning Luna acts as if she is happy to see me. It's cheesy, but I still blush and smile.

"Good morning, Luna." I reply. She is one of those people who are actually happy in the mornings. I don't get it, but whatever. She hands me a couple of burritos, one for breakfast and another to take with me for lunch. I'm not ready to sit down with the whole family for breakfast yet, and they don't push me on this. I dive into the burrito stuffed full with scrambled eggs, cheese, and refried beans as Luna talks with me. I chew, listen, and nod all at the same time.

"New tourists arrived last night. I will need some fresh fish, maybe a lionfish, and a couple lobsters if you find some today." Luna tells me.

"Sure, no problem." It's good to know that I need to catch extra fish for the new people.

I start walking away when Arturo stumbles out into the morning sun. "Hey, Ugly," he smiles, and gives me a fist-bump.

"Hey, Stupid." I give my normal reply. It doesn't matter that we have been using this same greeting since we were six years old; we still think it's funny.

"So, what are we doing for your birthday?" Arturo starts in on me. "I mean, you're turning twelve and we have to figure out something to do for your party other than fish."

I still think last year's fishing party with only a few guys was great, but whatever. Maybe I should plan a proper party with more friends. "All right, fine. I'll think of something cool for a group of us to do. Hey, maybe we can have a bonfire on the beach."

Luna halts our planning when she tells Arturo he better start cleaning the beach; it's one of the many jobs he has. I guess that's what happens when your family owns a business. He works at the hotel and I supply some fish to the restaurant.

I've been fishing by myself for about six months now. Grandfather started letting me go out alone just a little way at first, and eventually he let me go further. He was a fisherman long before I came along and much is still done the way he remembers; but there are new ways that make it easier. The motor on my boat allows me to fish further out along the reef and still be home before dark. My speargun has not totally replaced spearfishing by hand, but it does let me catch the fish without them having to be directly below me.

I make some money by selling fish to restaurants and to other village people and my parents send money to Arturo's family. I like to think that I'm contributing to them, at least a little bit. Today I'll look for lionfish and lobster as Luna asked, but I'll also be on the lookout for other fish, especially since grilled grouper is my and Arturo's favorite dish.

Grandfather once told me that invasive lionfish are relatively new to Caribbean waters. Their spines are poisonous and must be expertly removed without contaminating the fish meat. Tourists find this story as appetizing as the fish itself. And, of course, everyone relishes fresh lobster.

I can't imagine a life without the ocean; it's a part of me. And,

I love this island. I can name every waterfall and all the trees, plants, and birds. I know every reef around this island and the best fishing spots. I make sure to never over-fish an area, since a healthy reef is vital to everyone on the island.

I like living on my small island; I don't want to live where people don't know each other, where it's cold, or where I can't see and smell the ocean. Nope, I'm happy right here and don't want to move anywhere else. We have all the fresh fruits, vegetables, and fish right here on the island that we'll ever need. The weather is perfect, and school is *finally* out for the summer.

While I prepare my gear, I go over the list in my head. I need my lionfish bucket, lobster bag, spearfish gun, extra line, swim fins, mask, and lots of water.

I grab my lunch burrito, untie the boat, and hop in. Pushing out into the canal, I pass the last of the homes before motoring into the Caribbean Sea. On the last sea wall, I see that guy in the black suit from this morning. I don't wave at him, and he doesn't bother with a greeting either. I forget about him as soon as he's out of sight.

I stop the boat on the first fishing spot of the day and prepare my speargun. I clean my mask and get ready to dive in - until I notice an odd-looking cloud moving in my direction.

That's weird; how can only one cloud be hovering on the water and moving directly towards me? I wonder if it's a swarm birds or insects. Grandfather told me that swarms of insects would migrate past the island in the old days (you know, like the 1980s); maybe they're back.

It's not a white fluffy cloud but more of a circle of haze. It's getting closer, but I still can't make out what it is. The cloud stops about five feet from my boat. It's not insects or birds, and I'm more than a bit nervous. But I've been fishing these waters on my own for a while now. I've faced sharks, barracudas, and stormy seas. Grandfather said kids are too pampered today. He started fishing when he was only ten years old and fed his entire family. I fight back the shakes and try to act brave, just like Grandfather would.

No way! There he is again - the tourist guy in the black suit. He's right in the center of the haze, raising his hand in a greeting.

What the heck? Now he decides to wave hello? How did he get here? Where's his boat? Who is he? What does he want? Confused questions bump against each other in my mind.

He and the haze come closer. I grab my spear in case he tries something weird. Well, weirder than this already is. "Good morning. My name is Jordie." He introduces himself as if it's perfectly normal to hover just above the water.

I'm stunned. "Who are you? What are you?" Maybe not the politest answer, but I don't think manners are important right now.

The cloud moves forward to surround me and the boat. It feels like heavy mist, but with no water. How is that even possible? I turn in a full circle, but I can't see outside of the cloud.

Holy Neptune! I almost fall overboard in surprise when I turn back and find Jordie standing in my boat! I'm about to jump into the water and get the heck out of here when I suddenly find it all very funny. Like, really, really funny. I'm laughing so hard that I have to sit down. Tears are forming and I think I actually snort laugh at one point. I'm still laughing as Jordie sits next to me.

He doesn't say or do anything particularly funny, but he's just so hilarious.

And that is the last memory of my final moments on Earth.

CHAPTER 2

"Who are you?" Grandfather would have thumped me on the back of the head for talking like this, and I try to hold my tongue before I say more. I feel as if I've taken too much cold medicine and my brain is foggy and sluggish.

The man looks familiar and I search my mind to figure out why. This guy is sitting next to me and I don't like him. I don't know him, but I still don't like him. The last thing I remember before this is that I was fishing when some strange guy showed up. Not just showed up, but floated on the water towards me - like upright, walking on water - floated towards me.

My eyes dart around to scan my surroundings. I'm sitting in an over-sized chair in a bedroom - sitting room. There's a twin-size bed in the far corner and a round kitchen table in the other.

"My name is Jordie. You saw me on the water while you were fishing."

Okay, wait, I'm beginning to remember things.

"Where am I? Where's my boat?" Trying to stand, I wobble and sit back down.

"You are in an orientation facility. You are no longer on your island." He barely stops to take a breath. "I am a Finder and it is my job to match my clients with compatible pets. Humans make ideal pets for species on other planets. I have been watching you for some time and have determined that you will make an exceptional pet for my client, Jutte – a Mari from the planet Oonala."

¡Dios Mio! I've been kidnapped by a psycho stalker!

I stand up and square my shoulders, pretending I'm not afraid of him, as Grandfather always advised. "Look, I don't know who you are, or why you think it was okay to take me, but you need to let me go right now."

Jordie remains seated. "Marco. Please sit down so we can talk." How can he say this with such a calm attitude? I'm totally trying not to freak out.

He is sitting at the table, so I walk over and stand close to his chair, giving him my best scowl. "If there is no problem here, then show me the way out. Now."

"Marco, please have a seat and we can discuss this. I am not going to harm you. Besides, you are not on Earth anymore and have nowhere to go."

I'm the fastest runner in my class and I'm sure I can outrun this guy. I make a break for it and dash for the door. Before I make it across the room, I feel a stinging in my legs and they completely give out.

The rest of my muscles become useless too and I slump to the floor like a jelly fish - no muscles and no way to move, although I'm still fully conscious.

Jordie sighs as he walks over to me. "I know this can be unsettling, but I really need you to keep an open mind. I will not hurt you; I am here to help you. I'll teach you about your owner and what your life as a pet will now entail. I know that few humans fully accept the fact of life on planets besides yours, but we do exist. Few species live in your solar system, but there are hundreds of other solar systems out there with many other living beings. We generally leave you humans alone, since you are a new species and startle easily." I flop onto my back to look at him.

What? Did he just say he is an alien and I'm going to be a pet to other aliens? I'm a charming kid and can relate to most people, but how in the world do you reason with someone who is completely bonkers?

"So, if you're looking for pets, why not monkeys for your clients? Or elephants - they're smart. Or octopus, they have amazing problem-solving skills. Why have you taken it upon yourself to capture humans and decide their fate?" I don't even stop for a breath. "What gives you that right? What gives you *the right* to try to make me a pet?" Panic rising causes my voice to come out in a weirdly high level.

Jordie squats beside me and quietly looks at me for a moment. He then says "In your world almost every little boy and every little girl grows up with a puppy, or kitten, or bird - some sort of pet. As children you capture frogs and turtles, you keep reptiles in glass cages and rodents in wire ones. You decide daily how to treat these other species. You decide if and when they receive life sustaining food and water. You choose to shower them with love or take your anger out on them; you are in complete control of their lives. You find it perfectly normal for humans to keep pets and you use them to teach your children responsibility for another living being. And now you sit here with such indignity and ask me why? You ask me what gives me the right? For the exact same reason you believe you have the right to keep all other animals as pets: *because we can*."

Holy Neptune, that completely humbles me. It also scares me to my core and a thin sheen of sweat breaks out over my entire body.

"Being a pet is not a bad thing. Your friend, Arturo, has a dog. Is that pet unhappy? People on your planet accept their pets as part of a family. Their dogs or cats are taken care of, fed, walked, and given toys and love. So, you see, being a pet is not a bad thing. It just means you will now be a part of a different family."

Arturo's dog would dig a hole in the sand under a palm tree and spend his day sleeping in the cool sand. Often, he would sleep on his back, mouth open and paws hanging at his sides. I remember thinking how nice it would be to sleep instead of go to school.

I'm speechless. Jordie gets back to business. "You will stay in this orientation facility for roughly two weeks. I will teach you about your new planet and new owner. A groomer will tend to your hair to make you look your best for a good first impression on Jutte. I will be there for your daily trainings of the Mari language. Other Finders take humans immediately to their owners without orientation. But I am compassionate and I hope you will come to see that it is in your best interest not to fight. As I said, I've been watching you and I know you are quite intelligent for a human your age."

My tongue refuses to work, but I have no idea what I would say anyway. I want to run, fight, kick, and punch. My arms and legs have completely betrayed me, and I'm still on the floor.

A door opens and two big guys come in. They each grab me under an arm and drag me to the large chair in the middle of the room. Once they deposit me there, they turn and leave. I guess this is better than being left on the floor.

Jordie points to a doorway past the kitchen table. "There is a restroom with a shower in there. To turn the water on, simply wave your hand in front of the panel, and then do the same to turn it off. You will find clothing to fit you. Unfortunately, I will have to lock the doors until you accept your situation." He picks up what looks like a computer tablet from the table. "You will be able to move again in a couple of minutes. Please shower and change your clothing. I will be back soon to answer questions."

With that he turns and walks out of the sliding door, leaving me alone and still unable to move.

CHAPTER 3

You know that tingly feeling when your foot is asleep but begins to wake up? Yeah, that's how my entire body feels right now –painful tingling. I'm slowly able to move my arms and legs again. Attempting to stand sends jolts through my legs that momentarily stop me, but as soon as I can stand, I stumble to the door - and nothing.

I expect it to automatically open, like it did for Jordie, but nothing happens. I try to pry it open, bang on it, look for buttons, and wave my arms in hopes of a sensor. Nothing. I'm locked in here.

I pace the room, looking for cameras, other doors, maybe some windows, anything that will get me out of here. While crawling on the floor and looking under the bed I realize something - I stink.

How long has it been since my last shower? I decide to check out the bathroom and I gotta say, it's nice. I'm used to my rustic accommodations, and this is the kind of bathroom you'd find at a fancy resort. It has a single sink set in a cool, smooth countertop. The walls are the same soft green color of cashew tree leaves. Large plants sit in pots on the floor and smaller ones on the counter. Fancy.

The shower takes up the entire back wall. I strip down and look for the shower head, but again I'm coming up blank. I find no handles to turn on the water either, but there is a metal square where a handle should be. That Jordie guy said something about waving my hand in front of a panel. Okay, let's try it. I wave my hand in front of the metal square and just about jump out of my skin as the water rains down from the ceiling. I move to the back of the shower where I can get a good look at this without getting soaked.

It's a true rain shower, letting me move in and out of the water just by stepping towards the front or the back of it. I hate to admit it, but I like this. It feels good to wash away where ever I am where ever I've been.

A dispenser on the wall has soap - shampoo combined into one. Not a problem. Grandfather and I were never particular about buying brand name products. I wave my hand under the lip and it drops a thick liquid into my hand. I lather up and take my time rinsing off. While here, I need to figure out what my next move is. We never had enough hot water back at home, so I'm hanging out in this shower for a while, taking advantage of all the hot water.

So, this Jordie guy truly believes that he is going to sell me to aliens as a pet. I know Grandfather believed in aliens, or other life forms, or spacemen, or whatever he decided to call them. But I'm not sure I believe in them. I suppose it's possible for life to exist somewhere out there. I mean, why not? But I've never seen a UFO, or met any spacemen, so I can't say I really believe in them. Besides, Jordie looks human. If he were an alien, wouldn't he be little and green? But then again, he did float on water.

Wait, why am I thinking like this? I need to get out of here. I turn off the shower and find a plush towel conveniently placed on the cabinet next to the shower. As I dry off, I notice pants and a shirt folded on a small bench.

I check out my new outfit and toss it aside, grabbing my regular clothes instead. As I slip my shirt over my head, I remember why I needed a shower: my clothes stink. Fine, whatever, I take my shirt back off and leave it on the floor and try on the new clothes.

The pants are snug but not tight and the shirt fits but isn't too loose and hanging off me. They are actually comfortable. I bend and stretch to make sure everything stays in place. Great, escaping will be easier in comfortable clothing.

I wander back into the main room and try to figure out what to do next. Grandfather always told me to stop and think about the problem at hand, and work towards the best solution. The only solution I can think of is to get out of here. I want something to happen now, and calmly sitting around here is not my thing. The only time I'm able to sit still is while fishing or whittling.

Speaking of which, I get up and look around for anything of mine. My bag is sitting next to the bed. I open it and see what I have. I take everything out; my mask, fins, some wood, my whittling knife, some flip flops, and my swim suit. I know I didn't put all this in my bag, and I wonder why they are here now.

Did Jordie pack a bag for me? Was he stalking me?

CHAPTER 4

While I'm contemplating the contents of my bag, the door slides open and Jordie walks in like nothing is wrong, or even a little bit weird. I suppose it's not for him. He's sipping on something in a cup in one hand while carrying a tray that he sets on the table. I stalk across the room and meet him there.

"Hello, Marco" Jordie states as he sits at the table. "Please, sit down and we can try again to discuss your situation." I give him the stink eye as I sit down. I bet he can still paralyze me, and that hurt. I don't want that to happen again.

"I see you have showered and changed. Good." He is looking at his tablet and I'm surprised he even noticed what I am wearing. "I'm sure you are hungry. I brought you food and water."

Well, isn't that nice of him? I guess he isn't ready to kill me yet.

The food in the bowl looks like slop. Great, I get to eat prison gruel. Is that where I am, in jail? I lean forward and sniff it; it doesn't smell like anything. How good can food be that lacks any tasty smells wafting up? When I cook, I know food is ready by touch and smell. Doing most of the cooking for myself and Grandfather, I learned my way around the grill. We didn't have a microwave, and I rarely used the stove. I prefer fresh food on the grill.

"Please eat. You need to keep your health." Jordie nods towards my bowl. I look at the bowl of mush and wonder if I'm not better off fasting.

"Don't worry; it has all the required nutrients. It is designed to taste like anything you are hungry for. Simply think about what you want, and take a bite."

Yeah right, like this is going to taste like lobster. There is a deep spoon sitting next to the bowl, so I pick it up and scoop up some of the slop. I'm not letting him think I'm afraid of this food or anything else. But I do close my eyes for a moment and think of the taste of fresh lobster.

Whoa! It tastes exactly like lobster! Grilled lobster; like fresh lobster with butter running down my arm. I don't know how he did it. I gulp down my food, aware that Grandfather would make me slow down. But right now, I'm starving. Jordie nods and smiles, but doesn't tell me to take it easy.

I finish that bowl and look around for more. Arutro's mom, Luna, used to say I had a hollow leg, and I could eat enough food to fill that and more. Since my food is gone, I push the bowl and spoon to the side. I cross my arms and stare at Jordie.

"Now, what questions can I answer for you?" He asks as he sets down his tablet and looks at me.

What questions do I have? Where to even begin? "How did I get here?" I start tapping my middle finger and thumb together.

"I took you while you were fishing. We were out of sight from everyone and we simply flew here. They found your boat floating above the reefs."

"What?" I'm not sure what I was expecting, but that was not it. "You kidnapped me and made everyone believe I died?" Even as I say the words out loud, it sounds like a low budget sci-fi movie. "How long have I been gone, been here, been unconscious?"

"I took you roughly two days ago. We ran tests to ensure your health; you must have recently been bitten by a mosquito and may have soon developed a fever, but we took care of that. We still need to check your sight and hearing, but otherwise you are healthy and perfectly acceptable."

I look Jordie dead in the eyes, "I don't believe you. I don't believe that you kidnapped me for aliens and are going to turn me into a pet. I'm not talking to you." With this I get up, walk to the bed, and sit with my back to him.

Jordie stays at the table. "We are currently located on a large ship and are outside of your galaxy. If it would help you, I can show you the outside, or as you say, outer space."

Wow, this guy is really keeping with his story.

"Given your history of trying to run away, I must restrain you. You will be able to move freely until I deem it necessary to stop you. Shall we go for a walk?" He asks.

Nope, I'm not talking to him.

"Please come with me. I think seeing outer space will help you accept where you are." He actually seems sincere. I turn to glare at him, but then curiosity gets the best of me.

Okay, I'll pretend to play along, but I'll actually be looking for a way to escape. I stand up and walk towards him with my wrists out and together.

"Let me clarify," Jordie says as I approach him. "I'm not going to tie your wrists together. I will simply place this small, round button on your arm. If you try to escape it will deliver a jolt that will leave you unable to move. As you can see, it will stay on until I remove it. Now please, do not try to run. Besides, I think you will want to see this." For the first time, I note a hint of a smile, like he is excited to show me outer space.

I bet he'll have me look out some window with a hokey picture of space in front of it.

I try to pick the button off my arm, but it's completely stuck to me. I give him a nod. "Okay crazy man, let's go." I have to add that last part to let him know I'm not as gullible as he thinks I am.

We step up to the door and it instantly slides open. "Hey, how come the door wouldn't open for me?"

"It is programmed to open only for me. Once you come to accept your surroundings, and I do not fear that you will try to hurt anyone or run away, the door will be programmed to open for you as well." Jordie walks out the door and turns right.

So, if I'm a good little pet I'll be able to roam this place freely? Whatever.

I walk beside Jordie to show him that he is not my superior

and I refuse to trot after him like a dog. Grandfather always said that actions speak louder than words, so I'll act equal to Jordie.

The walls in the corridor are a soft yellow color and are without pictures or painting anywhere, not even a fake plant to be found. We walk past numerous closed doors and around corners. Well, I guess this means that I'm not locked in the basement of a house somewhere.

We walk without speaking for several minutes until Jordie stops before two large black doors. "We'll go into a holding room first. Then I will open the next door and you will see into outer space. Please do not run, because I will stop you. You will see other species, but do not approach them. You are here merely to observe. Are you ready?"

I'm not so sure anymore. My middle finger and thumb are tapping rapidly together.

Jordie turns towards the doors which glide apart, opening into a small empty room that is barely wider than it is long. We walk in and Jordie opens a panel on the wall. When he presses his palm on it, a compartment door opens. He moves me towards the center of the next door.

"All right Marco, here we go." With that, the doors behind us close and the ones in front of us slide open.

¡Dios Mio!

CHAPTER 5

Okay, either I'm totally sleeping and dreaming this, or Jordie is telling the truth. Because I see aliens actually walking around. Like, real, live, from somewhere else, aliens! Tall, short, blue, yellow... all just walking around, working, and talking with each other. Two aliens about 20 feet tall with bald heads with designs painted on them walk by, holding a small device between them, obviously in deep discussion. Beyond them aliens work on spaceships, some climbing into the tall, skinny space crafts, some underneath, calling out to each other in noises that I can't even comprehend.

One creature walks by so fast, his olive-green fur ripples from the wind he makes. Or maybe it ripples with anger because he has now raised his voice and motions to a three-foot tall alien with huge hands. His hands are so big and flat that I wonder if he uses them to slap other aliens. Imagine all the mosquitos he could kill in one thwack.

I can't comprehend anything I'm seeing or hearing. This is all so... alien.

No one pauses to look at me. It's like they either don't see me or they don't care that I'm here. It makes me wonder if this is real or if I'm looking at a movie screen.

I don't know why this Jordie guy is going to such extremes to convince me that kidnapping me is acceptable, but I'm not falling for it. I walk forward with my hands out in front of me, expecting to hit a wall or screen. So far, nothing. I step into the hangar area with the aliens. Jordie stays by my side, and the door behind us slides closed. I jump and spin around, worried that we are locked out. "It is fine; we can be here as long as we stay out of their way." Jordie explains. Of course, he would say that in order to make me believe all this. To me, these aliens seem unreal; I bet they are movies or robots. I want to touch one, just to confirm this idea.

I keep slowly walking forward until Jordie touches my arm and stops me. "We cannot go any further; it is dangerous to be in the working area." He tugs on my arm. "You must stay behind the yellow line." He points to the floor at a yellow line that marks a three-foot space between the door and the working area.

"But, how do I know this is real?" I ask. "It could just be some scheme you've worked up."

Jordie sighs. "Wait here." He then approaches the closest alien working alone and talks to him for a moment. I don't know what they are saying, but Jordie points to me and they both walk my way.

I back away until I bump into the door we just came through. Thankfully it doesn't open or I probably would have fallen backwards.

The alien is a dark reddish color and has really long spaghetti arms and legs, and barely a body and head to hold them together. Why would an alien need arms and legs that are like six feet long? It stands about eight feet tall and makes it to me in two strides, with Jordie following behind him. The alien stops directly in front of me and merely stands there. Is it waiting for me to do something?

I don't breathe. I don't move. I stay plastered against the door.

Jordie finally arrives. "Marco, this is Stan and he is from the planet Tribina. He works here." Jordie then turns to the alien, "Stan, this is Marco. He is from the Earth and has never seen a species besides those found on his planet. Please excuse his staring, he does not mean to be rude."

I continue to mouth-open stare at this thing.

The alien makes some noises to Jordie, who nods in return. "Did he understand you? Do all these aliens understand English?" I ask. If so, then it really means this is all fake.

"No," Jordie answers. "When I speak, all species understand

me in their language. When you hear me speak you hear it in your language; when another species hears me speak it comes to them in their language."

Okay, well that's pretty cool.

I look up at Stan. "Can I touch it?" I don't believe this is real; it can't be. Jordie nods to him and he stretches one of his long, red arms toward me. I step forward and poke it with my finger, half expecting to pass right through it like an illusion.

I jab at the alien again. Just one finger at first, but then I use my entire hand to really feel his arm. I can almost believe I'm petting an animal. I look for fur but don't see any. I tap the creature a couple more times before I step back and look up at him, it, whatever. Jordie thanks him and it turns and walks away in really long steps. I bet he gets where he's going pretty fast with those spaghetti legs.

I realize that no dressed-up human could walk with strides like that. I think I'm going to be sick, and I never get sick, not even sea sick.

"Well," Jordie says. "Does this satisfy your questions about whether aliens exist?"

I don't know how to answer that. All my life I've rarely given aliens a second thought. I figured they were possible, but not probable. And now, I not only saw and touched one, but I'm standing here looking at a whole room of weird species. How do I even wrap my head around this?

"Let's go back to your holding room." Jordie turns and walks through the doors as they slide open.

I follow him, looking over my shoulder as we walk out the door. The same weird aliens are still talking and working with each other.

What do you do when fairy tales and ghost stories come to life?

Once we're clear of both doors, I focus my attention on Jordie. I can't think straight, so I focus on a completely irrelevant fact.

"Hey Jordie," I pause, looking around. "Why are there no pictures on the walls?"

"*That's* your only question?" He asks as we turn a corner.

I shrug, why not?

Jordie doesn't even break stride, so I jog to catch up with him. "Not all species enjoy the same artwork. In fact, some don't have or even understand pictures. It's best for everyone to simply not have any."

How can someone not understand a picture?

I assume we're going back to the room where I'm being kept. I'm not paying attention to where we are going, my mind is still going back to the aliens, their colors, and … Wait!

"Jordie, I forgot to look at outer space!" I panic. My one shot to look at outer space and I blow it. "Can we go back? I want to see space." I'm facing sideways in the hall, looking back and forth between Jordie and the way we just came from.

"It's all right," Jordie assures me. "I will let you see space on another day."

I look back down the hallway, then at Jordie again. I look backwards one more time before I jog to catch up with him. Next time I won't freeze up. "Why are spaceships grey, or black, or white? I mean, cars come in all different colors, why are spaceships so boring?"

"You really do have some interesting questions, Marco. They certainly are not what other humans ask." Jordie is peering at me like I'm a freak alien with two heads. I stand my ground and wait. He finally decides to answer me. "Spaceships aren't for decoration; they are to get us from one place to another. There is no need for various colors."

"So are cars."

"Okay, Marco that is a question I can't answer. I don't know why all spaceships are neutral colors They just are."

Ha! I won an argument. See, Jordie doesn't know everything. But I still say a purple spaceship with flames on the side would be cool. Wait, you can't have flames in airless space; okay, a purple spaceship with stars all over it would be cool too.

We continue down the yellow hallways, turning here and there until I'm completely lost again. Jordie finally makes a right-hand turn as a blue door opens. I peek in and see the room where I woke up.

Normally I would take this opportunity to run, but my mind is still swirling with what I thought I saw. Once the door closes, Jordie reaches over and removes the round button from my arm.

I sit down and look up at Jordie. "How do all those aliens work together?"

He sits across from me at the table. "What do you mean? Why wouldn't they all work together?" He is looking at me with a confused, squinty look.

"Well, how do they understand each other, and how do they know each one's job?" I'm not sure how to say what I mean; I'm still partly amazed and totally confused.

"It is similar to you humans working together - each one knows their job and goes about doing it. They have learned other languages, and it's always easy to find a common one." Jordie waits for more questions.

"But, isn't it weird for aliens to work with other aliens... I mean, they're aliens! They didn't seem freaked out by working with other species." I pace, struggling to put my thoughts and words in order.

"I understand your confusion." Jordie says. "Humans are not aware of other species living just outside your solar system. Other systems have many, many planets, and multiple species of life. We visit other planets and work and live with other species. We don't view each other as aliens and are comfortable with each other. We know who to work with and who to avoid. It really is quite simple."

"Wait, are *you* an alien? You said 'we', like you're one of them." I take a couple of leery steps away from him.

Jordie smiles, "I am not a human, Marco. I look like you, but that is where the similarities end. It does work to my advantage for my job. I move freely on Earth without drawing unwanted attention."

Shut up! This guy actually thinks he is an alien. But then I remember that Stan, so maybe Jordie really could be an alien. I don't know, I can't figure any of this out. My head feels like I've been holding my breath too long.

I cross the room and reach into my bag, pulling out my whittle knife and feel around for some wood. I come up with a branch that I have been carving into a palm tree. I ignore Jordie and start to whittle. Grandfather said doing something you know well will help you figure out the things you don't know.

I think I need to whittle a lot.

What's happening here? Am I really on a spaceship? Were those actual aliens that I saw walking around like nothing strange was going on? Is Jordie an alien? If I accept any of these as true, then does that mean I really have been taken to be a pet on another planet?

My head begins to hurt and I walk back to the table.

"Jordie," I say. "Why take humans when dogs already know they are pets? It wouldn't bother dogs at all."

Jordie looks up from his tablet. "Do they really know they are pets, or do they accept their role because they are raised with you? If you see a wild dog, do you naturally pet it? Do you tell it to sit and stay? If it is wild, it does not automatically assume you are its master. So, no, it is not instinct for dogs to know they are pets. The same could be said for you. Your species does not automatically accept being a pet only because you were not raised so. But once you realize that other species are far more advanced than you and they will love and take care of you, you will begin to accept your role in their family. It is hard for humans to accept that they are far from the most advanced species around, because on your planet, you have been raised to believe you are above all other animals."

He continues. "But now you, Marco, must change your way of thinking. Aliens do exist and they are more advanced than humans. And frankly - humans make cute and wonderful pets."

Did he just say that humans make cute and wonderful pets? Like a fluffy kitten or a rabbit? "I have a headache." I drop my head on the table, making a loud thunking noise

"Wait here." Jordie says. He goes into the bathroom and comes back with what I assume is some sort of alien aspirin and water. Why didn't I see those? Whatever, I swallow the pills with a gulp of water and thunk my head back onto the table.

"I will leave you alone for a while. Marco, I know this is hard for you to understand, but we do have a schedule. In about an hour I will show you a hologram of your new planet and owner so you will be relaxed the first time you meet him. You are encouraged to ask me questions, but I'm also leaving you with paper and pen so you can write down your questions when I am not around." He gives me a quick pat on the shoulder.

With that, Jordie sets a pad of paper and a pen on the table and leaves me alone to try to figure this all out.

I ignore the pen and grab my knife. I begin to whittle again.

CHAPTER 6

"This is the simulation room." Jordie's voice comes over speakers as I stand in the middle of a large, empty, dark grey room. I turn in a circle, looking for a way out.

"You will be shown a hologram of the planet Oonala as well as a hologram of your owner. It is best to prepare you ahead of time so that you will understand what to expect. I know this is new to you, but please wait until the end of the presentation to ask questions."

With that the lights dim and suddenly I'm on a beach. I'm standing on sand with trees behind me and the ocean in front of me. I turn to inspect the trees first. Unlike swaying palm trees, the trees grow straight up, and all the branches are straight out with a type of palm growing out from the end of each branch. Another tree is shaped like a square, which makes no sense at all. I turn around and look at the ocean. The water is a blue, but it's unlike any ocean blue that I've ever seen. It actually seems to be various shades of blues all swirling together but not mixing. I'm not sure which I find more interesting: the trees or the water.

I walk towards the tall trees first. A voice, not Jordie's, speaks. "Those are Haja trees, the wood is very hard and used to make dwellings for the Mari people."

Cool, okay, but now I want to see the water. I walk towards the shore's edge. The voice speaks again. "The Mari live both on land and under water. They breathe air similar to that on Earth, but there is very little land on Oonala. Therefore, the Mari have created underwater living environments. They have a few cities on land but more markets underwater. They have adapted to their surroundings. Your owner is quite well off and has a small piece of land for himself."

Whoa, this is way cool. I expected the holograms to be shaky and see-through. But this feels like actually standing on a beach. This must be virtual reality. Like, really good virtual reality.

"They have constructed domes roughly twenty feet below the surface; each dome has air circulated through it, so you simply swim to the entrance you need." The hologram changes. It's as if I'm floating in the water and can see the clear domes. These are not small domes either; they include entire parts of cities down there. The scene zooms through one of the domes and into a small shopping mall.

I exhale, I guess I didn't realize I was holding my breath underwater. I walk around and look at all the strange items. The colors are intense, but most have some sort of blue tinge to them. It's as if I'm in a foreign market, with shops full of foods and goods. It's completely overwhelming. I try to touch a square block with a round hole in the top, but of course, my hand passes through it.

I know I'm supposed to wait with questions, but I can't stop the words. "Can we go back into the water and see the different domes from above again?" The world around me zooms out and I'm floating above a series of seven domes, all different sizes, but all large enough to hold several farmers' markets. I'm stunned into silence. I could have never imagined an entire society living below water. The domes are clear, but I can't see clearly into them. I wonder if the water here distorts my vision like it does when I free diving for fish. Maybe I need my mask to see clearly.

The oddest-looking fish swim by me. At least I assume they're fish since they are swimming outside of the domes. One is so close that if it was real, I could touch it. Another is half the size of me and has a brown base color with glowing blue spots. It's round and flat in shape, like a Frisbee, and I can't help but wonder how it's swimming so well without fins or a tail.

The voice guy continues. "The air on Oonala is quite similar to that of Earth, but there is no humidity, so it is not thick and heavy. You will be able to breathe on land without the use of a mask or other aid. The average temperature where you will live is 80 degrees Fahrenheit, so you will be comfortable. The water is normally a few degrees warmer than air, so you won't need a wetsuit.

Okay, I can breathe and swim comfortably. Good to know.

"Please stand in the center of the room again and you will see a hologram of your owner." The underwater scene disappears and I'm near the wall in the empty simulation room. It leaves me off balance a bit, but I move to the center and wait. I don't know why I have any sense of anticipation; I'm still not fully convinced this is real. I start to tap my middle finger and thumb together, waiting for the next hologram.

"You are about to see your owner. He is a male Mari and has never taken a mate. He is looking forward to having you as a pet. The Mari are not encouraged to breed due to the lack of land on Oonala, so it is not unusual for a male or female Mari to stay single."

The lights dim again, and suddenly an alien is standing in front of me. I fall backwards, landing on my backside. "You could have warned me." I mumble as I get up. I know that he actually did warn me, but I wasn't expecting it to be almost on top of me.

Even though I saw aliens earlier today, it's strange to see another. There's an alien, right in front of me. I remind myself that this isn't real, it's just a hologram. But it looks alive; it's even moving a bit as it breathes.

"This is Jutte, and you may address him as such." The hologram alien gives me a slight nod of his head.

I jump back. "Can it hear us?" I ask in almost a whisper.

"No, he cannot hear us, but the hologram is programmed with a few simple moves." Thank goodness, that would have just been too creepy if he could see and hear me. I step forward again to inspect this alien.

The voice explains "The Mari are dark blue in color with light blue vertical stripes to help camouflage them while in water. Attacks by fish were more prevalent in the past, but not as much anymore. Their bodies are streamlined to aid in swimming. As you can see, they have two sets of hands. One set of hands are larger and have webbing, this allows them to easily swim to the sea bottom. The smaller set of hands is used for more detail-oriented tasks." The hologram spreads out all four arms.

Okay, they have two sets of hands. That's so smart!

"Their feet are also webbed, allowing them to swim quick and smooth."

So, he has built-in flippers. Way cool. But how does he walk without tripping?

"The male and female of the species each average about ten feet tall. Their body is covered with a fine sheen of hair, but it is barely noticeable. These hairs allow them to sense a change in water movement and air temperature, alerting them to anything coming near."

I can't stop the words from coming out, "So wait, are you saying that there are creatures that can go after the Mari and eat them? You're telling me I'm going to be a pet to something that is constantly on guard about being mauled?"

At least the voice doesn't sigh in exasperation like Jordie does. "No. This was a concern in the past, but the Mari have evolved over many, many years. They now live in harmony with their surroundings, but they still have some primal features that they use to their advantage. This is actually a good stopping point." Jutte nods a goodbye and disappears. The room lights up and I feel disoriented. I almost forgot I was in a room, on a spaceship, in outerspace.

Jordie walks in. "We can now head back to your holding room. I'm sure you have questions."

You're darn skippy I have some questions. I follow Jordie out the door and we walk side by side down the hallway.

I begin babbling, not bothering to wait until we get back to the room. "I thought they would be little and green, with big eyes. I thought they would be able to read my mind and try to hurt me."

"That is understandable. Your movies and television shows have portrayed alien species in a very specific manner, and it is often wrong. I have yet to find a species that can read minds; most are not out to harm humans. You only inhabit one planet which is not worth the trouble of taking over."

Huh? He goes from talking to me in a normal, educational manner to insulting me without a pause. I decide to let it pass.

"Do they know English? How will I talk with them?"

Jordie answers, "No, they do not speak English or any other human language; you are expected to learn the Mari language."

I think about my questions. "Why is it normal for them not to marry and have kids? Don't they worry about the continuation of their species?"

Jordie patiently answers this question too. "They have minimal land to live on; therefore, it has become common to regulate their numbers. They have enough room so as to prevent too many living large cities. Some Mari, such as Jutte, even have their own pieces of land."

We're back at my holding room, but I'm not done yet. "So, why don't they just live underwater? Why do they sleep on land and go about their days underwater?"

Jordie sets down his tablet and sits across the table from me. This feels like the first real conversation we've had. "The air on Oonala is filled with nutrients that the Mari require. While they have filtered air under the domes, it is not the same. They also require the light from the sun and living in both environments gives them everything they need."

I'm not sure if I believe that this is actually true, or if this guy is going all out with this delusion of aliens.

I nod to let Jordie know I'm out of questions for now.

He smiles as he stands up. "You can rest for several hours. Your next appointment is to have your teeth cleaned and hearing checked. We have already tested your eyes, and you have excellent vision.

How has he already checked my eyes?

Jordie walks toward the door.

I don't think, I don't plan it, I simply act. I jump up and run behind Jordie, knocking him out of the way as I run out the door.

TIFFANY JO HOWELL

This is too much.
    I need to escape.

CHAPTER 7

I run headlong down the yellow hallway. I'm making the turns that I think will take me back to the alien landing area with the space crafts. It's time I figure all this out once and for all. Is this real or some giant hoax?

I turn right at the third hallway, then take an immediate left. I slow down and stand in front of doors, hoping one will open. I know Jordie said they are not programmed for me, but that's fine, I'll sneak in when someone is coming or going. All I know is that I have to get out of here. The door doesn't open so I move on.

I stop in front of a pair of double doors; they also refuse to open. Should I wait a moment or keep running? I look behind me, expecting to see Jordie come around a corner. I'm just about to leave when the door slides open. I'm momentarily stunned to see a tall, orange alien glide by me. It lacks feet, or else they are hidden. He simply floats and glides at the same time.

At the last second, I dive through the doors before they slide closed. I think I'm in the right place, because there is a second set of doors – I'm in a small holding area. I don't understand the reasoning for both doors, but hey, I don't understand anything that has happened lately.

I look for a button on the wall that will open the other doors. I'm hitting and slapping all over the place, hoping something good will happen; and miraculously, it does. The second set of doors parts and slides open.

I have found the landing area.

I don't move inside. I stand there, mouth hanging open, staring at the scene in front of me. Once again, I see aliens of all shapes and colors walking around.

When the doors begin to close, I dive between them. My right foot gets caught. I'm stuck!

I yank and pull, trying to free myself. I pound the door and run my hand along the inside edges of the doors, hoping it's like an automatic door that opens when it senses an obstruction in the way. I'm trying hard not to panic, but who could blame me? My foot is stuck between doors and I might be noticed by aliens at any moment.

With one final heave, I pull my foot hard, freeing it. I can breathe again. Whew, that was close!

I barrel roll to the side of the door, landing on my belly to avoid been seen. I crawl behind some boxes and peer out. It's a scene similar to what I saw before, aliens walking around, talking, and working on ships… I half expected the room to be empty, that it was all just a show the last time I was here.

Maybe this is a movie, a hologram like I saw earlier.

Grandfather always told me that if you look like you know what you are doing, most people won't question you. I wonder if the same holds true for aliens? I heard somewhere that you only have to be brave for ten seconds. So, I take a deep breath and grab a piece of debris lying near me. I step out from behind the boxes, pretending I'm supposed to be here. No alarm sounds and no one is yelling and pointing. I make my way along the edge of the area, walking as with a purpose, and no one pays attention to me.

Oh crud, an alien about three feet tall is heading straight for me. It's either going to call me out or keep going. I give a quick nod as we approach each other. It simply blinks at me with all three of its yellow eyes. Thankfully, it doesn't make a scene. As we pass each other, I reach out to see if my hand will pass through it, telling me it's all fake.

I touch it.

It's real.

Holy Neptune, it's real!

It stops to look at me but I keep walking, pretending that I didn't just reach out and touch it. It doesn't holler, so I walk up to every alien I can and poke them.

They are all real.

"Marco." Jordie calls out from behind me. I spin around and run for a spaceship. My plan is to fly away before Jordie or anyone else can stop me. At a full run, I throw myself into the nearest ship. I've seen the movie *Guardians of the Galaxy* enough times that I believe I can figure this out. I make my way to the front seats and choose the one on the right. I sit down and push every button I see. Lights flash, sounds beep, but the machine doesn't move.

"Marco, please stop that." Jordie stands right behind me. "The ships are here to be repaired; it is not going to take off." I keep pushing every button, I bet he'd say that whether this UFO works or not.

But still nothing happens.

Jordie places a hand on my shoulder, "We need to go back to your holding room, it's almost time for your grooming." I turn stare at him. *Really?* Aliens are walking around, I'm sitting in a spaceship, and he's worried about his precious schedule?

My shoulders slump, "I thought this was fake," I whisper. "I thought maybe they were holograms and this was all fake." I sit back in the seat and stop trying to start the ship.

"I know." He quietly states. "I know you want this to be fake. But let me assure you, this is very real. You are in space and these are species from other planets. Please believe me that I would never lie to you, it is counterproductive to your training for me to do so."

I follow Jordie out of the ship and towards the double doors. But I keep poking aliens as I pass by them, still hoping that they're just pictures.

"I can't accept that this is real, that aliens are real, and most of all, that I'm going to live with them for the rest of my life. I want to go home." Walking beside Jordie, I talk out loud to both him and myself as I try to make sense of it all.

"I know it can be difficult to accept, but you must. Marco, this is your life now, and soon you will be at your new home. It will make everything easier on you once you finally accept this."

Jordie actually stops and is looking at me as he says this.

"I can't." I tell him as I stand up tall and look him in the eyes. "I can't forget my home, my parents, and my grandfather. I can't just roll over and accept this life that someone else has decided for me. I will never be a timid little pet that pads along behind my owner. I am a human, I am free, and I do not accept this."

Jordie stares back at me. I'm hoping he will see that I mean business and agree to send me back home. Instead, he quietly answers, "I am not asking for your permission. On Earth, a human does not ask permission from a dog to be your pet. I am not asking you what you want, I am telling you that this is your life now; and working with me will make the transition much easier on yourself. It is completely up to you how you choose to handle this, but understand this - it does not hurt me or your owner if you fight and pout, it only hurts you."

I don't care who it hurts, I'm not giving in to this.

Jordie begins walking again. I catch up and walk next to him.

We keep walking through the hallways. He says, "You are scheduled to begin learning the Mari language tomorrow. It will benefit you to understand some simple words and commands. I encourage you to learn as much as possible. Some pets have picked up the language and can fully converse with their owner; it makes them feel more connected."

Commands? Like 'sit' and 'stay'? No way.

"I see you tensed up, please do not fight this before giving it a chance." Jordie barely glances at me.

"Fine, I'll keep an open mind." I say only to appease him. I totally don't have an open mind about this, but I'll pretend to go along with it…for now.

CHAPTER 8

We walk into a room with a single chair in the center. Grandfather would remind me that nothing good comes from so much quiet and lack of color. This just doesn't feel right.

"You will first have your hearing checked, then your teeth cleaned. Both are painless and we will be done quickly." Jordie places his hand on the arm of the chair.

I assume he wants me to sit there, but I stop beside the chair. "You're not going to stick needles or anything in me, are you?" I mean, if I'm really on an alien spaceship, who's to say that they are not going to poke and prod me like you in the movies?

"No, there will be no needles during your teeth cleaning, and of course none during your hearing test. Really, it will be fine. Please, sit down and we can get started."

"Are you going to clean my teeth?" I definitely do not want Jordie poking around in my mouth. He sighs. "No, I will not be performing the teeth cleaning or checking your hearing. We have professionals for that. Now please, sit."

I'm still not sure about this whole thing. I consider running again but the button on my arm reminds me that's not an option. I wonder why he didn't taze me earlier. Whatever. I slide into the chair. Soon enough a team of people come in and set up trays of equipment that I'm not sure I even want to see. Wait... are these people really people? Like, human? Can they help me escape? I glance at Jordie making sure he's busy with his tablet and not paying attention to me.

"Psst..." I try to get the attention of the nearest lady. I'm betting she is in her mid-twenties. "Psst...Hey." I whisper. She comes to the chair, not saying anything, simply looking at me.

"Hey, why are you here? Can you help me escape?" I'm still whispering, trying not to rouse any attention. She looks at me for a moment, then turns away. Maybe she doesn't speak English.

Jordie speaks up instead, "The workers here are not human, Marco. They look similar to your species to keep you comfortable, but they are not from Earth and will not help you escape."

He heard me? Wow, he must have bionic hearing or something. "What do you mean she isn't human, she looks human? Maybe she's French or something."

Jordie lowers his tablet. "If you look closely, you will see that she is not human." Jordie nods and the lady comes to stand near me. I look at her, like really look at her. If she is an alien she may not be offended by my blatant staring. I now notice small irregularities: her skin has a slightly orange tinge, her eyes are set too wide apart, and her hands each have only three fingers and a thumb.

"OMG," I breathe. "You're an alien too?" My mind hurts.

Without a word, she turns and goes back to work setting up the tools. I grip the arms of the chair. Before I can fully freak out, a male about forty years old gets my attention. "We will first test your hearing. I will place these small receptors into your ears. Please respond when you hear a beep." He places small metal pieces into each ear before I can tell him no.

I don't see a computer, or even a tablet like Jordie has, but I hear a tone pitch in my right ear. Instinct causes me to raise my right hand. While the sound continues at different tones and different volumes, and I continue with this pitch and hand raising hoopla for about five minutes before he nods and removes the 'receptors'. He and his assistants gather their tools and leave the room.

What the heck? That was it? I wonder if I passed. I assume I hear okay but I'd like to know for sure. Before I can ask Jordie, a new group of people, aliens, whatever, enter the room and set up their equipment. I don't bother to try to talk to them, but

I do look closely at them and notice strange things. One guy is taller than normal; another lady has arms that reach almost to her knees - I can't stop staring at her. She reaches across the trays and grabs items that others would have to walk around the table to get. This is weird and kinda cool.

Just when I've worked up the courage to try to escape again, a different lady comes next to me and explains that they are about to clean my teeth. Wow, a one stop shop - everything done right here. Okay, I'll wait for a better moment to bolt out of here.

Is there really the right moment to escape; or should I be ready to run at every moment?

When the long-armed lady taps my lips, I open my mouth wide. But it's the other lady who's talking. "We will place two trays in your mouth that will surround your teeth. A gentle vibration will clean them." She tells me while peering into my mouth. "You won't feel any pain or discomfort." This new lady assures me.

Great, because I don't like pain or discomfort. She nods and the long-arm lady motions for me to open my mouth again. I do so and she puts plastic forms around both the upper and lower rows of teeth. I try not to gag. The vibrations make my lips tingle; I scratch them and wonder how long this will take.

I study the alien people. The tall guy and long-arm lady move smoothly about. I have always imagined tall and gangly people to be uncoordinated, but these two aren't awkward at all; well, except that they might not be human. I'm totally engrossed in looking at all the people around me and trying to pick out what stands out as different about them. Another guy is overweight and doesn't have a neck. One alien, I swear, has a third arm hidden under his shirt. I don't know how much time has passed while I study these alien people when the dentist lady comes back, "Please open your mouth, you are done." Done with the form part of this or done with the cleaning? I guess the whole cleaning because they all grab their equipment and leave.

Um, okay, bye.

I hop out of the chair, ready to get out of here. "Is that it? Is that all there is to cleaning my teeth?"

Jordie leads me out of the room. "Yes, that is all there is to it. Again, your species is not as advanced as others. You still manage to do things the hard way."

I pause at the door. "You know, we aren't simpletons. You don't need to keep talking down to me and about humans." I don't know why, but he's really beginning to irritate me.

He actually stops to consider this. "I do not mean to talk badly of your species; I am actually quite fond of humans. But you are unnecessarily hard on your bodies - cutting for surgeries, cutting your eyes to see better, and drilling into your teeth. You will find such things do not happen here. Your owner will bring you back to this orientation area every six months for hair grooming, teeth cleaning, and an overall check-up."

Wait, what? he's talking long-term? I never really thought past the immediate future. We come back here? "You mean my owner can just fly here whenever needed? Like a weekend trip or something?"

Jordie smiles at me. "I'm glad to hear you actually beginning to accept your situation. But think of it more as a day trip. We will now have your hair groomed, your nails trimmed, and a general clean up."

What does he mean 'general clean up'? I showered today. Or was it yesterday? Whatever, I recently showered. I mean, I smell clean. I do a quick sniff test to make sure. Yep, all good.

We walk about three doors down and turn into what I assume is the barber. It's actually nicer than I thought. I'm used to the open-air room of my barber on the island. No frills, no girly salon, just a good barber chair and a good guy to cut my hair. But this is kind of nice. I see one barber chair in front of a mirror, but the neutral colors of the room are soft. There's even soothing music playing. A line of three comfy chairs with tables in between each are against the wall to the right. On the left the other wall is one big, quiet waterfall flowing. It's a small room, but very peaceful. Of course, the walls are empty of artwork.

Jordie introduces me to Simon, who studies me before

saying anything. "Hello Marco. Let's see what we can do with that wonderful mop of yours." He looks human and speaks English, but maybe he's the same species of Jordie. Either way, I immediately like him.

Jordie sits in one of the comfy chairs while Simon leads me to the barber chair. "Let's see what we should do here." Simon is gently picking at my hair while talking. "You have thick hair, so let's keep it full but just clean it up a bit."

I shrug, whatever. My hair isn't all that important to me. Not like my friend Arturo, he was constantly brushing his hair and worrying about his looks.

"Here, place both hands here." Simon wheels a table in front of me. two blue curved boxes with five holes are set on the front on the table. I stick my fingers in and feel a slight heat and vibration. No pain, so I'm okay.

Simon trims and talks. "How are you handling this new life of yours? It's pretty exciting, yes?"

I snort. "Exciting isn't the word I would use. More like a sham. I mean, I miss Grandfather, but generally I was happy with my life on Earth. I want to be back with Arturo and his family. I want to be fishing on my island."

Simon nods and is still working the scissors through my hair. "Yes, yes. I can understand that. But this must be exciting too. You are one of the lucky ones that gets to live on another planet. You will see what it's like to live with other species. The newness is what I find most enticing. All right, here we are."

With that I take my hands out of the boxes and he spins me around to face the mirror. Wow, I look good. But then again, I'm Marco. I smile at that thought, and at how great he has tamed my hair. He turns me towards Jordie for his approval. Of course, Jordie doesn't gush about it or anything, but he does give a slight smile and nod. Hey, that's pretty good in his book.

I stand. "Thank you, Simon. I really liked meeting you. Are you who I'll see each time I come back here for my check up?" The thought of seeing someone I know is a bit of a relief.

"Yes, I'll be here when that head of hair of yours needs

attention. Have a great new adventure in your life." Simon waves goodbye as Jordie leads me out the door.

"Is Simon the same alien species as you? Or is he really human?" I ask Jordie. Maybe Simon is a human who works here instead of being a pet. Now that would be something unusual.

"No to both questions. Simon is from the planet Beltha. He has the ability to change his appearance and adapt to different species. This way he looks human when grooming you."

Ohhh, a shape shifter. Cool.

We get back to my room, the holding room, the place I stay. That's how I'll think of it – the place I stay. We must have been close because we quickly get back here. Jordie sits at the table.

Am I beginning to accept all of this? I believe there really are aliens working here and that I'm on a spaceship. "Are there any other humans on this ship? How many people have you kidnapped? Is this what happens when people go missing and are never found again?"

Jordie explains "My job is a Finder, and I take my job seriously. I have studied humans for several years and have placed a good number of humans with their owners. I am very selective of which clients I accept to work with me, and which humans I find for them. I match your personality and living location with that of your owner. I chose you for your owner due to your comfort in water, your strong swimming abilities, your intelligence, and the fact that you are industrious; you are always working on something. Your owner looks forward to meeting you." He continues. "Other Finders use other selection processes, or lack thereof. They do not let the pet become accustomed to their new surroundings. Imagine your confusion if you woke up on another planet with an alien trying to speak to you. I work hard to ensure a smooth transition for you. So yes, sometimes when people disappear, they can be taken by me or another finder. But usually, it is another human who has done them harm."

I don't think I've ever heard him say so many words. "So, you watched me and specifically decided to kidnap me? How long have you been spying on me and planning this?" This makes me nervous.

"I wasn't spying on you; I was simply doing my research to find the best match for my client. Please do not become offended by this, this is not a bad thing." Right, he's not the one who was snatched off his boat and is being told he is about to become a pet.

"Please stop brooding." He doesn't get it and he doesn't stop talking. "Take some time to relax. We will start your language training later. You have time to relax, sleep, or work on shaving your piece of wood. I am confident that you will pick up this new language quickly."

With that, Jordie pats me on the shoulder and walks out the door. I'm left sitting here, still trying to figure this all out. I miss Grandfather.

Any doubts I had about this being real are pretty much gone for good now. I mean, who would or could go to this extent, right? If all he wanted to do was kidnap me, he would either demand a ransom (which my parents could never afford) or kill me, which seems less and less likely with each day. So, I need to accept that I'm stuck on an alien spaceship with apparently no way off, for now.

Okay, change of plans – learn everything I can in order to escape.

I can't sit still. I walk to the door not really expecting it to open, but it does. I peak around the corners and eventually step into the hallway. I wonder if Jordie accidently left the door unlocked, or maybe he trusts me to escape. Either way, I'm out of here. I need to move, to walk, to get away. I walk out of the room, heading in the opposite direction from Jordie. I want nothing to do with him right now.

I need to clear my head. I miss the smell of the ocean air. I want to dive into my own planet's water and swim with normal fish. I want to eat food that looks like food. I want people around me to be people instead of people-looking. I'm tired of being scared.

I want to go home.

CHAPTER 9

I manage to make my way back to the hangar area that I found the other day. It's something I know; I feel comfortable here. I walk through the two sets of doors and stop, my feet refusing to move further. This place is unreal. People and aliens walk all around, working and talking with each other. How are they not all freaked out by the different species?

Maybe it's like us humans not being freaked out by different hair color, tattoos, or piercing; although I did stare a bit when someone with purple hair arrived on the island. Actually, all of that freaks me out a little bit. I guess I need to work on that.

I stand in the doorway, looking right and left. No one seems concerned that I'm here, no alarms are going off, so I walk forward.

I glance down and notice the same yellow border line, thankfully I'm standing on the right side of it. I don't have a specific destination, just strolling the perimeter while watching and listening. There are curious languages, whistles, and hand gestures. Do all these guys understand several languages? Or do they learn as they work here?

I stop and listen to see if I can understand anything. A small group of three aliens talk together. They are about 10 feet tall, light blue colored with jewels and paintings on their bare heads. I move closer to listen. They fail to notice me, or are unconcerned as I stand next to them. I step closer, not wanting to be rude and interrupt, but really wanting to understand what they are saying.

I have so many questions.

I have to touch one of them. Unable to stop myself, I gently poke the one nearest to me. They stop talking and simply stare at me.

I try to be cool and casually wander away.

I hear and swoosh... *¡Dios Mio!* Huge, and I mean HUGE, doors are opening. I think I'm about to see outer space!

Will the air leave? Do I need a mask? I grab a hold of the wall in case I'm sucked out into the void.

Everyone seems unconcerned, but I'm not taking a chance. I find a rope connected to the wall and wrap around my arm, clutch with both hands, and hold my breath.

No one gets sucked out, in fact, some don't even take a second glance towards the door, like this is normal or something. I stare in amazement at a UFO flying toward us. It slows to almost a stop and is waiting for the doors to open all the way, then continues slowly forward.

The UFO is about to enter the hangar area. The air surrounding the UFO shifts, almost like it's passing through an invisible wall.

That is probably the coolest thing I've ever seen.

Ever.

A whistle escapes as I slowly let out my breath. The ship floats forward into the center of the area, fitting into an open spot. There weren't any guys with orange vests or guiding wands. It went directly to an open spot. I bet it's computerized.

Okay so, there must be an invisible shield that keeps the air in, that's convenient. I rock back and forth on my feet, I want to see more outer space before the doors close, but I also want to see what kind of alien gets out of the spaceship.

Outer space wins.

Keeping along the outer perimeter of the area, I dash toward the doors. I get close without touching anything. Knowing my luck, the barrier would be electrified and I would be zapped if I touch some invisible shield-wall-thing.

Holy Neptune. There it is: outer space!

Back home I would lay on the beach and look at the stars and the Milky Way. I felt like I was there, among the stars; but this is different. This time I really am here with the stars. I move to the center of the doorway. All noises stop, everything drops away, and it's just me and the whole wide universe.

There's color. Not just blackness with white dots, but actual color in outer space.

Some of the stars are changing colors - fluid and changing. I can see lots of stars and planets and objects, not a vast emptiness. I feel small, insignificant, yet somehow important.

I wish I could tell Arturo and Grandfather about this.

When the doors begin to close. I move out of the way, watching as long as I can. I turn and look at the newly arrived UFO.

An alien climbs out of the ship. The creature has a square body with a circle head sitting on top. No neck to speak of and no arms. It walks on two legs towards a waiting alien. The square guy stops and its legs disappear. It hovers in front of the other guy when an arm comes out from the middle of its body and hands the alien something. I squint to get a better look. It seems the square alien is handing the other guy some sort of small, thin tablet. Maybe it's similar to paperwork we would use on Earth.

It has retractable arms and legs, that is so cool! I can't imagine a day when looking at aliens won't surprise me.

The square guy sees me staring and raises his hand to me. I assume it's a greeting, maybe from meeting another human before. I give a polite wave back before I turn and run.

OMG, I just waved at an alien!

Never in my life would I have imagined this happening to me. I don't get it. My mind can't keep up with everything. I feel like all my thoughts and emotions are in a blender turned on high. I want to go home; but then again, I just watched a spaceship enter and land, I stood on the brink of outer space, and I waved to an alien.

Who can say they've done that? It sucks that I can't tell Arturo all about this. But it's still pretty amazing. I want to go home, but I can only imagine what will happen tomorrow.

CHAPTER 10

"I will say the word first in English then in the Mari language. I ask that you repeat the Mari word after me." I'm back to sitting in the center of the simulation room. The voice explains the process over the speakers. Living in the Caribbean, I already speak English and Spanish, but I have no idea if I'll be able to learn this new language. What if it's a just series of grunts, clicks, and whistles? I click my tongue to practice.

He starts saying words in both English and the Mari language. Okay, they are words I can pronounce. I repeat each word. If I'm going to escape, I better learn the language.

After about the third round, I'm beginning to figure out the words before the voice translates them. He changes the routine and says a word in Mari and I translate in English. After we finish the list, the voice then recites the words in English and I translate them to Mari.

Well, this is boring. I lay on back and make up my own game. With each word he says, I translate it to English, Spanish, and Mari again. Growing up speaking two languages must have prepared me for learning a third.

I fully understand some basic words such *as hello, come here, wait, yes, no, swim, walk*, and *sleep*. Plus, I learn a few easy phrases such as*: let's go, be careful, I will return,* and *are you hungry.*

We continue this for at least two hours, or forever - they both seem to be lasting about the same amount of time. Finally, when I'm overloaded and begin forgetting what I've already learned, the voice stops talking. Jordie walks into the room, "Very good, Marco. You are picking up the words quite well. We can stop for today and continue your training later. You are a very fast learner and soon you will be speaking full sentences."

I'm not used to compliments from Jordie and not sure how to respond. I give him a slight nod as we leave the simulation room.

When we get to my room, or rather the place I stay, I see food on the table. I lift a lid to find the same ole' porridge. I decide that today I want fresh grouper with sea salt and a squeeze of lemon. "So, is this the food that I'll be eating on Oonala? I mean, it's good and all, but it gets old after a while."

Jordie nods. "Yes, this is the food you will have. It contains of all the nutrients you will need to keep you healthy. Jutte will occasionally give you snacks.

So, like, treats if I'm a good boy? Forget that, I'll just eat this food. I don't need *treats* from him.

"Do the Mari eat fish? I mean, they practically live in the water. I lived near the water and ate fish daily. I can't imagine they have cows roaming their land."

Jordie sets down his tablet. "No, they don't eat fish like you did. This is an entirely different species from humans, they do not need to kill and eat for sustainability. Sitting down to eat several meals a day is completely foreign to the Mari. But your owner understands that you will be on a different food schedule and will make sure you are kept fed and healthy."

This confuses me. "What do you mean they don't eat? How do they stay alive if they don't eat?" How can something live without eating?

"The Mari take in nutrients through their skin from the sun, the air, and the water while swimming. While humans center much of their life around food, it is merely a side thought for the Mari."

Wow, that's interesting. It's like photosynthesis that happens in plants, but without needing roots to stabilize them. Mr. Jameson, my science teacher, would like to hear this.

"Marco, as a human you attempt to understand new concepts by relating them to what you already know. You must stop that. You cannot compare what you know to what you are about to encounter. Everything will be new and different. I want you to understand this."

"I suppose you're right; aliens are different from humans." I like riling Jordie a bit by referring to other species as aliens.

I clamp my mouth closed so as not to laugh as he raises his voice an octave. "You must stop referring to us as aliens. You are the odd one on the planet; you will be the one the Mari want to watch and maybe touch."

That got my attention. "Whoa, wait. You never said anything about aliens touching me. You mean they will want to stop and pet me like humans do with dogs?" It never crossed my mind that I would actually be treated like a dog or cat. "I will not walk on a leash. And I absolutely refuse to be petted." I cross my arms and flop back against the chair. I dare him to tell me otherwise.

"Marco, you will be a pet; have I not made this clear to you?" Jordie asks, exasperated. As if all his work this past week has been wasted.

"Well, yeah, you said I would be a pet, but I guess I never *really* thought about what 'a pet' would mean. I figured I would still be me, but living with aliens on another planet."

"Perhaps once I explain more, you will understand better. You will be a pet to your owner - his companion."

Nope, I've changed my mind again, and this is not happening.

Without another word, I get up and leave the room. I know my way to the hangar area and I go to the only place I enjoy here. It doesn't bother me now that the hallways are so plain, I make the turns like a pro.

I easily enter both sets of doors and see a Mari person walking around. I duck and hide: what if that's my owner here to check on me? Or watch me through a two-way mirror? What if he wants to take me sooner? Surely Jordie wouldn't let that happen. While I watch from between some boxes, he stops and talks with other workers

I only have to be brave for ten seconds.

I step out from behind the boxes and walk towards the tall, blue Mari. He notices me, but does not show any recognition. Whew, he's not here for me. I decide to try out my new words.

"*Hello.*" I say in his language.

"*Hello.*" He answers. He says more words, but I'm not sure if he is asking how I am, or if they have other pleasantries on Oonala. Or maybe, he is telling me to leave him alone. Who knows?

He doesn't seem angry with me, so I'm going with the pleasant greeting.

I smile and tentatively reach out to touch him. This is my chance to actually touch a Mari alien. If I'm going to live with them, I should know what they feel like. The hologram doesn't let me actually feel anything.

He glances at me as I gently poke him. He reaches down and pokes me back. I wonder if I unknowingly told him that this is how humans greet each other. I laugh at the thought that I could start an alien incident if I'm not careful.

His skin is cool to touch. I suppose it has to be if it's breathable and takes in air and water. It's pliable like a soft dough. I was expecting something more along the lines of what a dolphin feels like.

I tell him more words that I learned. *Hello, yes, no, wait, swim, walk.* That's all I say I've forgotten everything else I've just learned. He smiles and nods. He keeps talking to me in Mari, even though I can't fully understand him. But by his hand gestures, I can guess what he's saying. I bet he's telling me that my Mari language is quite good, because, well, you know, I'm Marco and I'm great at learning languages. I have so many questions I want to ask.

We talk in my limited words a bit more before he tells me *goodbye.* That wasn't something I had learned yet. I raise my hand and tell him *goodbye* as he walks away.

I'll have to ask Jordie if a real Mari can teach me the language instead of me simply learning odd words from an unseen voice. A dog can understand simple commands. I can do better.

I'm not ready to go back to the room I'm staying in just yet, so I simply wander around the hangar and watch the activity.

I think I'm only gone about an hour, but then, I guess time really doesn't matter here.

Okay, I've decided my earlier idea was right. I'm not going to be a stereotypical pet. I won't be kept on a leash and paraded around. I refuse to be petted and looked down upon. I'll be different; I'll be the exception. Just because I can't escape doesn't mean I have to roll over and show my belly.

And to do this, I need to speak the Mari language, not just a couple of commands.

I head back, ready to learn more.

CHAPTER 11

"Hey Jordie, how long have I been here?" The days are a blur of sleeping, eating, and training. I never know if it's day or night. Do they even have day and night here? I mean, are we circling a sun?

"You have been at this facility for a week and a half. You will spend the next few days continuing to learn the language and learn more about your owner and the planet of Oonala. We will also go over what is expected of you those first few days of your arrival."

Holy Neptune, next week I'm going to live with aliens on another planet. How did this happen to me?

"Does everyone assume I'm dead?" My voice is barely above a whisper as I look at my hands, twisting them in my lap.

Jordie stops what he is doing to answer me. "Everyone assumes you were lost at sea; they found your boat without you in it. Arturo now uses it to find fish."

Wow, it seems everyone went on without me. I look at Jordie, and try my hardest not to cry. He lowers his voice. "They searched for you, they miss you, but life must go on. It is not as if they have forgotten about you, they are only now learning to live without you there."

I feel good that they miss me, but I still wish I was there.

So that's it, I'm gone from Earth, but not to Oonala yet. I felt lost and in limbo since Grandfather died. But at least I still had the people of the village, I still had Arturo and his family, I still lived on my island and I knew my place there. That's completely and utterly gone now.

My father named me after Marco Polo for a reason: to go

and explore. But what happens if you don't want to live up to your name, if you don't have your father's dreams? I don't want to explore a new planet, and I've seen enough aliens to last a lifetime. I'm ready to escape and go home.

Before I can spiral too far into a funk, Jordie tells me that it's almost time for my next appointment in the simulation room. "We will work more on your language skills today."

I interrupt him. "Hey, do you think I can learn more than just words, I want to know how to actually talk in the Mari language. I met a Mari man and I wasn't able to say more than just a couple of words. I couldn't say actual sentences. Do you think that one of them can come and teach me how to carry on a conversation with them?"

Jordie looks at me for a moment. His expression never changes, so I don't know what he thinks of my idea. "Yes, you are picking up the language quickly. But we cannot interrupt the other workers so please don't take too much of their time while talking with them. We all rent space on this station and all have our own jobs to do. The voice you hear running the holograms are fluent in the Mari language and will customize the lessons for you."

"Can you sit in the room with me and talk in Mari, like we are doing now? It's odd sitting in a room by myself." It would be weird to carry on a conversation with a bodyless voice. Maybe the voice isn't human and that's why I've never seen him. Maybe he is some terribly fearsome creature, monster alien. Maybe he would eat me if he was in the same room with me.

Jordie interrupts my scary thoughts. "I do see your point. Let me reschedule. Normally I work on other projects while you train. If only you and I talk we can do that either here or in your holding room. I will speak in the Mari language rather than English for these final few days."

Now that excites me. I can practice talking with that Mari in the space hangar when I see him.

Jordie is furiously typing on his tablet. "The room is already reserved and I cannot push back my other work right now.

Instead of your language training today, would you like to see the galaxy of N391 and the planet Oonala?"

"Sure! I love to see some more of outer space. Wait, what other work do you have? Are you planning on kidnapping another human? Do you have other ones? Can I talk to them? How many humans have you stolen?" I jump up, almost yelling. If there are others, maybe we can all escape.

"Please sit down. I have told you that this is my profession; I match humans as pets with other species. But I have much more to do than this orientation. No, there are no other humans attending orientation at this moment; I prefer to give my full attention to one human at a time."

I return to the table, doing my best to calm down. I was so wrapped up in myself that I forgot to think of others. "Are there other humans on Oonala? Will I get to see and talk with any of them?" I shrug and try to sound casual, like it doesn't matter to me. I tap my middle finger and thumb together under the table.

"There are several humans on Oonala, but they will be a great distance from you. Will you see them? Probably not. Humans as pets is still fairly new. You are quite special."

Funny, I don't feel so special.

"Now come, let us go see your new galaxy and planet."

I follow Jordie out the room. As we walk, he talks to me in the Mari language. I watch his mouth while listening. It's like listening to someone speak Russian or some other language that I've never really heard. He talks and points at doors and the hallway in front of us. I try to pick up repeated words.

"I was telling you that we are walking past doors used by other renters. And that we are nearing the simulation room." I nod, keeping quiet in case he starts talking again.

At the simulation room. Jordie talks to me in Mari and translates to English. "I will be in the other room, but please listen without interrupting too much."

Is joking with me or completely serious? Whatever, I just want to see space again.

At the center of the room, I wait, and wait more. I suppose

Jordie is telling the hairy scary voice creature that we are changing up the schedule. Now I picture a space monster when I think of that voice talking, no longer assuming it's human. I laugh. I crack myself up sometimes.

Finally, the lights dim. I'm in total darkness. Then slowly, pinpoints of lights appear. More pinpoints light up and become stars and planets.

I'm floating in outer space.

CHAPTER 12

I know I'm in the simulation room, but I pretend I could be anywhere. I lie on my back and stare up at the stars like I did on the beach back home. "Let's start in the Milky Way galaxy, and then move to N391," The monster voice says. The sky shifts and changes until I'm looking at our sun and its moon.

There's Earth. My Earth.

It's odd looking at the planets and stars as if I'm actually in space. I'm not on Earth anymore, only viewing it from a distance. That tug of longing for home hits my chest again.

Come on Marco, enough with the sappy stuff. I hear Grandfather's voice giving me a pep talk. He never was touchy-feely, but I knew he cared.

The voice speaks in English. "Here are your planets, moons, and stars. As you know, they all revolve around the main star you call the sun."

It's amazing to watch the moons circle Jupiter and our one moon moving around Earth. I wonder why we have named Jupiter's moons but not our own. Maybe it does have a name and I don't know what it is. I've always looked towards the sky and stars, always appreciated them; but never thought I would be here. I never dreamed of being an astronaut and never, in my wildest dreams, imagined that I could be here among the stars, and the planets, and the galaxy.

"We will now move towards the first worm hole that takes us to N391. The speed and movement tend to unnerve some humans, so be ready for this." The stars fly past me as I float towards a place I didn't see before. It's a vacant space between some stars. Looking closer, I see not just empty space, but a movement to the blackness: a hole.

I'm hoping a worm hole takes me someplace, unlike the black hole that would rip me apart.

I brace myself against the floor as I'm sucked into the worm hole at warp speed. White lights and blackness flashes by so fast that I seriously think I'm falling. This is some great virtual reality! I should talk to Jordie about the technology on Oonala. I wonder what other cool things they have.

The picture stops so suddenly that I would have hit the windshield, if there had been one. I can understand how some people could get freaked out. Living on water and waves, I'm not as prone to motion sickness as others might be. I always felt bad for those tourists on my island who spent their time throwing up over the side of the boats they hired. I mean, it was almost funny, but I still felt a little bit bad for them.

Now THIS is cool! Planets and stars of all shapes and colors. I can't figure out if I'm sitting still while the planets move, or if I'm moving and they're sitting still. It is a freaky feeling.

Once everything stops moving, I get up and walk around. Walking while floating is a new experience for me. I put my arms out to balance. Here's a purple planet, and another made up of shades of blues and greens, all swirling together. I wonder if the aliens see their sky as swirling colors. Whoa! Talk about motion sickness.

"You are now in the galaxy of N391. Your planet, Oonala, is right here." The voice talks as we zoom in on a small planet. Well, smaller than the ones around it; I guess it's big enough to have aliens living on it. Do planets exist that are too small for humans? If so, do other, tiny life forms live on it?

Stop overthinking everything. I look behind me, because this time I swear that once again I have heard Grandfather's voice. I still miss him every day.

Oonala is dark blue and perfectly round. I would call it a midnight blue... not that I'm comparing it to something I already know...

As we get closer, I notice bits of yellow, maybe small islands in the ocean. It's as if the planet is one big ocean and just specks land here and there. At least I'm not going to an ice-covered planet.

The voice starts again. "The three suns in this galaxy are lined up in a row. Oonala rotates around the first sun, is pulled towards the middle sun and passes on top of it, and then completely circles around the third sun. After its rotation around the third sun, Oonala is pulled back past the bottom of the second sun, and eventually around the first sun again. Therefore, each lunar year, your planet will be circling all three of the suns."

Huh? Of course, I have a question. "Can you draw that?"

The voice pauses the planets. Which, by the way, is totally awesome to see. He doesn't seem the least bit peeved for me interrupting him, like Jordie probably would. A line is drawn back and forth around the planets. Making a figure eight path.

"Oh, a figure eight with three planets. Why didn't you say that, it's much easier to understand? For future reference, you can just say 'a figure eight around three planets and humans will understand that." I try to be polite since he answered me without a heavy sigh first.

"Duly noted. Now, when in between the suns, you will be able to see both of them. But when rounding one of the end suns, you will only see that one. The planet of Oonala is currently circling the middle, or dominant, sun of Juja and the other two are Epax and Troxi. Each Oonala year is similar to two and a half years of Earth time. Due to the fact that the planet is usually close to one of the suns, Oonala has near constant sunshine. The temperature of the air and water is warm, and there is more water than land on Oonala. The only dark is when the planet is traveling between Juja and the other suns.

Well, okay. That just answered several more questions.

The planets start moving again and the monster with a normal voice continues. "You will have daylight and darkness and you will adapt to the timing. You will learn to sleep when you're tired rather than only when it's dark. Your owner understands that it may take a while to adapt to your new schedule."

In the quiet, I watch the planets move and spin.

Okay, so I'll live on a new planet with three suns, and I'll be living with an alien.

My plan is to still get back home. And I still stand firm that I'm not going to behave like a good little pet that answers to commands such as *sit, stay*, and *roll over*.

The stars and planets fade when the light comes back on. At the center of the room, I sit cross legged while Jordie talks over the loud speaker in the Mari language. I understand a few words and get the gist that we are done with training for the day.

We walk back to my room with Jordie talking in Mari. I assume he has asked me how my training went. I search my mind for a way to answer with *great*, rather than just a *yes*. It turns out that there is no need to answer since he keeps talking.

This is exactly what I wanted: conversation. I listen and echo his words, learning more as we go. I'm excited to chat with an alien. Maybe I'll see that Mari guy again, and that tall blue alien.

What should I ask? Or rather, what should I ask first? I have too many questions for just one.

CHAPTER 13

"Hello, how are you? Let's go to the store. I'm tired, can I sleep now? I'm hungry." I feel a bit like a child relearning basic greeting, but saying them in the Mari language is pretty cool. I understand the words and Jordie is teaching me full sentences. "We will stay in the present tense for now, and you can learn future and past tense once on Oonala with your owner, Jutte."

I'm not about to ask permission from anyone to sleep, so I formulate sentences on my own. *"I'm tired and do sleep,"* is as close as I can get. Hey, he'll get the point. Especially when I walk away and to my... wait, where will I sleep?

"Jordie, will I have my own bed?" Many of my friend's dogs simply slept outside where it was always warm enough, and they sure didn't have their own beds. "Will I have my own bed or will I have to sleep outside?" What if I'm expected to have a pet bed in the corner of the living room?

"All right, Marco, now is a good time to explain what you can expect. Jutte lives in a modest home, where he has made a separate room for you. This is something required by all owners. In your room you will have a bed, a seating area, and a bathroom. You will be comfortable in your room, but I encourage you to limit your time there. You should be with your owner most of the time. He understands your need to sleep and eat, so you will have a tentative schedule that can change depending on yours and Jutte's needs."

I like the idea of having my own room, but not about being fed on somebody else's schedule. "I don't wait now for someone to feed me. I'm not a child, I should be able to eat when I want."

Jordie stared straight at me. "No, you are not a child, but you are a pet. Your owner will decide your feeding schedule."

I think about this. Arturo didn't leave food out for their dogs all day, but that was mainly because all the neighbor dogs would eat it if they did. I'd rather starve than be put on a schedule of when I can eat. At least I'm not expected to scratch at the door to go out. Or wait, how will I get in and out of the house?

No, this is becoming too real and I'm not liking this at all. I get up and start pacing.

"What's wrong Marco?"

"What's wrong? You have the nerve to ask me *what's wrong*? You tell me I'm a pet and put me on a schedule for feeding. I'll probably be trapped in the house and have to scratch, clap, or do cartwheels to go outside. And you ask *what's wrong*?" I think I'm hyperventilating.

"Marco, I have been telling you for two weeks that this is now your life. I don't understand your surprise at this."

I stand over Jordie. "Okay, let me see if I can explain this. Two weeks ago, I was on my boat fishing when I was kidnapped by a psycho stalker." I hold up one finger to make my point. Then two fingers. "Then, I wake up to you telling me you're an alien and you have two big guys attack me and drug me." Finger three goes up. Jordie tries to speak but I don't let him. "Next, you tell me we are on a spaceship and I'm here so I can be a pet for some alien. At this point I didn't believe in aliens and was sure you had me in a bunker under some scary house." I put up the fourth finger. "But wait, there's more. So, I meet aliens, I see spaceships, and I see a hologram of who you say is my new owner and family. Point five. I'm taken to have my eyes and hearing checked and my teeth cleaned, like some animal having a check-up." I raise my other hand to show a sixth finger. "You teach me some weird foreign language, and now, now you tell me I will be a kept animal, that I will be given food and water on some alien's schedule. And you ask me *what's wrong*? Are you flippin' kidding me?"

All my fingers are up, and I'm definitely hyperventilating. I cross the room and sit on my bed. Nope. I can't sit still. I'm up and moving again.

I've got to get out of here.

Jordie stands up and steps between me and the door, he knows I'm about to run. "I know you are upset. Please wait a moment. Let's talk about this." Ha! He wants to talk, easy for him to say. Jordie continues, "I know this may be overwhelming, but that is why we talk first, so we will be able to see your new home and meet your owner without running away."

Darn skippy I'm running away, at the first possible moment. But for now, I stay here, in this room with Jordie.

"Now, please sit down so we can discuss this. I've learned from watching you that you are intelligent. You know there is no escape. You know this is real. It's time you stop the outbursts and discuss it with me like an adult."

I stay standing, arms crossed, glaring at him.

"Soon we will leave here and fly to Oonala." He continues

My arms flop to my sides. "Wait! I get to fly in a spaceship? Why didn't you say so?"

Jordie does his normal sigh. I know he hates my interruptions, but I don't care. "Yes, that is how we will get from here to Oonala. You do realize we are on a spaceship right now, don't you?"

Ohmigod, I'm going to fly in space! It's like a dream I didn't know I had. Flying in space, on a spaceship. Oh, I wish I could tell Arturo - he would be so jealous. Maybe I could be the captain, and talk into the radio.

"Marco." Jordie interrupts my thoughts of warp speed, of pretending to be Captain Kirk, and for some odd reason, the phrase *Danger Will Robinson* comes to mind.

"Marco, please, we have more to go over today."

I snap back to reality.

"Let's go back to our initial conversation. You will have your own room, and together you and your owner will figure out your schedule." Jordie picks up where we left off. "Once you become accustomed to your surroundings, your owner will take you outside to swim. Both of you will dive to the stores and shops, although you may not be allowed in the shops, but soon he will take you out and show you how to get around."

"Why can't I go in the shops?" That one confuses me.

"Not all stores allow pets inside. It's nothing personal, just what it is." Jordie is looking at me to make sure I understand what he is saying. Yeah yeah, I get it, I'm a pet. La tee da.

"Now, Let's move on. Let's go over what is expected of you."

What could possibly be expected from me? I'm the new one here, I'm the one that was kidnapped and turned into a pet.

"You will be expected to behave properly. You cannot keep running away. You are to be polite and not constantly interrupt your owner. I understand you cannot always be happy, but control your anger. No one wants a pet with a bad disposition."

Did he seriously just say that to me? Did he just tell me how I'm expected to act?

I'm out of here.

I storm out the door and head for the hangar area. I got this path down. That's it - I'm finding a spaceship and figuring out how to get back to Earth.

"Marco." Jeez, I didn't even hear Jordie come up next to me. I now understand the phrase about jumping out of your skin. "Marco, stop walking. I understand that humans do not like to be told what is expected of them. This part seldom goes over well, but that is just how it is. You need to accept this."

I keep walking, staring straight ahead and ignoring him. Jordie pauses and lets me continue on my own. Good, this is how I like it, by myself.

Once in the hangar area, instead of stealing a ship, I sit and watch the aliens. They work together, talking, laughing, and working hard, much like happy humans.

So, this is it; in a day or so they'll call me a pet. How do I get out of this? I can't control where Jordie takes me, and that's probably the hardest part of this whole thing, that I have no control over my life.

This sucks.

I continue to hang out here. Get it? Hanging out in the hangar? Arturo would laugh. Sitting here is kind of like sitting around, people watching, just more interesting.

I finally get up, stretch, and head back to my room.

I may not have a say in where I live or who/what I live with, but I can control my actions. I'm not completely helpless. I'm going back to my first line of thinking - I may live with an alien, but I refuse to be a cute little pet. I'm going to learn the language because I want to know what people around me are saying – not because Jordie says I have to. And I'm not living my life so that Jutte will feel less lonely. I'm going to do what makes me happy. And I refuse to be completely dependent on Jutte; I've already been pretty independent even though I'm only twelve years old.

Jordie somehow knew I was on my way back, because he is sitting at the table as I walk in. "All right," I say. "Let's go fly a spaceship to this new planet."

CHAPTER 14

I pack my bag with my new clothes, mask, swim fins, and whittling knife. I see that Jordie also included the flip flops, a bathing suit, and a beach towel when he decided to kidnap me. I still have my notebook and pen that I slide into the bag and cinch it closed. It's sad that this is all I have left to my name.

I sling the bag over my shoulder, take one last look around the room, and nod to Jordie. We walk out the door for the last time, and head towards the hangar area. It's weird; I was finally getting comfortable around Jordie and in my room, now I'm off to somewhere new again.

I admit, I'm a bit excited and nervous at the same time. I have no idea what's in store for me on this new planet, or what the alien expects of me. But I am excited to fly in a UFO. I wonder if it will be one of the spaceships that I have been seeing.

The double doors to the hangar area open and once again I see the colors against the backdrop of space, but this time I'm going there. Everything around me fades away as I stare into outer space.

I get to fly in a spaceship.

Jordie has been quiet this entire time. Which is good because I really don't feel like talking.

I stop to see which ship we are taking. Jordie leads the way to a smaller ship that opens as he approaches. I stop to admire the machinery before climbing the stairs. Two seats are at the front of the ship with storage room in the back. I guess you don't need a lot of room when capturing humans.

"Is this your ship or is it a rental?" I wonder out loud.

Jordie barely glances at me. "This is my ship. Please have a seat right there. The seat will secure you."

What? What does he mean 'the seat will secure me'? As soon as I sit down the sides of the seat conform to my body and somehow, I'm stuck to it. I can move my arms and my head, but my body is suctioned to it. I guess this is what he meant.

I watch the aliens out the window move around and get out of our way for take-off. What do they call it when we leave? Take-off? Exiting? Ready for go? Is there space lingo?

Whatever, I watch Jordie. When I escape, I'm going to need to know how to fly one of these. I watch him punch buttons; of course, none of them are in English. I wonder where Jordie is from and what language he naturally speaks.

A bar comes out from the console in front of Jordie, and expands to a t-shape. I assume that is the steering wheel.

Jordie talks but not into a headset or microphone, just talking out loud. "C254 to flight authority, we are ready for departure." I look around to see where the speaker is. I hear an answer in gibberish that I don't understand. They must have cleared him, because we start to move forward.

The aliens are out of the way, but not really caring that we are leaving. I look out the window and see Stan. When I smile and wave, and he actually waves back. Well, an arm comes out of his body and he holds it up to me. I take it as a wave. Smiling, I look forward again and watch as we move towards the outer doors, towards space. I can't believe this is actually happening. I think I'm going to puke.

I hold my breath as we slide through the first force field. We roll through the chamber in between the two invisible doors and easily slip through the outer force field.

I quit breathing.

Jordie glances at me. "Are you ready?" He actually looks a little excited to show this to me. All I can do is nod as I stare straight ahead.

Wham! We take off like we're being shot out of the building. I'm pushed back into my seat. But I'm stuck to it anyways so that's okay.

We bank right and I can see where I have been for the last two weeks. The space station is shaped like a large rectangle. It's huge, probably the size of a ten-story building laid sideways. We exited from the end and are flying next to it. I'm looking everywhere; right, left, above me – everywhere. "Do other humans like this flight too?" I can't stop wondering how others reacted, and when I'll see another human again.

Jordie turns to me. "I don't normally allow humans to be awake during the trip to their new planet. But I've had one or two humans that I think can handle the flight. It will only take us about two Earth hours before we arrive at Oonala."

I wonder if he has the ship on auto pilot, since he is watching me closely. But then again, I guess there's nothing to run into.

"Don't worry," I assure him, "I'm not going to freak out. This is really cool."

It is a smooth ride. The roads on my island were full of holes and bumps. But this feels as if we're sitting still and the stars are gliding past us. They're large masses of blues and whites - glowing, blinking, and folding within themselves. This must be the blinking that I see from the beach at night.

I think back to lying on the beach, admiring the stars. It's funny that I never imagined I would be flying among them, and here I am. I never really wanted to. I'm amazed to see this, but I'd still rather be back at home, and I wish Grandfather was still alive.

Jordie pulls me out of my thoughts. "That is the first worm hole we will be traveling through. It will bring us to the solar system of Umpta where we will fly for a while before taking another worm hole to N391, your solar system."

"Why doesn't the solar system have a name? I mean, the next one is called Umpta, and I'm from the Milky Way, but the next one is just a number. Is it new or something? Like no one has named it yet?" Sometimes my thoughts slip out before I can stop them. Jordie looks at me like I just asked the strangest question he's ever heard.

I thought it was a legitimate question.

"Honestly, I don't know why it doesn't have a name other than N391. That's simply its name. It's not new. In fact, the Mari species have existed longer than you can imagine." Jordie answers while fiddling with some knob on his other side.

So, there are buttons and at least one knob to deal with in order to fly. Got it.

I've already forgotten to care about the name of the new solar system. I mean, I never thought about the Milky Way, so why worry about N391?

I spot movement ahead and try to lean forward for a better look. I know I saw something move. There it is again, a black shadow with edges expanding and moving like a wave.

"That is the worm hole you are seeing." Jordie tells me.

Wow, they really do exist. And we're heading straight for it.

"Are you sure this is safe? Going through a worm hole, I mean?" How can he be sure where we'll end up? What if there is already a ship in there coming our way? What if we collide?

"They are perfectly safe if you have the right equipment and know how to maneuver through it." For some reason, Jordie's statement doesn't make me feel all safe at all. I can't pull my eyes away from this inky hole of death. I don't trust it. Jordie is unfazed and steers the spaceship directly into it.

I dig my hands into the arm rests, and press back into the seat. Jordie notices. "Do you remember going through the worm hole in the simulation room? It will look and feel just like that."

Yeah, well, that was a simulation room; this is real. I don't think I'm out of line by freaking out a little bit. At least I'm not in a total melt down and completely losing it. Well, just a little bit. But then again, I'm Marco. I can handle this.

"Look." Jordie points out his window. "A shooting star. Not something we see often but must be on the lookout for."

I watch as the blue and white mass streaks by. Holy Neptune, I just saw a shooting star while in space. I close my eyes and make a wish. Guess what I wished for? Yep, that this worm hole would take me home. I could happily die now. I bet I've seen more in the past two weeks than most people see their whole lives.

I don't really want to die. I kind of want to see what will happen tomorrow – heck, what I'll see in two hours.

As soon as the shooting star is out of sight, I remember the worm hole. We are still moving closer towards it. I don't want to go there, but I really don't have a choice either. The entire last two weeks are summed up right here – I don't want to but I don't have a choice.

The closer we get the tighter I grip the arm rest and the faster I'm breathing. In two, three, four. Out two, three, four. Nope, it doesn't work.

My heart pounds so hard that I might break a rib. Is that even possible? Oh great, one more thing to worry about.

I feel Jordie studying me. I don't look his way. I couldn't even if I wanted to. I can't look away from the worm hole. I try to blink, to turn my head, to duck, but nothing happens. I have a front row seat to zoom through a worm hole.

"All right Marco, it's just like the simulation room. You will be perfectly fine. In fact, you might even enjoy this." That is the only warning I get as the ship enters the pull of the worm hole of zooming death.

Eyes wide open and body froze in place.

Here we go.

CHAPTER 15

I hold on tight as we fly through a tunnel of white and black. Not just spots of white like stars, but streaks of white among the nothingness of black.

Jordie's right, it is just like being in the simulation room, except for one teensy little detail - this is real!

I loosen my grip on the arm rest and slowly exhale. I swivel my head, looking at the lights passing from every angle. It's scary, but in an awesome sort of way.

We turn through curves and keep shooting forward. I forgot to ask how long this will last. I mean, how long does it take to get from one galaxy to another?

I look at Jordie; he's steering us through this thing. He doesn't look concerned, but then again, he never looks concerned. I'm afraid to ask him anything, I don't want to distract him and cause us to crash into the side. Would we actually crash or go through the side of the worm hole and end up in the middle of nowhere? Like, for real, nowhere.

I keep my mouth shut. Looking straight ahead helps me see the curves before we get there. I've never been on a roller coaster, but it's what I imagine it would be like. I lean with the corners and straighten out when the tube does.

I break into a smile. I'll never admit it out loud, but Jordie was right; this is fun.

Just as I'm getting comfortable, I see the end. I see where the streaking lights stop.

I brace myself. As we exit the worm hole, the ship instantly comes to a complete stop. The seat holds me in place as my head and legs keep accelerating forward.

I'm having trouble with the sudden quiet and stillness. Nothing for two heartbeats.

"Whoo hoo! That was great!" I holler as soon as we stop. Jordie jumps at my outburst, which adds to my excitement. He's not easy to scare.

I look around at the new galaxy - or at least new to me. Planets of green and yellow circle several suns. Purple spots dot the yellow planets, and the green planets are varying colors of green; some are solid, deep colors of green while others have lighter and darker shades making up the planet.

Umpta – interesting galaxy.

I didn't realize we are moving again; instead, it feels like the planets are moving closer to us. I guess that could be possible, but since Jordie is steering, I assume we are the ones moving.

"How long before the next worm hole and then my new galaxy?" I ask. Not that I'm excited to get to Oonala, but I'd rather get this over with than drag it out. It's like a band aid, you have to pull it off quickly and be done with it rather than peel it off in a slow and excruciating way.

"Less than half an hour, then we will take the next worm hole to N391." Jordie glances my way. "Fun, huh?" He's actually smiling. I smile back and continue to look out the windows.

I'm mesmerized by the rotation of the planets; I can't blink or look away; it's amazing. I didn't know I would actually be able to see movement. I mean, when I would see pictures of Earth, I couldn't tell it was rotating and moving around the sun. I wonder if I would get motion sickness on these planets since they seem to move so fast. Wouldn't that be weird to try to walk around but keep falling because the planet is moving so much? Maybe I wouldn't fall since I can stand and fish in my boat. Or, I used to be able to do that.

I finally blink and take in the rest of the galaxy. I feel small moving among the stars and planets. I didn't know that being in space would humble me.

I press my hands and face against the side window. I see stars blinking in and out. Is that a star being born or dying? Or do they just always exist? I look further to the right and see a planet with rings... is there a Saturn in this galaxy? Does that mean there's an Earth too? I mean, if Oonala has an atmosphere that can support humans, why can't there be planets in all galaxies that have air? Oh, what if I just discovered more humans? I'm a genius.

Jordie starts tapping on the ship's computer. I watch to see if I can figure out what he's doing. Okay, he pushed the button on the left side, and the screen lit up. Got it, I have to turn it on first. I wonder if the computer is programmed for several languages, and I just need to find out how to change it to English. I don't know what he's entering since he is also steering, I mean, if he was entering coordinates, wouldn't it fly on auto drive? And how is their technology supposedly so far advanced but he still has to manually drive?

I have too many questions that I can't answer, so I go back to looking out the windows. The view steals my concentration away from the computer panel.

Fixated on the stars and planets, I almost miss seeing the worm hole in front of us. It's not right in front of us yet, but I see it in the distance. It's odd, how do you see nothing? Maybe what I'm seeing is the absence of stars and planets. These thoughts are too deep for an afternoon drive.

"Is that the next worm hole that we are taking?" I point forward as I ask Jordie. I guess the pointing is unnecessary since it's the only worm hole in sight, and we're heading straight for it. Thankfully, Jordie doesn't feel the need for a sarcastic remark. Personally, I would have answered with "No, it's the worm hole behind us," or something just as witty. I don't think Jordie has a humorous side to him. Maybe no one in his species is funny.

"Yes, we will take that to N391. We will be to Oonala shortly. Are you ready?" My mouth goes dry and my forehead sweats. I'm surprised how I instantly go from fascinated to terrified. I'm not scared to go through the worm hole again. I'm scared of what's on the other side. Of what my life will be like once we actually get to Oonala.

I push back in my seat, hoping to slow the ship down.

Jordie watches me for a moment. "It will be all right Marco. We have gone through what you can expect; nothing should surprise to you. Your owner is excited to meet you and show you his world. This is a good thing that is happening to you."

We are almost to the worm hole, at least I know what to expect. I try to enjoy the ride again. Grandfather always told me that worrying never did any good, but how do you stop from worrying? Breathe in two, three, four. And out two, three, four. This time it helps.

"Hold on, we are about to enter this worm hole." Jordie tells me the obvious. I tighten my grip on the arm rests again, but this time, my eyes stay open, and I'm actually a bit excited.

The suction starts and we pick up speed. Once again, we are zooming through the tunnel. I'm ready this time and wide-eye watch as we twist and turn through the tube of black and white. Before long, I see the light at the end of the tunnel. Actually, I see the darkness at the end of the tunnels since the streaks of white will stop. I anticipate the sudden stop and it doesn't faze me at all.

I could so totally drive a spaceship.

"Here we are, in the galaxy of N391. And there," Jordie points to our right, "is the planet of Oonala."

Total and complete panic takes over. I fumble trying to undo the seatbelt and try to get up. I don't care where I go, but I need to move, to leave, to go somewhere.

There is no seatbelt and I can't make the seat release me. I try pressing the sides of the seat, I look for a bar between my feet, like in Grandfather's car that moves the seat forward and back. I check for a lever to my left where a handle would be in a normal vehicle.

Nothing. I'm stuck.

Breathe in two, three, four. And out two, three, four.

Jordie notices me flopping around but doesn't say anything. He lets me ride out my panic attack.

I close my eyes and picture a palm tree. Just one lone palm

tree. It helps to calm me down. I open my eyes and look at Jordie. "Are you well?" he asks.

I nod, "I'm better now, thanks." He gives a slight inclination of his head and continues steering and punching buttons. Wow, does Jordie actually care about me? I bet he does.

My vision clears and I look out the window.

The air catches in my throat. There it is, the galaxy of N391 and the planet of Oonala. *¡Dios Mio!* It's right there.

The three suns (Epax, Juja, and Troxi) are lined up, and the planets are poised around them. Mid figure eight, I guess. How am I supposed to handle it when a movie I saw in the situation room turns into real life?

Oonala is currently on the far side of one of the end suns. I really don't care which sun it is, it will all change when I see them from the ground, or water.

My dark blue planet is sitting out there among other planets, and stars blinking between them. Okay, I gotta admit that it's beautiful.

Everything fades away. Jordie is gone, the ship is gone, the other planets are gone, all I see is Oonala, the deep blue color with yellow spots that become more noticeable the closer we get. I wonder which speck of land I'll be on.

I come out of my trance to hear Jordie talking. "... all right? Please remember this."

Wait, what? I have no idea what I'm supposed to remember. "What? I wasn't listening. What am supposed to remember?" I stare at him; worried I missed something important, like a special code word.

"I was saying that we will land on the beach near your home. I'll go speak with your owner and then come back for you. Please mind your manners and be polite when you first meet Jutte. Tell him hello and be personable."

Clearly, I didn't miss anything important. But Jordie is watching me, so I shrug to let him know I heard him. I'm not going to gush or come out running and hug this alien. I'm not a puppy. But then I think; what if I did run up to him and start licking his face? Would he be grossed out and tell Jordie to take me home? Again, I crack myself up.

We get closer and my insides freak out. My stomach drops to my toes, my tongue dries up, and my feet tap out their own song.

We enter the atmosphere and fly lower. I look through my window, and see the ocean. It's dark blue but stunningly clear. I can see waves break on reefs, even though we aren't near land. It's vast and empty, a feeling I know well. When fishing I would normally stay within sight of land, but looking out towards this sea reminded me of how tiny my boat was.

We glide along when I spot land in the distance.

I try to swallow but my dry throat sticks to itself. We're almost there; we're almost here; we're almost to everything new. I don't like this. I didn't ask for it and I'm leaving as soon as possible.

I notice the trees first. Unlike jungle I'm used to, it's more like a cluster of trees; maybe they will be bigger when I'm walking under them.

The ship slows and almost hovers above the beach before gliding into a smooth landing. That was nowhere near as jarring as coming out of a worm hole. How cool is it that this ship can fly like a plane and stand still like a helicopter? I'm definitely going to enjoy stealing one and taking it home.

We land near a large hill made of wood and sand. "Oh my God, is that an ant hill?" I whisper. I shudder to think of ants the size of me swarming in that hill.

Jordie looks at me as if I've totally lost it. "No, that is your home."

Wait, what? I'm living in an ant hill?

Thankfully that stays in my brain and doesn't come out my mouth, because Jordie continues to explain the house. "You will live here with your owner, on the edge of the water. Not far below the surface is the town. You will spend much of your time down there as well as up here."

I guess I didn't think about what the house would look like. I expected a hut like mine back home. Every now and then I'm hit with a wave of reality, and I just got typhooned.

Jordie pushes buttons until the steering wheel disappears and the seat lets us go. "Please stay seated until I return." He stands and is looking at me, waiting for an answer.

"Fine, whatever. I'll wait here." I'm hoping I sound bored when I say it because I don't want to admit how freaked out I am.

Unfazed, Jordie turns and walks to the back of the ship and out the door. I throw myself against the window, straining to see this alien that I'll be living with.

A space on the hill opens and a Mari walks out.

CHAPTER 16

The alien bends down and reaches one of his small hands down to shake with Jordie. I saw how tall he was in the simulation room, but seeing him stand next to Jordie emphasizes the immense size of him and his hands. His webbed hands sway by his side while his small hands are gesturing to me and his hut.

The blue of his skin absorbs the light around him. He is not shining in the sun, he is not glowing, but the opposite. It's as if the light around him is sinking into his skin and never returning.

They both turn and look my way. I duck out of sight so they don't see me.

Run. The thought crosses my mind and before I fully contemplate the idea, I'm on my feet looking for the door. I press the frame surrounding the exit, I push the door itself, and nothing happens.

Then I get a better idea.

I jump into Jordie's seat and start pressing buttons. The panel lights up and the hum of the machinery is no match for the pounding of my heart. I keep pressing buttons until the steering wheel appears.

Score!

I squeeze the handle as I pull it towards me. I feel a slight tremor from the ship, but it doesn't take off. I push more buttons.

Out the front window, I see Jordie walking towards me. Why isn't he running and why doesn't he seem worried

I punch more buttons.

The door slides open.

I kick the area around the steering wheel.

Jordie is standing by my side.

I use my entire hand to bang on all the buttons at once.

Jordie sighs.

"Really? Given your history do you think I would leave you unattended in the ship without locking it down?"

I give up and shrug. "You know I had to try."

The right side of Jordie's lip twitches upwards, almost into a smile. "I would have been surprised if you didn't."

I smile too. We have finally come to an understanding and now everything is about to change again. I don't want to stay in the orientation place, but I'm really not ready to move to a new planet. But here I am, with no choice at this moment.

I take a deep breath and nod to Jordie. "Okay, let's go meet this Jutte alien." I purposefully throw in the word alien so as to poke fun at him one more time. I smile – he turns and walks away.

Jordie leads me out of the spaceship and towards what I assume is my new house. I'll never call it my home. Home is the planet Earth, my little hut on my island that I shared with Grandfather. This is just a stopping point until I can get back home. I sling my backpack over my shoulder and walk out of the spaceship.

The alien stands in his doorway, waiting for us. I walk next to Jordie, letting this guy know that I refuse to cower behind Jordie or him. I need to let this alien know right away that I'm not a scared little pet.

We stop in front of the alien and Jordie speaks. "Hello, Jutte. This is Marco." No flourish, no big introductions telling him my likes and dislikes, just straight to the point. I step forward and speak in the Mari language. "Hello, my name is Marco. It's nice to meet you."

Jutte nods and his mouth opens in a huge way. Seriously worried, I take a step backward. "Holy Neptune, does he bite?"

Jordie stifles a laugh. "No, that is how he smiles."

Well, okay then. Wide open mouth means a smile; got it. It's a little scary, but I got it.

Jutte answers me and I think I understand pretty much everything he says. "Welcome Marco, it is nice to finally meet you too." I look at Jordie who doesn't respond to me at all. Jutte steps back into his house, allowing Jordie and me to walk inside.

I'm used to the small home Grandfather and I shared. We spent most of our time outside and never need huge master bedrooms with en-suite baths. But this house is deceiving. It doesn't look like much from the outside, but, holy moly, the inside is something else. The ceilings are so high, it's as if there should be a second floor in between me and the roof.

I'm looking up at the ceiling trying to figure out what is different about it when I bump into Jordie. I didn't realize he had stopped walking. He glances at me, but I'm too busy looking around. The walls and ceiling are all varying shades of blue with a hint of green. The floors are a darker blue that gets lighter as it goes up and the ceiling is a soft blue with hints of white. The green colors are worked in so subtly that I almost don't realize what I'm seeing.

This house reminds me of being underwater.

Jordie nudges me to pay attention, but I don't. *You pay attention, I'm looking around.* I want to explore this place; I've never seen anything like it. Well, duh, I've never been to the planet of Oonala before.

"So, what happens now. Do you sign me over to him or something?" I don't bother to keep the snarkyness out of my voice.

He doesn't flinch. "No, the paperwork is already done. I'm here because I've learned it helps the humans to have me here for a short while. Once you settle in, I'll be on my way. Don't worry, I will stop in to check on you from time to time and see if you need anything."

"You're leaving me here today? I was kind of hoping this was a meeting and we would come back another day." My heart pounds. I start looking for the door.

"Marco, you knew today was your day to move to Oonala

with Jutte. I'm not leaving yet. Let's have Jutte show you around the house, and to your room. I'll wait here for you. I won't leave until you are comfortable."

I stare at him for a moment. This guy may have done a complete upheaval of my life, and sold me as a pet – but he has never lied to me, so I believe him when he says he won't sneak away when I'm not looking.

I let out my breath. Okay, I can do this.

"Please, come here." Jutte's low voice comes from behind me. I jump and spin around, fists up. I completely forgot he was here. And now my heart is pounding again, just when I had begun to calm down.

Jordie lets out a true full-belly laugh. I should be mad but I'm surprised to see him show an emotion other than exasperation. Actually, that was pretty funny of me to forget about a ten-foot-tall alien. I start laughing too. It must be true that laughing is contagious, because Jutte's mouth is wide open again, which makes me laugh even harder.

I laugh so hard that I sit right there on the floor. I lightly pound Jordie's leg, since he is still laughing too. Arturo would have loved to see me jump like that.

Jordie calms down and resumes chatting with Jutte. I finally pull myself together, wipe my eyes and nose on my sleeve, and stand up. I nod to Jordie to let him know I'm okay now. It's still a bit hard to understand their conversation, but I get the gist of it.

"I'll let you... his area ... sleep... talk with him..." Jutte nods as Jordie gives out advice.

Jutte looks my way and speaks slowly to me. At least he doesn't talk louder like people do when they think you don't understand them. "Come...you... sleep." I miss the middle of what he said. I wonder what they call a room? Maybe they just call it the place where you sleep. Whatever, I follow him.

There isn't much difference between the ceiling, the walls, and the floor. They all blend together with rounded edges. There are no doors, we simply walk around an S corner to get to other rooms. Huh, that's pretty cool. It's as if there is no need for a door when you have a couple walls that go back and forth to give you privacy.

Jutte steps aside and swipes his large arm around. "… You sleep… you be…" He said some words I don't understand. I guess he means this is my room. It's as big as our entire house back home. I have no need for all this space.

Except I don't see a bed. "Um, thank you." I say. "Where me sleep?" Jutte does his open mouth smile thing and points to a red square block the size of two suitcases standing upright, next to each other. "Here." He happily announces.

Yeah, I still don't get it.

Why isn't Jordie here to help me with this?

"I… no…." I confess.

Jutte uses his small hand and taps the top of the cube. With that pat, the box unfolds itself into the size of a bed.

That is so cool. I smile at Jutte and his mouth opens even wider.

When I push on the bed, my hand oozes into it. That's weird. I push down again and my hand is absorbed into the bed.

I shrug out of my backpack. I'm going in.

If a water bed and a bean bag chair had a soft, squishy baby, I think it would feel like this bed. I sink into it as it wraps around me. This is really comfortable. I'm not able to roll around, or flop onto my stomach, but I don't think I need to. Just like my hammock, I wasn't able to toss and turn in that, but I still slept well in it. Now how to get out? I've sunk down so that I'm eye level with the edge of the bed.

I roll to my side and grab hold of the edge. As I pull myself up the bed seems to almost help ease me upwards. I roll out and end up on the floor.

I jump up laughing, "Yes!." I try to fist-bump Jutte, before I realize he has no idea what I'm doing. I drop my hand. "How does go?" I don't know the words to say fold back up, so I search for words that hopefully he will understand.

He uses his large hand to gently nudge me two steps back, and reaches behind the head of the bed with a small hand and lightly taps it. With no noise at all, the bed folds itself back into the cube.

I study it for a moment, then reach out to tap the cube. Nothing happens. I try again, but this time I give it a good slap. It unfolds itself into my bed. I feel around the head section, as Jutte did, until I feel an outline of a square the size of my hand, I push and the bed folds itself up again.

Okay, this I can totally handle.

Looking around, I notice more shapes and furniture. I'm on a hunt to discover everything in the room. There are a table and chair in the far corner, and a soft chair along the wall to my right. Everything is laid out in perfect angles. Odd, I wonder if Jordie is OCD and told Jutte how to set up my room.

I walk toward a slit in the wall on the other side of the bed to see if it's another hall/door opening, and walk into a bathroom. Now this I recognize right away; it's similar to the bathroom at the orientation place. Good, at last, something I recognize. It has the light green walls with grey accents and a shower at the far end. I look close at the shower wall and see the same panel. I wave my hand in front of the sensor and the shower turns on to the perfect temperature. Back in the bedroom, Jordie is standing next to Jutte. "Oh my God, did you see this bed? This is like, the coolest thing ever." I say in English while pointing at the cube.

"Yes, I have seen a bed like that before, I'm glad you like it. You will have plenty of time to explore your room and the rest of the house. Let's go to the main area to talk."

He sure knows how to suck all the fun out of a room.

Since both Jutte and I automatically understand what Jordie says, Jutte leads us back to the main area.

This must be when Jordie says good bye. I won't miss him, but I'm still trying not to freak out too much. I know Jordie. I don't know this alien or what happens next. I start tapping my thumb and finger together. What happens after he leaves? What will I do all day every day? Will I be allowed outside? I need sunlight.

"All right," Jordie breaks the tension. "I'm glad you two have met and seem to be getting along well. Marco, Jutte knows you are still learning the language and he will help with that. He also understands your eating and sleeping schedule. You are free to sleep when you need, so you can adjust to Mari time. Please remember, to be respectful. I will be back in about a week to see how you are settling in." He turns to the alien. "As you know, this is all new to Marco, he may sleep more in the beginning, he may not talk much right away, but I am confident you two will work things out." Then Jordie says something in a language that I don't understand. Jordie chuckles and Jutte opens his mouth wide.

What the heck? Are they making fun of me?

"What was that about?" Again, this man can stop fun from happening at any moment.

"I told him to keep an eye on you and that you may try to run away." Jordie shrugs.

I glare at him.

First of all, why is that funny? And second of all, now I know not to tell him any secrets.

Jutte walks Jordie to the door, using his small hand to shake Jordie's. I stay behind. Just for that comment, I'm not going to try to run right now.

At the door, Jordie turns to me. "My apologies, I do not want us to part on bad terms. I did not say that to him to make you look bad, it was simply a matter of fact. Again, I would be disappointed if you didn't try." He actually smiles and gives a small shrug.

I relax a bit. It's hard to stay mad at someone who is that honest with you. Jordie reaches out his hand, and I shake it. "Be thinking of items you may need. I will do all I can to make this transition an easy one."

"I can't say thank you for being abducted by aliens. So, I guess this is 'I'll see you later.'" That's about the best I can come up with.

Jordie nods, "Yes, I will see you later."

With that he turns and walks back to the spaceship. Jutte and I stand in the door way and watch him fly away.

We look at each other, unsure what to do next.

He steps back into the house, holding the door for me.
I don't try to escape, not yet.
Here we go, the first day of my new life.

CHAPTER 17

Jutte walks back to the main area. It's not that I'm following him, I just happen to be going that way too. He crosses the room and sits on an oval piece of furniture. As he leans to the side an arm rest miraculously appears. Wow, it automatically knows what you want.

I stand in the middle of the room, shifting my weight from one foot to the other. I don't want to be here. I want to go home and joke around with Arturo, heck, I'd even go back to school.... Anything to be home again.

Jutte opens a basket next to the couch and pulls out some long, tan pieces. They almost look like palm fronds. "It's just you and me." He says.

Um, okay captain obvious. Unless you have other human pets somewhere, it's just you and me. "Yes." I choose to say that out loud. Wait, he can't understand English, I can say anything I want and he won't know. But he beats me to it and starts rambling away in the Mari language. I think he is talking just for the sake of talking. Maybe he thinks I'll pick up on his language better if he keeps talking. *I'm not a plant and can't learn through osmosis.* Whatever, I guess it's better than silence.

Instead, I pay attention to what he is actually doing with the palm fronds. I step closer and he slows down to show me. I know he is explaining what's going on, but I don't understand most of it, I just watch. He is weaving the fronds within each other, pulling them tight close together. I wonder what he's making? Maybe he's crocheting a scarf. Even I have to laugh at that.

"See… this…." Jutte motions me closer. His long arm reaches into the basket, pulls out a bag and holds it up. I touch it, looking to Jutte for permission. "Yes, here." He hands me the bag. Huh, it really is a bag made of palm fronds. It has a long flap that wraps around itself two times and the ends fold over, tying it closed with two straps to hold it by. Interesting. I think he's explaining what it's used for, but I don't get what he is saying. He stands, slings the bag over his shoulders, resting it on his front like a baby carrier.

"Wait, please." I run to my room and snatch my backpack off the floor. I stand in front of him and put on my backpack, turning to show him that I have one too. "How do you say?" I ask and point to his bag. He tells me the word for that bag. I show how my bag snaps closed and rides on my back instead of my front.

He sits back down and returns to working on his bag. I go back into my room, drop off my backpack, and decide to grab some wood and my knife. I don't know where I'm supposed to sit in the living room, so I simply sit on the floor and whittle while he is making his bag.

If this is the most excitement in my life, I'm going to die of boredom. Please not let us be like an old married couple that sits and weaves and whittles every night. I need more.

But for now, I guess I'm fine.

Jutte looks at me, "What is?" he asks.

I hold up my wood carving that I've been working on. "It's a dolphin." I say in English. How do I explain a dolphin in Mari? What's the word for fish? "It be in water," I tell him in my stunted version of the Mari language. I hand him the dolphin. He uses his small hands to turn it over and examines it from every angle. I bet it's like seeing a carving of an alien for him.

"Very good." He tells me as he hands it back. Yeah, I know, I wasn't asking for his approval. But I still can't help smile; it really is pretty good.

I also have a spotted eagle ray that I'm working on, but I focus on the dolphin for now.

I lose track of time as we sit here. Jutte finishes the bag and starts another. How many bags does one guy need? "You make bag?" Jutte asks me.

He wants to teach me to make bags? Um, okay. I stand next to Jutte while he shows me how he folds the fronds over each other. He hands it to me and shows me how to use my fingers to hold the fronds apart and maneuver them together. I get the idea of it, but it's hard to make them line up straight.

Jutte adjusts my fingers and soon I think I have it. Not all that great, but at least I know how to make one straight line, even with spaces between the fronds in some places and bunched together in others.

Jutte opens his mouth wide and pats me on the head.

"No." I tell him. I am not a dog that gets a pat on the head. I make the motion of patting and say again. "No." I'm putting a stop to that right now.

Jutte looks at me with his head tilted. I don't think he likes me telling him no, but I don't care. Instead, I hold out my fist. He uses his small hand to make a fist, and I bump it. "Good." I tell him and smile. I can handle fist-bumping with him, but I will not be patted on the head.

"Good." Jutte repeats and fist-bumps me again. Hey, maybe I can teach him tricks instead of him teaching them to me. I can't help but smile at how smart I am. Okay, fine, Jutte's a pretty good guy.

He continues to show me how to weave the bag; he shows me how to move from one row to the next, how to count the length of each row; and how to make the next row longer than the last. After a bit I understand that we are making the flap of the bag larger.

"Why bag?" I ask Jutte. I actually want to know why he makes several bags. Doesn't he really only need one or two?

He shows me that he puts items in the bag, ties it closed and straps in to his front. "When swim." He tells me while using his long arms with the webbed hands to make a swimming motion.

Ah, to hold your items while you dive down and go shopping - got it. "Water out bag?" I ask, wondering how the water stays out.

Jutte opens his mouth and holds his fist out for a bump. I guess he liked my question. "Come." He gets up and walks toward the front door. I set my fronds down and follow him outside. He heads to the trees behind the house.

I step outside and stop.

I'm outside.

It's just like the hologram, but better. I can smell the salt water and feel the heat of the suns on my skin. The water is such a part of my life, and I've missed it while in orientation. The ocean is straight ahead, and it's beautiful. I look up and see two suns in the sky. I'm not sure I'll ever get used to that.

Jutte pauses, watching me. Probably remembering Jordie's warning that I'm an escape artist. I decide to prove Jordie wrong, and walk to where Jutte is waiting.

Maybe he'll give me more leeway if I earn his trust first.

He walks past the first trees and stops just inside the grove. He waits for me to catch up and points to a tree. "Here." He says.

Um, okay, it's a tree. So what? He uses his long arm and touches a piece sticking out of the tree. I watch as he breaks the piece of wood off, and sap flows into a bucket he grabs with his other hand.

"Yes." I nod. I understand that he is collecting sap, but then what? He grabs some clay dirt from the ground and puts it onto the hole to stop the flow of sap and starts toward the house.

"Come." He tells me again. I don't like being told to follow, so I run and catch up and walk next to him instead of behind him.

Jutte lets me in the door and heads to the bags. He takes a mat of sorts out of the basket and lays it on the floor. He then lays the bag flat on the mat. From the basket he pulls out a flat paddle and uses it to scoop the sap out of the bucket and spread it onto the bag, making sure to fill in each hole and seam.

He is using the sap to waterproof the bag. How smart is that?

"No water." I point and smile at the bag he is working on.

"No water." He replies, and keeps spreading the sap.

Once done, he tells me "No touch." I wasn't planning on touching it, but now I want to, just because it's forbidden.

So, I get that he makes waterproof bags he uses when diving down to the underwater town, but why does he make so many? I try again to ask. "Why three, four, five bags?" I'm frustrated at being unable to say exactly what I want.

He answers me, but I don't understand what he says. I shake my head and shrug. He tries again to explain why he makes so many bags. All four arms are moving while he is talking, but I still don't get it. He sighs at my frustration.

"We swim?" he asks.

Sure! I don't know why the sudden change of subject, but I'm up for a swim. I want to see this underwater world Jordie told me about. I jump up, run to my room, change into my swim trunks, and grab my mask and fins.

Back in the main room, Jutte is folding bags and putting them inside a larger bag. He ties it closed, straps it to his front, and nods to me. He's using his bag to carry bags? What is this guy is doing?

We walk outside to the water's edge. I put on my mask and fins. Head tilted; Jutte watches me. I point to my flippers, then to his webbed feet. "Swim good." I tell him. He opens his mouth and nods. He gets my meaning.

We wade into the crystal clear and warm water. There are no waves, just the smooth, silky feeling of calm waters. I'm already swimming while he is still wading out. Jutte looks to me. "You good?" he asks.

I don't know if I'm 'good', my mouth has gone dry and my hands are shaking. I can hold my breath longer than just about anybody back home, but is that enough? What if we go deeper than I can handle? I keep paddling out. I stick my face in the water to see what's below me.

Holy Neptune, I can see domes in the distance below us.

I spit out my snorkel and start hollering. "Omigod, do you see that? There is a whole village down there! It's just us up here, but down there is so much more." I know I'm babbling in English, but how can I not?

Jutte is smiling, mouth open, at me.

"Swim?" he asks. Heck yeah, I'm ready. I nod, take a deep breath, and we dive down.

CHAPTER 18

I swim head down, my fins paddling hard. Next to me, Jutte keeps looking my way. His blue skin definitely camouflages him underwater. I can see him, but I understand how the Mari easily blend it with the underwater world. The sun and movement of the water perfectly match the blue lines of his skin. We get deeper, the colors of the water still mix with his colors. The water is crystal clear, warm, and current-less. I think I'm doing pretty good following him on one breath. Not that I can take another breath underwater, but still. He swims ahead of me to show me the entrance.

He reaches a doorway and pulls himself through a huge arch. I follow, making sure to grab the sides of the room so I don't float to the ceiling. I hold my nose and blow, popping my ears. He points to a button at the back of the cavern. Okay, so he's showing me how to open the door. A clear door slides up and we swim into the next room. He pushes another button which closes the door. As soon as the door is sealed tight, the water starts draining away. I swim upwards to catch a breath rather than waiting for the water to go down.

I gulp the air, thankful to make it without panic. I actually could have held my breath longer, but I'm glad I didn't have to. I sink to the floor as the water continues to drain away. I'm able to stand and take off my fins and mask to look around. This place is huge, and so cool. The walls are clear, allowing me to look through them at the sea around me.

Schools of strange-looking fish swim overhead. They are probably the size of me. I wonder if the dome makes them look bigger, or smaller than they really are, which is a scary thought.

The fish have bright yellow, long lean bodies. They remind me of barracuda, except they each have two heads, and almost smiling faces.

Jutte is watching, waiting for me to finish looking around. I'm not sure I'm finished, but I'm ready to see more. I hold up my swim fins and my mask, wondering where I should put them. Jutte takes several bags out of his main one, hands them to me to hold, and puts my stuff in the bag still on his chest.

He points to a button. It's located on the wall and above my head. I stand on my tip toes, just barely able to reach it. I push and nothing happens. I try jumping up and slapping the button; that works. The next door slides upwards and opens into the center of the market.

Again, Jutte leads the way. I glance around his legs to see where we are going. About twenty steps into the market, another Mari guy comes charging at us, yelling pointing at me.

What the heck? What did I do?

I jump behind Jutte. The way this guy is shouting makes me think he just might hurt me. Jutte stands up tall and hollers back at the man. Holy Neptune, these guys are scary! They are talking loud and fast, leaving me completely in the dark about what is said. Lots of arms wave around wildly, and the other guy keeps pointing at me and saying the same words over and over. I try to make out what he's saying, I think it's something like 'no pets allowed'. Is he saying I'm not allowed in the market place?

Now Jutte fiercely gets into this guy's face, talking to him in a quiet and threatening manner. Crap, I know not to make Jutte mad.

The other guy leans around Jutte and grabs me by the arm! With his small hand, he snatches me and drags me towards the exit door, yelling at me the whole time. Once I gather my senses as to what's happening, I try kicking his shins and hitting his arm. I've already been kidnapped once, no way will I let another alien take me.

I manage to turn and bite his arm, hard. I put everything I have into it, and really chomp down on his rubbery skin. He roars and lets me go, which is probably good for him, because Jutte is right there, ready to fight for me.

Jutte grabs my arm and pushes me behind him, and begins pushing the other guy away. A crowd has gathered, and I stay close to Jutte in case someone else tries to steal me. Pretty soon, the other guy steps back, he points at me again, yelling. "That... bite... you...saw it... bite me." He spins around, looking at everyone before storming away.

I'm completely surrounded by aliens. I nudge closer to Jutte. I don't know if they are staring at me or the crazy guy. Now that he is gone, they all seem to be pointing at and talking about me. I wonder if they've ever seen a human before.

I don't want any of them to pet or pick me up.

Jutte watches him go before he turns and bends down to me. "You good?" he asks.

No, I'm not good. I just had an alien yell at me and try to kidnap me, or throw me out into the ocean. But either way, no, I'm not good. I don't answer right away. Instead, I take a couple of deep breaths. In, two, three, four; out, two three, four. After about three deep breaths, I'm calm again.

"Yes, I good. Thank you." I want to say for protecting me, but I don't know the words yet. "Why mad?" I ask. Jutte pats my shoulder. "He bad... not you... stay me." Are the words I understand.

Um yeah, you don't have to tell me that twice to stay close to you.

Some of the other aliens have left, but some are still staring at me. Jutte opens his mouth to them, and several start asking questions. "Human?" is the first question. They all begin talking and coming closer. Jutte answers their questions without offering me to them. I silently thank him.

No one tries to pet me and eventually, they all wander off. Jutte turns his attention back to me. He fist-bumps me, and acts like nothing happened. Great, at least one of us isn't rattled. He begins walking through the market, and I make sure to stay close to him in case that guy comes back for me.

I think I understand the layout. Each stand has its own entrance, but also, its own clear dome, so I can actually see through several stalls at a time. Plus, I can look up and see the outside ocean. It's an eerie feeling to know I'm walking around on the bottom of the sea. I mean, I swam in it daily and was completely comfortable sitting on the bottom waiting for a lobster to come out of hiding, but this is different. I'm actually walking around and breathing down here.

The bright array of colors against the blue of the ocean makes me dizzy. I look down at my bare feet to regain balance.

Jutte puts a hand on my shoulder and guides me into a stall. A Mari lady walks up to Jutte, talking friendlier than the other guy. Besides the simulation room, this is the first time I've seen a female Mari. "Hello Jutte, I hope the water is good to you today." Huh? What does she mean that she hopes the water is good to him? I didn't learn that greeting in orientation. I should have brought my notebook and pen to write questions down for Jordie. What was that man yelling, and what does her greeting mean? I'll have to remember them until we go back to the ant hill house.

Jutte taps me and points to the lady. "... Marco... living with me...." The Mari lady opens her mouth really wide, smiling big. I'm worried she will pat me on the head, or pet me, or some freaky thing like that. So, I make the first move.

"Hello, it is nice to meet you." I say in the Mari language,

She steps back and starts clapping her small hands with her larger ones. That's funny, the hands on the right side of her clap together and the hands on the left side of her clap together. I would have thought she would clap her two small hands together in front of her and the two larger hands together. I can't help but stare as I step behind Jutte. I think he tells her I'm shy. Whatever, I'll play shy if it means she won't touch me.

Jutte holds up the bags to show her. They start talking seriously, I catch words like, *looks very good, yes,* and *thank you.* She takes the bags from Jutte and hangs them on the wall. She then walks away and shortly returns and hands something to

Jutte. They smile, nod to each other, and we leave.

"Jutte," I tap him on the leg. He stops and looks at me. "You give bags her?" That's the best I can do, asking why he makes so many bags. "Yes." He answers. "Mari swim with bags. Look." He starts pointing to other Mari walking by. Sure enough, some have his bags strapped to their front. Other Mari people have different bags, but many of them look like the ones he makes.

Got it, he makes and sells the bags for a living, or for a part time job, or for fun. Whichever, Jutte makes and sells bags.

We continue to another stop and Jutte pulls smaller bags out. A Mari male is working this store, and they greet each other. "I hope the water is good to you today." The guy says. Once they are done saying their hello's Jutte introduces me to this guy. "... human Marco."

They guy squats down to my level. "Hello." I tell him, and hold my fist out. He tilts his head and looks to Jutte. Jutte fist-bumps me to show the guy what to do, and tells him "It is his good."

The guy fist-bumps me and stands up, talking with Jutte. I know I should be listening to them, but I can't help looking around at everything. The merchandise in this store is so weird and I can't figure out any of it. I wander away, looking at the dome above me. I don't get far before Jutte taps me on the shoulder. "Go home?" I'm torn. I want to explore this market place and watch the aliens, but I'm also nervous the mean guy will come back and yell at me again.

"Yes, we go house." I tell him. Jutte slightly opens his mouth, and turns me towards the exit.

I can't believe I'm walking around these aliens. I have to watch out for their flipper feet. Some of them get too close and almost step on me.

We walk back to the inner door. Jutte lets me jump up and press the button to open the door. As we step inside, he brings my mask and fins out from his bag and hands them to me. He waits in the middle of the room while I put on my flippers, and spit into my mask to make sure it doesn't fog up. "I'm good." I tell him. Once the first door is completely closed and we are sealed in, he pushes the next button, which is good, because I'm not sure how high I can jump in flippers. The floor begins to flood with water.

I look nervously look around, I want to be near the ceiling, breathing until the last moment. Once the water is about chest high on me, I start treading water. My breathing is fast and I'm flailing around here. I know I'm not trapped in this room, but it sure feels like it. Jutte reaches over and holds me up with his large flipper hand. Just having something to hold onto calms me. I close my eyes for a moment, steady my breathing, and begin to float instead of flopping my arms.

In, two three, four. Out, two, three, four.

We are at the ceiling, and the water is still filling in fast. I take a deep breath and dive down. Jutte swims ahead of me and pushes the button to open the outer door. We swim out and I head straight up towards the surface. Jutte follows me.

My head bursts out of the water as I inhale deeply. Okay, maybe I'm more panicked than I need to be. I mean, it was barely a minute that I was holding my breath, and that's usually no problem for me. I look around as Jutte surfaces. He points behind me. "House there." He tells me. I see that we are further from land than I thought we would be. I guess I should have swum upwards at an angle and come out closer to the house. Oh well, I turn around and start swimming backwards towards land. With my fins on, it's easier to swim backwards if I keep my head above water. I push my mask onto my forehead, lay back, and kick-swim to the house.

We start the long trek back to land, but hey, at least I'm breathing. It's easy to swim in this ocean without large waves. Do they not have a moon that causes the pull of the tides? Of the two suns, Juja's the only one I can pick out. This is all so weird: living on an alien planet, talking with Jutte, being a pet. But, Jordie said there are other humans on Oonala, so maybe one day I'll run into one. My luck they'll speak Japanese or some language I don't understand. I guess, then we would both revert to the Mari language.

My mind is running in circles as we swim back to land, but what I'm thinking most is that as amazing as it is here, I still want to go home.

It's finally shallow enough for me to touch bottom. I slip off my mask and flippers, drop them on the beach...and run.

CHAPTER 19

We came ashore in front of the house, so I break left and dash down, along the beach. I figure Jutte can surely outrun me, so once I'm past the house, I turn and sprint into the woods. I can duck and jump through tighter spaces than he can.

"Marco!" I hear him calling behind me, but he sounds far enough behind to let me know I have a good head start. I barely notice that the trees are different here. The trunks have streaks with different shades of red, and branches or foliage are sparse until towards the top of the tree. This makes it much easier for me to run, but it also makes it easier for Jutte to run through.

I swerve back and forth rather than run a straight line. My goal is to lose Jutte, then find my way to a town and maybe stow away on a ship, or steal a spaceship. Hardly a fully formed plan, but hey, it's all I've got for now.

I debate on hiding somewhere, but decide to keep running. I need to find a safe place first, then I can hide and devise my escape plan.

I can still hear Jutte crashing through the odd forest behind me, but not as fast as I'm running. Maybe the Mari aliens can't run very fast with their flipper feet. This just might be my advantage. Escape on land, because they can outswim me. Well, that, and the fact that I can't hold my breath as long as they probably can; their lungs must be huge.

Focus, Marco.

I slow down a bit and look around. The trees changed, some are shorter and have wider, and perfectly square trunks. That makes me stop. Here's a square tree like I saw in the hologram. I tentatively touch one, who knows if it is poisonous, or will come to life? Strange things can happen on an alien planet.

Thankfully, it doesn't come alive, and my hand doesn't go numb. I place both hands on the tree to try to figure it out. The edges are perfect right angles; there is no slant to it at all. I decided to name it a box tree.

Focus, Marco.

I snap out of it and try to figure out which way to go. I see an opening in the trees and run to the edge, stopping before I expose myself to aliens that may be walking around. I'm on another beach with no aliens in sight, not even Jutte.

I turn left again. Up ahead, the beach curves. I duck into the woods to avoid being seen. I peek around the curve and again I'm met by an empty beach.

I didn't see any spaceships underwater, but then again, I didn't look around much because I was focused on holding my breath long enough to get to the market.

After walking for about twenty minutes without seeing anyone, I'm beginning to wonder how I'll survive here. I don't have food or water and I'm really thirsty. Back on Earth I always brought lots of water on the boat when diving. Being under water seemed to make me more thirsty than normal; and now, walking in the hot suns (two of them), I'm really wishing I had grabbed a bottle of water. Does Jutte have bottles of water for me? I know Jordie says I'll have food and water when I want, but will it be in a cup, bottle, or what?

It's funny how your mind can wander without noise to keep you distracted. The trees are the same tall, red, skinny ones and short square ones, so nothing new to look at there. The water is crystal clear: I wonder if markets exist below me no matter where I am, or if they are only in certain places. Did Jutte build his hut near the stores or just near the ones he likes?

I look up and down the beach to make sure I'm alone, and wade into the water. I put my face in and look down. Everything is distorted but I see that the bottom of the ocean is flat. A couple of sea creatures walk along the bottom. They are the strangest things I've ever seen... and lately I've seen a lot of strange things.

I see five or so of these little guys. They're about the size of my hand. They are diamond in shape, all different colors, but what I can't look away from is their five eyes that are looking all around them. One spots me floating above and somehow alerts the others. I suddenly have a ton of these diamond-shaped creatures start to float towards me.

I turn and swim back ashore. What the heck would they have done to me? I think it's best to stay on land for now.

I turn another corner of the island, and see Jutte's ant hill house. So, basically, I walked in a circle and his is the only building I've seen.

Great, I forgot that I am assigned to an alien that lives on a deserted island.

CHAPTER 20

I take a deep breath and walk to the house. Using the side of my fist, I pound on the door. I don't know what kind of trouble I'm in, but I guess I have to face the music.

I brace myself as Jutte opens the door. Is he going to yell at me? Spank me? Not let me back in? There's just no telling what's about to happen.

Instead, he simply holds the door open for me to walk in.

I step inside and wait. Without a word he walks into the main area, I follow. The silence terrifies me. When I was younger, I knew I was in big trouble when my mom would not say a word, but walk into my room and expect me to follow. The silence is worse than the yelling.

I stand in the middle of the room, waiting for the other shoe to drop. My nerves finally get the best of me, "I'm sorry." I blurt out. I debate whether to keep babbling or stay quiet.

Thankfully, Jutte starts talking to me. He sits down in front of me, looking me in the eyes. "I show you outside. I give you space. I understand this new. I no want Marco hurt. Only want Marco good."

I know he thinks he is giving me a great home, but I wonder if Jordie has told him that I already had a great home. I never wondered if puppies miss their mom and their siblings when we take them as pets; the question never crossed my mind.

I haven't given up hope of going home one day.

All this flashes through my mind, but stays inside my head. I'm not ready to share my feelings with someone I don't really know. Instead, I look at my feet and nod. I'm still waiting for my punishment.

Jutte taps me on the chest. "I worried." He tells me. I kind of feel bad for making him worry. Instead of yelling, he asks me, "What did you see?"

I start talking quickly. "I saw trees that like…" I'm at a loss for words. "Wait, please?" I ask and run to my room and stop when I notice my flippers next to my bag. Oh, he was nice enough to save them for me. I shake away emotions and grab the notepad and pen and run back to Jutte; he still sits in the main area, waiting for me.

I draw a picture of the square tree. "This tree." I hold it up to show him. He looks at my picture, then gasps and leans backwards. I look at my picture and back at him. I know I'm not a great artist, but I didn't think my drawing of a tree would scare him.

Jutte reaches out with a small hand and tentatively touches the picture, cocking his head as if to figure it out. I try to avoid any fast movements.

"I see this and I see this" I draw the tall tree now, and again hold it up to him. "These trees." I say, pointing to the pictures. Maybe I'm saying the word trees wrong; my luck I'm probably saying something bad like a dirty slang for women's breasts or something. I wonder what the Mari find offensive.

"Tree? Is that the word?" I ask.

"Yes, tree." He softly utters, still staring at my drawings. Jutte takes the notebook away from me and flips through it. There is nothing exciting in there, just some questions I asked Jordie, written in English, of course; and some doodles here and there.

It all fascinates him. He points to one of the sketches, "What is this?" he asks. I have some other sketches that are better than this 3D box that I drew one day while thinking of other things.

"A box." I explain slowly. My bed is the shape of a box, how does he not know what it is?

"No, not box, what is all?" He looks up from the pad. I stare at him for a moment and decide he's not kidding, he's seriously baffled, which has me clueless, as well. I wish Jordie was here to answer him.

I shrug. "I doodle" I say the word 'doodle' in English. I realize I'm speaking part English part Mari more and more. "I not think, I just doodle. I know not good." I take the notebook back and try to hide it away.

"You make tree?" Jutte asks. Is he asking if I can actually make one, or what? He points at the book and says again. "You make tree right there."

Um, okay. I can't deny it, since I already showed it to him. "Yes, I make tree." I don't know the word for 'draw' or 'paint', so I say 'make', like he did.

"How?" he looks at me so seriously.

I open the notepad again and draw the square tree again. He scoots forward so he can watch as I draw. He touches the picture, and then the pen. Looking at me, he asks "More?"

I decide to quick sketch the outside of the house. When done, I hold it up for him to see. "House!" he exclaims. He grabs the pad away from me and runs outside. I follow, not wanting to miss whatever's about to happen.

Jutte stands near the water, looking at the house. He has the notepad in his small hands and is points at the house with a large flipper hand. "House!" he exclaims again, this time his mouth his wide open. Good, at least he likes the picture of his house.

He looks around and points at a small sea creature scurrying in the water past his toes. "You make this?" He asks. I peer down to see another new animal. This one is flat, perfectly round, with stripes of purple and red. As I'm looking at it, the whole creature blinks. I jump back. Holy Neptune, is that an eyeball swimming around! I cautiously step forward; it blinks at me again. But this time it's blue and green, as if it's trying to hide.

I decide not to touch it.

Jutte is holding the notepad out to me, so I take it and sketch the eye fish. I have only one pen, so I make lines to show where the colors would be, and shade in some areas. It doesn't take me long since I'm not trying to create a masterpiece. I hold it up to show off my art work. Duly impressed, Jutte stands there with his mouth open wider than I have yet seen.

Hey, maybe he forgot that I was supposed to be in trouble.

I wonder if what I'm about to do will freak him out. I turn my back so he can't see my drawing. He tries to look over my shoulder, but I keep turning and use my body to hide it. I take a little more time with this one since I want to get it right. I draw, shade, and try to make it realistic. Not perfect, but realistic.

Jutte taps me on the shoulder, but I ignore him. I want this to be a surprise. When I'm done, I step back, holding the picture against my body. Jutte is practically hopping up and down with anticipation. "Ready?" I ask.

"Ready!" he almost yells.

I flip the book around and show him a picture I've drawn of myself, well, at least what I looked like the last time I saw myself.

Silence.

I was expecting some kind of response, at least a smile. Jutte is staring at the drawing, speechless.

Maybe he doesn't recognize it. I point to the picture and then to me. "It's me. It's Marco." Now I'm looking back and forth, hoping I drew a semblance of me. Jutte whispers something and lightly touches the picture. I look back and forth between the pad and him. What?

With a huge smile but no other warning, his large hand swoops around and hits me square in the chest, knocking me over backwards. "Hey!" I exclaim in English. "What the heck was that for?" It really didn't hurt, but I'm sitting in the sand, rubbing my chest.

"So sorry," Jutte says as he comes towards me. I'm not sure if I should duck or not. "So sorry," he repeats as he picks me up, completely off the ground, and sets me back on my feet. He's smiling again. "It's Marco, you make Marco!"

He's more concerned with the drawing than with knocking me down. "How you make Marco?" I'm too busy brushing the sand off my backside to answer him. He taps my chest. "How you make Marco?" he asks again.

How do I answer this? I don't know the word for mirror. I look at the water again, and can see a faint reflection. I point to that and tell him. "I see Marco and I make Marco." He stands over me, peering down at the water. I can barely make out his reflection. "I make Jutte?" I ask him.

He jumps back, touching his own face. "You can make Jutte?" He asks almost reverently.

"Sure, I can make Jutte." I tell him. This is actually fun. I walk back onto the sand and sit down. "Please sit." I tell him. Jutte plops down in front of me and looks expectantly at me. Drawing a picture of a person is hard. Sometimes people see themselves differently from how others see them. I wonder if this is true with the Mari.

I start with his mouth, sketching it open in a smile. I move on to his eyes, and the rest of his face, glancing back and forth between him and the drawing. Maybe I shouldn't have done this. What if he doesn't like how I draw him and is mad at me again? Should I do just his face or draw his entire body? I opt to start with his face. I'm no Picasso, but I'm actually not that bad at drawing. I get my ability from Grandfather. When he could see, Grandfather could paint some amazing pictures that tourists would buy.

I draw the last line and look up at Jutte. Okay, here goes nothing. I hand him the notepad and wait. He looks at the picture, touches it, looks behind the notepad, and back at me. "This is me?" he asks. Crud, I didn't think I did so bad.

"Well, yeah, I guess." I stand up and dig my toes into the sand. He hates it.

"I never see me." He hands the picture back to me.

Wait, what? "You never see you?" I ask, unable to comprehend such a thing. I slip into English. "What do you mean you never see you? How can you not know what you look like?" Totally not the response I was expecting. There is no excitement in his voice, no smiling, nothing. "Well, you look good." I say, pointing at the picture. "I mean, I try to make you, but you better." Maybe he isn't happy with the way he looks, in real life or in the drawing. How can someone possibly not know what they look like?

"You do very good. I am happy." He smiles as he pats me on the back, again almost knocking me over. "Let's go in. You run away."

Great, we're back to that. I guess the excitement has worn off and I'm back in trouble. I nod as he walks behind me towards the house, a hand on my shoulder so I don't run away again. Inside, he closes and locks the door, and gets serious.

"No run away, it is dangerous for Marco. Many animals hurt you. I want Marco good here. I give food and water. I keep Marco safe. You no run away."

Wow, he went from being excited about the drawings, to nonchalant about the picture of himself, and now to ordering me not to run away. I can't keep up with his emotions. Did he just order me not to run away? I guess it's better than locking me in my room.

I know Jordie said I'm the pet, but I still don't like being told what to do, but I'm smart enough not to argue about it right now.

"Go to your room we talk later." Jutte says as he walks away.

As I trudge back to my room, I notice something: there are no pictures on his wall. No artwork, or photographs. I expect to see at least a statue or something. Is it just him, or do the Mari not have pictures of any kind anywhere on this planet? That would explain why he was surprised by my drawing. Maybe they appreciate the beauty around them and don't try to capture it. How can entire species not appreciate art? I know Jordie mentioned it, but I thought he was exaggerating.

I contemplate this while I whittle in my room.

CHAPTER 21

I'm hungry, thirsty, and bored. I fell asleep shortly after being sentenced to my room. I don't know how long I've been out since there aren't any windows for me to see if it's day or night. When does Jutte sleep? *Does he sleep?*

I'm tired of waiting for him to come get me so I take it upon myself to go find him. I can't promise him that I won't run away again, because I'm still planning on returning to Earth, but at least we can work out a truce.

Do the Maris hold grudges? For how long?

He actually seemed more disappointed than mad. I didn't do it to hurt his feelings, I just want to go home.

Jutte is making more bags, so I sit on the floor near him and begin to work on a bag as well. I figure I can help with this. After about one row, my stomach loudly rumbles. Jutte looks up. "What that?" he asks.

"I'm hungry," I point to my stomach. "And thirsty too, please."

Jutte nods. I follow him to the other side of the room where he rummages around. I realize that I still need to explore the entire house. I guess the Mari don't have kitchens since they get nutrients from their surrounds rather than food.

This area is just a place consisting of different storage spaces. Open shelves hold odd-looking items, all too high for me to reach. A bench my size is under some lower shelves, still taller than me, but lower than the others.

In the far corner I notice one of his home-made bags on the floor. I walk over and unwrap it, peeking inside. I can't see what's in there, and I'm just about to reach inside when Jutte grabs me. "No, no go in there." He states and wraps the bag back up and sets it on the ground.

What the heck?

Will something in there cut me? Kill me? Be lots of fun? Now I really want to know what's in the bag. I stop when I'm distracted by food.

Jutte is holding a bowl and spoon for me to take. I tentatively look at it, what would he feed me? Thankfully it's the same stuff Jordie gave me during orientation.

I close my eyes and imagine banana pancakes. I take my first bite and moan happily at the most delicious pancakes ever. They are exactly like Luna, Arturo's mom, used to make; maybe she still does.

I look around but don't see a table. I wonder where I'm supposed to eat. Jutte points to the bench along the wall. I guess that's my where I eat. I'm good, I don't need a formal dining area.

"Can I have water?" I ask. I'm so thirsty that I just might shrivel up and fade away. He opens his mouth wide and digs among the shelf again. "Water." He proudly holds out a cup to me. I have to set my bowl down next to me on the bench and use two hands to grasp the huge cup he hands me. I mean really, I think there's about two gallons of water here. Did Jordie even tell him how much water humans can handle. Maybe this is supposed to last me all day. Which, on second thought, is probably a good thing.

I set the water on the other side of me and go back for the food. I settle on the bench. I love warm pancakes with warm syrup. About half way through the food I change what I want. I close my eyes and imagine fry jacks. Some people like toast with their breakfast, I like fry jacks. It's a simple food, just bread fried to a puffy crispness outside, soft and warm inside. I also imagine some fresh mixed fruit jam spread inside the fry jack.

What could go wrong after a breakfast like that?

I'm loving the pancakes so much that I almost miss Jutte's exit. He's on the couch at the far end of the room. I look to make sure he is distracted; he's busy weaving bags. I put down my bowl and sneak to the bag that he ordered me to stay away from. Glancing over my shoulder, I quietly unwrap the bag. I still can't see what's inside, but I'm a little afraid to reach my hand in. What if something bites me? Instead, I hold the bag as close to the ground as I can and slowly pour out the contents.

Really loud bells the size of golf balls roll out, clanging, and ringing, and going everywhere.

Crap, crap, crap. Who has bells like golf balls? I scurry around, trying to grab them and get them back in the bag before Jutte comes in. I'm not so lucky.

Jutte comes running in, which is quite scary with his stomping flipper feet. I freeze with a couple of bell-balls in hand. He stops, and with a sigh tells me "Marco, I said no." He helps me pick up the bell-balls.

Once the noise of them dies down, I ask "What is that?" That's one phrase I've perfected. Jutte says a weird word. I don't really care about the name; I want to know what they do and why they're so loud. He slowly says the name again. Okay, fine, whatever.

"Be good Marco," he says as he walks away.

I try to be good, but I'm bored. I decide to investigate the rest of the house.

Okay, so we walk into the house at the main living area. Then to the far other side of that is the area with my food, shelves, and a storage closet with a bag of loud bell-balls. Got it. The hall is between the two areas, so I casually make my way past Jutte and down the hall. If I act cool, he may not catch me snooping around.

I pass my room on the right and see a regular door on the left. The straight handle is above my head, but within reach. I pull it down and the door actually opens. I was half expecting it to be locked, or to stay closed for some weird reason. I quietly open the door a little way, just enough for me to peek inside. The light automatically comes on and I realize it's a simple hall closet. A large disc sits on the floor. I tap it with my foot and nothing happens. I look around and decide that I'll have to come back one day when Jutte is gone or asleep to explore this more.

I quietly close the door and continue down the hallway.

The next doorway is similar to mine. I walk around the S wall and into a huge - and I mean huge - room. How can this anthill of a house be so big? This must be Jutte's room. In the very center is a large, bright red box twice the size of mine. That must be his bed. I wonder how hard I have to hit it to make it open. I bet his bed is so big that I'd get stuck in there forever. I leave that for another day as well.

Jutte has one big open room with open shelves along the far wall. I guess when you don't have clothes or artwork, you need very little storage. Okay, that's enough of his room.

Leaving the room, I look back and forth. That's it, I'm out of rooms and other places to go.

So let me get this straight, there's the main room with the area at the end with my food and shelves. Then down the hall is my room, a hall closet, and Jutte's room.

That's kind of uneventful.

I hear Jutte call me. "Marco. Marco where you?"

I scoot back into the main area before he knows I was snooping.

"There Marco. You want to go to swimming?" Jutte excitedly asks. I don't catch on right away that he's talking like a human asking his dog if he wants to go for a walk.

"Yes, I want to go to swimming." I run to my room to get my mask and fins. I'm waiting by the door when Jutte arrives with his bag strapped to his front.

When he opens the door, I race out first, stopping only to slip my fins on beside the water. I'm so busy getting my mask on that I don't see what grabs me.

I'm jerked sideways by my arm and thrown to the ground. I jump up, kicking off my flippers, and am ready to fight whatever is attacking me.

It's the guy from the market who was yelling at me.

I know for a fact that I'm allowed on this beach. So, I guess my question earlier about whether Mari hold grudges has been answered. This guy is definitely still mad at me.

He grabs me and pulls me into the water. Oh, this is not good. I start yelling "Help! Jutte help!" over and over. Where is Jutte? He was right behind me.

"Help!" I yell one more time before taking a deep breath and holding it as I'm pulled underwater. The guy has a strong hold on my arm. I'm kicking and hitting him, but don't take the chance of biting him since I'm underwater. He easily holds me while pulling me down deeper. He's drags me like I'm a rag doll.

I've lost my mask somewhere, but I open my eyes anyways. I need to see what's happening and where he's taking me.

I'm hitting and kicking while he is pulling me down. My ears pop and it's getting darker and harder to see. I try twisting away, but he's got a vice grip on me. This is as bad as my dreams of drowning. Is this how I'm meant to die, in the water?

I want to breathe.

I need to breathe.

My lungs are burning

He's dragging me towards a dome. Crap, is he petnapping me?

We get to the base of the dome; he pushes a button to open the outside door. He shoves me in.

Then nothing happens.

I turn around and see him fighting with Jutte.

Jutte found me!

I need to breathe.

My lungs have reached their exploding point, my brain is screaming to open my mouth and take a breath. Logically I know I'm underwater and can't inhale, but self-preserving panic believes otherwise.

I want to watch, to see what happens, but I can't. I swim towards the side of the door and find the button to close the outer entrance. I don't even wait for it to finish closing and I'm heading to the inner door, searching for the next button to let the water out.

My chest hurts from lack of air and my vision is growing dark around the edges. I'm going to pass out. I keep fumbling, smacking randomly at the wall, hoping I'll hit the button.

I keep trying, but I'm moving slower.

And slower.

Finally, my hand presses a wall where it moves, and the water begins to drain.

I can barely kick upwards and my head breaks the surface.

I gasp for air.

And pass out.

CHAPTER 22

"Wake up Marco. Open Eyes"

Why is Grandfather waking me so early in the morning? I ignore him, pretending I'm still asleep. Maybe he'll give up and go away.

"Marco good. Wake up." He just keeps trying to wake me. I try to open my eyes, but can't manage the chore. As I become more coherent, I notice two things: that's not Grandfather's voice, and two, my arm and throat hurt.

I moan, turning my head, but still not able to open my eyes. I would much rather go back to sleep, but that doesn't seem likely. For some reason, whoever is talking to me is making sure I get up.

I feel tapping on my chest. "Marco good. Open eyes. Hello." Wait, they're not even speaking English. How is it that I know what they are saying? Did I hit my head and am going to wake up speaking twelve different languages? What if I don't know who I am, what if I have… what's that word where you forget everything. Crud, I must have it if I can't remember the word for it.

"Hello. Open eyes." They keep trying, and I swear I must have swallowed razor blades.

"Water?" I croak out.

Someone helps me sit up and places a cup to my lips. I gulp the water like I've trekked through a desert and came across an oasis. I drink too fast and begin a coughing fit so bad that it tears apart my throat even more.

My eyes finally comply. A huge blue alien face hovers inches from my nose, with his mouth wide open.

I shriek and attempt to jump backwards, but only push my head a short distance back into a pillow.

My new life and the kidnapping come back in one swoosh. It's Jutte, I know him.

Jutte startles backwards, holding all four hands up. I guess that is to show he means well.

"Where am I? What happened? More water." I don't realize I spoke these thoughts out loud until Jutte holds a cup to my lips, offering water.

I take another swig, grateful for the way it soothes my throat. After three more gulps, I nod and push the huge mug away.

"What happened?" I ask again.

"Tratrvo took you. He... hurt you. I see. I come to Marco." Jutte is using easy words to talk to me. Thank you, because I doubt English would make sense at this time. But it comes back, the mean guy grabbed me and dragged me underwater.

Jutte rescued me.

He saved my life. "Thank you." I squeak, holding back my emotions.

"It's okay." He taps my chest with a finger on his small hand, and helps me sit up. I'm in a different bed; not my Earth bed or even my Oonala bed. I suppose he waited to bring me to the surface until I'm conscious. I look around at the blue room and see I'm on a body-size pillow with another behind me, propping me up.

"Why he mean to me?" I ask, seriously confused.

Jutte sighs. "He mad at me. He is mean. Now he hurt Marco to be mean to Jutte."

But why?

"When ready, we go home." Jutte nods and gets up.

I look around. Are all buildings on this planet blue inside? I look closer and realize that rather than blue, the walls are clear, and we're still underwater. Man, I wish my bedroom was like this. Sleeping with the fish would take on a whole new meaning. (Yeah, Grandfather and I liked mob movies.) A creature swims to the glass, peering at us, and continues on his way. Yeah, I would definitely like this as my room.

I'm not sure I can hold my breath right now, so I close my eyes instead. I could use a nap after that.

"Jutte, why he not like you?"

"Well," Jutte begins, "long time ago Jutte and him friends." I nod, keeping my eyes closed, but ready to hear this story.

"When children we lived close. I know Tratrvo long time. As children we swim and we work. Long time ago we good friends. We catch fish and let go, we hold on to end of the belerrota, it a very big mean fish, we hold onto them for fun. I know his family, he know my family. Long time ago we good friends.

"We got older and I move here. I not see him much, but happy when we talk. We still friends. I start making bags but he want the money. He said he think to make bags. He no work, but want money.

"I say no. I work and make bags. My money. He not nice anymore, and I stay away. Now, he want to stop Jutte. He say bags are bad and water in. Shop owners not buy bags, but I show them my bags are good. Because I say, Tratrvo not like me. Now they buy from me again. Tratrvo mad. He hurt Marco to hurt Jutte. Marco good. Tratrvo no hurt. Please no run away, Tratrvo hurt Marco. No run away, okay?"

Wow, it's sad to think that they were once good friends and the one guy grew up mean. I wonder why some people, or Mari, are like that?

Does Jutte think I was running away from him again? "I not run." I open my eyes and tell him. "I happy and go to water, not run away. Tratrvo grab me from behind. He take me underwater. I fight. He hold me hard."

Jutte holds out his enormous fist, and I bump it. "Marco good. Marco fight. I see. I happy Marco good."

Yeah, you and me both, alien man.

I stand up, stretch, notice the bruise on my arm, and turn to Jutte. "No market today." I tell him.

He nods and guides me to the door.

It's time to go home.

CHAPTER 23

Time passes; several days I'm sure, maybe even weeks? The days blend together, especially with so little nighttime. I sleep when I want, which is great, and Jutte has me on a flexible feeding schedule dinner.

I'm staying close to Jutte. I mean, being kidnapped and almost killed by an angry alien made me rethink about going off on my own. On a good note, I can make the bags almost as good as Jutte now. And my language skills are about ten times better. I mean, mostly I've just been sitting around listening to Jutte talk, so it's kind of hard not to get better.

We go together to the woods behind the house to gather palm fronds and sap. The air outside feels good, but I stay close to Jutte. No reason to get petnapped again.

"You want to go to market today?" Jutte asks.

You know what? Yes, I do. It's time to stop hiding and being afraid. I am fully recovered and ready to swim again. "Yes, let's go to market." I smile at Jutte who is smiling in his big, open-mouth way. We go inside to put away the bags we're working on.

Jutte taps me on the chest. "For you." he says, holding out a small bag, the perfect size for me to carry.

"You made this for me? Thank you so much." I'm not on the verge of tears or anything, but I am touched. It's odd to receive a gift from an alien. I look closely at the bag's awesome craftsmanship, and I know the time he took to make it. I nod and smile at him. Jutte taps me on the chest again with one finger and walks away to ready.

The bag is much smaller than the others he makes. But a big one could probably drag me to the bottom of the ocean.

I go into my room to change into my swim trunks. It's now that I realize that I've lost my mask. It's a bummer, but not earth-shattering - or would I say it's not Oonala-shattering? I liked being able to see clearly underwater, but I'll still be able to somewhat see.

As I'm packing, Jutte walks in. "What happened?" he gasps. I jump up, ready to fight whatever has upset him. I turn in circles trying to figure out what startled him. Everything looks fine.

"What?" I ask, truly confused.

"Your room, what happened here?" I can't tell if he is terrified or disgusted.

My room's a little messy, but not horrible. "It's my room, nothing happened; I just might need to pick up a little. It's okay"

"Ugh, it's dirty and smells bad." He shakes his head, waving all four hands around. I still don't get what he's upset about.

"Fine, I'll clean it when we get back." I tell him, gathering my swim trunks and flippers.

"No, clean first, market later. You clean it now. I wash your clothes; you pick up and close your bed. Always close your bed. Every time you wake up, close your bed."

"What? I never make my bed every day. Why bother when I'm just going to get back in it? No one sees my room but me. What does it matter?" This is just too much. I start picking up items and throwing them in the closet, as he is picking up my clothes. I swear, he would have a clothespin on his nose if he could.

"Always keep your room clean and bed closed. Those are the rules."

"I have rules?" What will it be next, no jumping on the tables and stay off the couch? Jutte is still gathering my clothes from the floor.

"Whatever." I tell him as I "pick up" my room. Jutte leaves with an armload of clothes, and I'm happy he is gone. It's a good thing he didn't look in the bathroom.

I reach behind the bed and press the button, causing it to fold closed. *There, bed is closed; happy now?* I still don't get the importance of it all needing to be clean.

I toss the last flip flop in the closet, close the door, and look around. The room is clean and pretty well organized again. Good enough. I grab my new bag, place a towel in it, tuck my flippers under my arm, and head to the main room.

Jutte is there, nearly finished packing all the bags into one. I haven't figured out how many he sells yet, but it seems to be a regular stream of work.

Outside, this time I walk with him. He waits while I put on my flippers. I look up to see him holding another gift for me.

"My mask! Where did you find it?" I grab it from his hand, happily inspecting it. I couldn't imagine he would have ever found another.

"After Tratrvo, another Mari found it and brought it to me. I forgot to tell you earlier that I had it. I know it helps you." Jutte shrugs and hands it to me, then straps his bag to his chest.

"Thank you, this means a lot to me." I tell him. He nods and stands up straight, waiting for me to finish getting ready.

I put on my fins and mask, swing my bag over my shoulders, and strap it to me like my backpack.

"No. It goes on the front, like this." Jutte pats his bag.

"Yeah, I know, but I'm more comfortable with a bag on my back. So, if it's okay with you, I'll wear it like this." I tell him as we walk into the water.

"It must go on the front for it to work right." Jutte seems adamant on this. *This guy is sure set in his ways.* I know it's not a big deal and I should just slide it around on my front, but after he made a big deal about my room, I want to stand my ground. "Just let me try it this one time. It's my bag and I will make sure it stays put."

Jutte huffs and snorts as he wades into the water. All right! I won that one and the bag stays on my back. I'm right behind him. I turn around swim backwards. When it's time to dive I flip around and expertly kick downward towards the market place.

Holy Neptune, I can't swim down.

The drag on the bag is so much that I'm only about half way

down and am starting to float upwards. I'm kicking furiously, and running out of breath way before I should.

Jutte sees me struggling and grabs me with one of his smaller hands. With his large fin-hands and feet, he gives a couple of good kicks we are at the doors.

I go in first and head towards the other button. Once the first door is fully closed, I drain the water and open the second door.

I sit down to take off my bag and hand my mask and fins to Jutte to put in his bag. He remains standing. "The bag goes on the front," is all he says. He's right, the drag was too much for me.

I don't want to give him the satisfaction of actually telling him he is right, so I shrug. "Whatever."

I stand up and let him lead the way into the market. This place is so cool. I look up as a school of fish swim by - at least I assume they're fish. While long like eels, they have fins and move their tails up and down to swim.

I'm distracted by a shop that displays black and white containers. They wouldn't hold food since the Mari don't eat; they are too small to hold their belongings and carry around like purses. Now I'm curious about what they're for.

"Marco." Jutte calls. He is a store ahead of me, so I trot to catch up. I check the crowd around me to make sure Tratrvo isn't around. The coast is clear for now.

We turn into the same store we visited that first day. "Hello. I hope the water is good to you today." The same lady greets us. She then turns to me with her mouth open. I smile back and say the greeting to her.

She stands up in surprise, and looks at Jutte. He simply nods, but lets me handle the situation. "Thank you, I hope the same for you." She replies. At least she isn't talking baby talk to me, or in a loud voice. Why do people talk louder if they think you speak a different language? It's not like yelling will help decipher the words.

I pay attention this time as she and Jutte negotiate the transaction. She inspects the bags and counts the sizes of each. "Six large bags and six small bags. That's twenty-four marigees.

I'll be right back." Jutte nods and we wait for her to return.

"How much do you get for each bag?" I ask Jutte. "I get three marigees for large bags and one marigee for small ones. The large ones are used more often, so I normally make more of the big ones, but I noticed she was low on the small ones last time we were here." I look around for his bags. "Over here." He points to the other side of the shop. Sure enough, the store displays a group of large bags for sale with only two small bags left.

"How many do you sell?" I'm curious about this business.

Jutte is already looking at something else. He shrugs. "It depends." Okay, I'll just have to keep track of sales on my own. I know about business from when I sold fish and lobsters to local restaurants back on my island.

The shop owner returns and hands Jutte something. I try standing on my tip toes to peer into his hand. To get his attention, I tap his leg. He bends down and opens his fist to show me. "These are marigees." He tells me.

Okay! The small, loud bell-balls, just like the ones I poured out of the bag that day. Well, now I know what those are. No wonder he was concerned about them, money was rolling around everywhere.

Jutte tucks them into his bag and leads me out of the store. We walk about a block to the next store. The owner guy greets Jutte and turns to me. He gives me a slight up-nod. I like that the shopkeepers acknowledge me, even if I am a pet.

Jutte pulls more bags from his big one and lays them on the table. The Mari guy counts out five large bags only - no small ones. I do the math in my head and know he should give us fifteen marigees. This guy makes a bit more of a production, inspecting each bag before saying anything. "They look good, as always. That's fifteen marigees for you." If they are always made well, why does he insist on inspecting them? I'm not so sure about this guy.

Jutte is unflustered by the ordeal and waits for the owner to return. I look around and spot the bags in the back of the store, half hidden by other items.

"If he put your bags out front, he might sell more." I say to Jutte.

"Wait." He tells me. I get he doesn't want to say anything in front of the guy, but maybe the owner should hear this. Maybe I should tell the shop owner. "Stay quiet." Jutte whispers. I see how serious he is. Fine; whatever.

The guy comes back and pays Jutte. They chat while I look around the shop. I stop to touch something that looks similar to a silk scarf, except when I reach out for it, it moves away on its own.

I snatch my hand back, wondering if that really just happened, or if I'm seeing things. I tentatively reach once more, and the scarf eases out of reach again. I try throwing my hand out fast, and it matches me, moving away fast.

What the heck is this?

I move to its other side. Am I behind it? Maybe it won't see me coming from here. I reach out to snatch it, and it beats me at the game and darts out of reach. I try to touch it twice more when Jutte calls me. "Marco, time to go."

I hurry up to him. "You've got to see this cool scarf-thing. I think it's alive. Come look." I run back before I even finish my sentence. I point and try to touch it as Jutte comes up behind me. "Watch, I can't touch it." I show him how it moves each time I reach for it.

Jutte opens his mouth, smiling. "You found a corobaa. Some like to wear it around their head to help sleep. It is programmed for the individual, and will move around to keep the eyes and head covered as the individual moves and turns in their sleep, but it will never cover their mouth. If it is not programmed for you, you cannot touch it."

"That is so awesome!" I say in English. Jutte gets the gist of what I'm saying and nods.

The shop man stops to talk with us. "The human found the corobaas. Perhaps he needs one?" He asks Jutte. Jutte smiles and tells the man no.

Well, I'm thinking I need one.

The guy shrugs and gives me a look like he tried for me. Jutte leads me out of the shop.

"Hey Jutte." I get his attention since he is walking so fast. He stops and waits for me to catch up. "Why does he have the bags way in the back of the shop. Should they be out front like the other store? Is he not as nice?"

Jutte pulls me to the side of the market place, out of the traffic of other aliens. "He is very nice. The other shop sells more, so he doesn't need as many. But he is fair with marigees and happy to restock when they run low."

Okay, I guess the guy is okay then. It's probably a good thing that I stayed calm and quiet. I have to remember to not talk too much in case I hurt Jutte's business.

"Are you ready to go home now?" he asks?

"Not really, can we look around?" This place is too cool to leave so soon.

"Yes, I will show you around." Jutte steps back into the walkway and heads in the opposite direction from the exit door. I suppose the market has other doors to the outside, but I only know the one. What would happen if one day I go out the wrong door? Where would I end up? I guess it's like getting lost on Earth: no big deal, you simply find your way home.

If that scarf thing is any indication, I bet these aliens have lots of cool gadgets here. I'm ready to explore and see them all.

CHAPTER 24

It's still weird seeing so many aliens walking around like normal. There are only the Mari people here in the market; I'm the only human, and I think the only pet. I would think pets are allowed since I'm here, but then again, Tratrvo was yelling about pets not allowed. Do Mari have other pets? What in the world would they be?

"Hey Jutte, do the Maris keep pets other than humans?" Now that this idea in my head I can't seem to let it go. Jutte doesn't miss a beat. "Yes, we have several species of pets, but you are special. Only a few have humans, and even fewer of those get to work with Jordie. You and I both are lucky."

So I've been told. Funny, I've only heard Jordie tell me how great he is. It's freaky coming from someone else.

Lagging behind Jutte, and no longer quite so happy, I dodge the huge Mari flipper feet of a guy who is looking up at the dome. Out of shear habit, I look up.

¡Dios Mio! What is that? I stop, gaping upward, not at all concerned about being stepped on. This creature is exactly what I imagine a dragon would look like. Flying above me and everything. Each scale is the size of half my body, and they sparkle in the light as he moves. He's shades of blue, but stands out in the water. I guess he doesn't need to be camouflaged since nothing is going to mess with him anyways.. And the claws, the claws scare me, even looking at them through the dome. I would hate to meet them up close and personal. It's leisurely gliding by, as if it doesn't have a care in the world. And I suppose it doesn't, it's probably at the top of every food chain.

Jutte notices that I've stopped and comes back to my side. He stands in silence, gawking as well. I wouldn't look away, even if I could.

I finally believe in aliens only to find out that dragons are real too.

Jutte speaks about the dragon reverently. "We call him Shamo Loonolo, it means The Old One. No one knows how old he is, but everyone knows stories told by their elders."

"He's amazing." I whisper.

In one flip of the tail, the dragon swims away. Noise returns to the market. It seems as if everyone was entranced watching him go by, and now have returned to their normal routines.

We walk past shop after shop of merchandise. What do the Mari need to buy if they don't eat or wear clothes? "What is all this stuff?" I ask, sweeping my arm past several shops.

"Mainly items for our homes, for swimming, and a occasionally for entertainment." He stops in front of one shop and points to an object about the size of a basketball. "That is a toy for young ones to play with in the water. You never know if it's going to float or sink, so you have to move fast once it's thrown."

Well now, that sounds like fun even for me, and I'm not a child. "Can we get one?" Jutte's on the move again and doesn't slow down at my request.

"Not today," is all he says without glancing at the toy again.

We meander through the market, with Jutte pointing out and explaining all sorts of items. My head is beginning to hurt from so much that is new and different. "I'm ready to go back to the house now." I tell him, wishing I was already in bed.

"Okay, we are near our exit door. We pass by the second shop that buys our bags. The guy is standing near the walkway, trying to draw people into his store. We give each other a polite nod as I pass by. I'm cool with him again.

Stepping through the inner door, Jutte reaches up to press the button as I put on my mask. I make sure to strap the bag on my front this time. Jutte doesn't say anything, but hands me my flippers as the water floods the room. Once it's almost full, I take one last, big breath, and press the button to the outer door.

Jutte lets me take the lead this time. I show confidence that I don't actually have. I hope I'm swimming at the correct angle - upwards and to the left. I suppose the worst that could happen is that we have to swim on the surface for a longer distance. Feeling the current of Jutte's paddles behind me, I don't need to turn to know that he is there.

We break the surface. I push my mask onto my forehead and look around. Hey, pretty good, we aren't as close to the shore as we are when Jutte leads, but we are fairly close. I turn and grin at Jutte, he nods and opens his mouth. He taps me on my chest and makes his way towards land. I proudly follow.

I can vividly imagine the softness of my bed. I drop my bag, mask, and flippers at the door and head to my room. "Marco." Jutte stops me. "Pick up your things and put them away, please."

All I want to do is sleep. "I'm so tired, I'll get them when I wake up." I mumble as I turn towards my room again.

"No, not later. They belong in your room, take them with you now." He insists.

Really! What is his problem with my things? He has the entire house and I have a couple small things by the door. I storm back and snatch my belongings off the floor. "Thank you." He says.

Whatever.

I drop my armful in my middle of the room and smack my bed to make it open. See, I wouldn't have to do that if I didn't have to make my bed earlier. I drop into the soft cushion, barely able to think straight. This is when it hits me... my bed lets me sink into it only about half way down, and I float there.

My bed is neutrally buoyant.

If you live near the water, you know that as you take a big breath you rise to the surface, and as you let it all out you sink. Being neutrally buoyant is when you breath slowly and barely move up or down. No wonder I sleep so well here, I'm actually floating.

~ ~ ~

I can't breathe. Water is everywhere, and I fight to figure out which way is up. I look for light; I try to spot bubbles rising. My lungs are ready to burst, but the net will not release its death grip on me. I fling the net around, looking for an end, a hole, anything that will allow me to swim to the surface. Blackness is creeping in from the sides, and my vision fades. This is it; this is how I die, caught in my own fishing net.

I snap awake, sitting up and wiping the sweat from my head. I hate that I'm still having this same dream.

I stumble out of my room to find Jutte making bags. Doesn't he have other hobbies? Several that have sap on them and are laid out to dry. My stomach grumbles really loud. Loud enough that Jutte looks up in amusement. "One moment and I will get you some food." He finishes applying sap to a smaller sized bag.

Having to wait for my food really sucks. I would rather just grab it as I need it. I work on my patience and sit with Jutte, watching him apply the sap in full, even strokes. Most of the bag is dry, and I assume I will have to wait for him to coat the entire bag. Now I know how dogs feel waiting for their meals.

I find the wood and knife I stashed earlier and go to work on the eagle ray. I'm almost done carving it but I wish I had sandpaper to smooth and something to seal it with once I'm finished. I wonder if Jutte's sealant would work or is it too sticky?

I'm lost in carving the tail of the ray that I jump a bit when my stomach rumbles again. Jutte must have forgotten as well, because he glances up, surprised that I'm still here. "Okay, let's get you some food." He stands and stretches. *I'm with ya man.*

I don't know how he prepares my food, but I use this time to decide what I'm hungry for.

Everything.

Before, I have imagined only one dish at a time, but I'm too hungry to choose just one. So I picture a full table of fish, lobster, and scallops with rice and beans on the side. My stomach aches just thinking of how yummy this will be. I grab my cup from the shelf and hold it up to Jutte to fill with water.

"Hey Jutte, do you think we can set something up so I can get my own water?" I drink a lot of water and want to be able to get it on my own. The same with food, but I better not push my luck.

Jutte pauses, tilting his head to one side. "We will have to find something small enough for you to handle" He says, looking around.

But I'm still starving. "We can do it later." I tell him. There is no need to interrupt him from getting my food.

"Yes, that's a good idea. I will figure out something for you."

I dig into the bowl of food before he has fully let go. I picture butter dripping down my chin. It works, I can taste everything all at once; this gives me more food ideas. All too soon, I scrape the spoon across the bottom of the bowl, trying to get every last bit. I'm not full, but at least I'm not starving anymore.

Jutte's already back in his spot on the couch. I set my bowl on the shelf and walk back into the other room, sitting down to whittle more while he continues to work on his bags.

"I liked talking with the shop owners." I start the conversation. "I'm learning what you do." It's pretty much the same as my business. "On Earth, I would catch food and sell it to shop owners. They would then sell it to customers too."

Jutte's hands stop mid-air and he stares at me.

What? What did I say?

"You had to catch food? It was not prepared for you?"

"Well, some was already prepared for us, but for really good food, I would have to catch it. The animals in the water, that is what I would catch and eat."

This surprises Jutte even more. "You eat water animals?" He recoils in shock. "Just grab it and eat it?" He shudders.

"Well, no, I would properly prepare it before eating it." Humans aren't complete animals. I don't know how to explain cooking and grilling fish, so I leave the details out.

He's still shocked and unsure about my eating habits. But he misses my point. "But like you, I would sell my products to shop owners."

"See, Jordie did good at choosing you as my pet." Jutte nods. Never mind. That kind of ruins the moment.

CHAPTER 25

"What I'm trying to say is that I enjoyed being with you when you sold your bags, and maybe I can help you make and sell them. What do you think?" All my life, I've worked with business owners and sold them what I have.

Jutte keeps working on his bag. I suppose it would be weird to have a pet helping with your livelihood, but, I'm no ordinary pet.

I hold up my eagle ray carving and contemplate what to do next. The body is done, it's balanced well on a small stick on a stand, the tail is near perfect, and the dots are carved all over. All I need to do now sand it and find a way to varnish or seal it. "What do you think?" I hold up the ray.

"What is it?" He asks as he squints and comes closer." It's a water animal, it swims on the bottom like this." I say as I glide the ray across the floor.

"Do you eat it?" He takes the ray from me for a closer inspection.

"Some people eat rays, but I don't. These are cool to watch swim by." I take the ray back and turn it over in my hands, wishing I had sand paper. How would I have known to toss sand paper in my bag that morning I was kidnapped?

"Do you think the beach sand would help smooth this out?" I mumble to myself

Jutte stands up. "Let's go try it." He heads for the door. I jump up and chase after him. I didn't know he heard me, much less would go right now to try.

Jutte strides out the door without a second thought. I, on the other hand, still remember being taken by the mean alien, and am a bit more hesitant. I run to catch up with Jutte and stay close to him while I look back, forth, and all around. Tratrvo isn't going to jump me twice.

On shore, I bend down and pick up a handful of sand. I start rubbing over my carving, but I find it awkward trying to balance it all. I sit down to steady the ray in my lap while I rub the sand on it. I try rubbing it all over, then I focus on just one spot, not sure which will work better.

This just might work.

I keep sanding my statue, running my fingers over it to feel if it's becoming smooth. I'm so lost in my work that I forget Jutte is there until he bends down, putting his face in my line of sight.

Holy crap! I jump back, dropping the ray.

"Sorry." Jutte says with his mouth open.

Yeah, real funny you big alien.

Jutte taps my chest. "Is it working?"

"I think so. Does it feel smooth to you?" I hold the ray up and Jutte takes it from me, stands up tall, holding it in his large hand and gently rubs it with a finger from his small hand.

"I think this is good." He hands it back to me. Does good mean smooth? I don't understand his answer. I wipe the sand off my hands and feel it again. It's not as smooth as I get them back on Earth, but it's getting better.

As I work on the ray Jutte wanders on the beach; not necessarily looking for anything, just looking around. I get it, there were many times when I needed to simply walk the beach and clear my head.

I look up and see JuJa straight above me - no wonder I'm so hot. I stand to stretch, and spot Jutte far down the beach. So far that he looks human size.

I try to stay calm. It's cool, Tratrvo is nowhere around. I spin in a circle to make sure. I'm okay. I start trotting to catch up with Jutte.

Checking the water, glancing behind me, still no signs of danger. "Jutte." I call out to him, trying to get his attention.

He doesn't hear me.

I get closer and try again. "Jutte." I holler, but with a semicontrolled voice.

This time he hears me and turns around. He waits while I catch up to him.

"Are you done?" he asks while looking at my carving.

"Yeah, I think so." I hold the ray up for inspection. He takes it from me, rubbing his finger along the back of the ray.

"Very interesting." He says and hands it back to me.

I like how it has turned out. I nod to myself and take one more look around.

"Then we can go home." Jutte states and turns back to the house. Huh, okay, I guess we're going home. It's just too weird not having a say in choices. What if I wanted to stay outside longer? I don't, but what if I did? Could I ask him to let me stay longer? What if he said no?

Whatever, I look at my carving and return to the house with him.

As soon as we walk in the door I head to my room. I gently place the ray on my desk, double checking its balance; I don't want it to tip over and break. Moving the dolphin a bit closer, I inspect them both.

Jutte has followed me into my room. "You are very careful with that. You put that away but leave your room a mess. Why do you do that?"

Are we on this again? I'm guessing my answer of: '*Because I care about my carvings. Keeping my room clean isn't important.*' would go over poorly. So, I don't answer. I totally understand why cats sometimes ignore their owners. I have more respect for cats now than I did on Earth.

He comes over to look at the dolphin closer. "This are new, I like it." I wonder if means new because he has never seen anything like it. I'm still amazed that they don't have art on Oonala.

"I'm fresh out of wood. I'm not sure what to do once these are done." I say as I glide my fingers over the dolphin.

Jutte picks up the ray and studies it more. "This touches the same as the linjali tree." He tells me as he sets it back down.

What? I can use the wood here? "What's a linjali tree? Is it close by? Can we try?" I grab the ray and hold it up to make sure we are talking about the same material. "Like, I can make animals from the linjali tree?" I start bouncing up and down on my toes. It will be amazing if I can keep whittling. "Can we look now?" I ask.

"No, not now. Maybe tomorrow. I have to make bags now. The linjali tree is the one shape like a square. You make it that one day." And with that, he leaves.

I never thought to touch the trees to see if they feel familiar. That would be great if I can carve from their branches.

This sucks. I was always bad at waiting. If Grandfather bought me a Christmas present early, I would find and secretly open it. I had to know what it was. My motto is: *why wait*? Well, maybe not my motto, but I like it.

How long do I have to wait? Will we go today or tomorrow? What if he forgets?

I take a deep breath. *I can wait. I can wait*; I keep repeating to myself. Nope, I can't wait.

I go into the main room. Jutte is lost in making bags. I get it and hate to interrupt someone busy working, so I try to be patient. I think it's all of ten seconds before I'm rocking back and forth and humming.

I miss music. Jutte either doesn't notice me, or is ignoring me.

I open my mouth to speak when there is banging on the door. Jutte somehow hears that, but doesn't acknowledge me humming.

He walks to the door with me trotting behind him. Who would come to his door? The Mari don't eat, so it's not a pizza delivery guy. There is no Amazon, so it's not going to be a box of stuff. I stand behind his legs when he opens the door.

I see the spaceship in the distance before I see him.

It's Jordie.

CHAPTER 26

"Jordie? What are you doing here?" I step out from behind Jutte's legs. Jutte greets Jordie as well, inviting him inside.

Okay, this is weird, Jutte is speaking Mari language and Jordie is talking in English, or whatever language he speaks; either way, I'm hearing English and it seems odd now. I wonder if I'll start understanding Jordie in Mari. I hate to think that one day I might forget English.

I snap back to the conversation to hear Jordie talking. "Yes, I am here to see how you and Marco are getting along. I hope all is well and you two are getting to know each other."

I'm curious to see what Jutte thinks of us.

"Oh yes, things are going well. Marco has tried to run away only one time, and other than his inability to keep his room clean, we are getting along very well."

Narc.

Jutte continues. "I am very happy with Marco. He is learning the language and we are learning from each other. I hope he is happy here as well."

I'm thinking he could have started with that. He didn't need to tell on me right away. Maybe I'll tell how we haven't figured out a set food schedule yet and how I don't have my own cup for water. I wonder if Jordie knows about Tratrvo kidnapping me.

I look up to see both Jutte and Jordie watching me. What? What did I miss?

"I'm sorry, what did you say?" I'm unsure about who to ask. I look back and forth between both of them.

"I wanted to know how you are doing." Jordie asks.

"It's going good. I help Jutte make bags. Did you know he

makes bags and sells them to the stores? I was trying to tell him it's similar to what I did on Earth; catch and sell fish. I doubt he understands the correlation. I actually talked to some of Jutte's store owners, and know how much money he gets for each bag. The market is so cool -we can swim down to it. I have no problem with the swimming, I can hold my breath long enough to get down there. I know how to open both outer and inner doors. And I saw a dragon! That was amazing, I didn't know dragons really existed, much less that they traveled underwater. Did you know they don't have art here? I showed Jutte my drawings and he has never seen anything like that. How does an entire species not know about pictures? I showed him my carvings too, I have a dolphin and an eagle ray. Oh, and I got kidnapped and almost killed."

I guess I have a lot to say.

Jutte's head is tilted, I didn't realize I was reverting to English. Jordie translates it all for Jutte, catching him up on what I said. Neither one of them has ever heard me say so much. Jutte's mouth is happily open, Jordie seems unfazed by my ramblings; but then again, Jordie rarely changes his expression.

Jordie takes control. "You have had a lot happen already. Let's start with the trouble with the other Mari. Marco, please speak in Mari as much as possible so we can all understand each other. I was made aware of the incident, but I would like to hear about it from both of you."

I say as much as I can in Mari. "Okay, we were going to swim. I ran outside to get my flippers on and wait for Jutte. I wasn't trying to escape." I slant my eyes to Jutte. "I was on the beach, right along the water, when out of nowhere this guy grabbed me and pulled me under water. Jutte was still inside the house and didn't see me get taken. This guy pulled me down and past the market. We swam far away. I held my breath as long as I could before I passed out. I might have even died a little bit."

Jordie looks to Jutte for his version of the story. "Yes, that is true." Jutte starts. "I was still inside but I heard Marco call out. Outside, I saw the ripples in the water. I thought he tried to escape again. I swam after him only to see Tratrvo had ahold of Marco and was taking him to a back entrance into the market, one that no Mari uses. I was able to push Marco through the outer door while I fought with Tratrvo."

I jump in, "That's right, I forgot that I was searching for the button to close the door and drain the water. I finally found it but couldn't hold my breath any longer. That's when I died."

Jordie corrects me. "You did not die Marco, you simply lost consciousness."

Whatever, it felt like I died.

Jutte continues. "Tratrvo eventually gave up. Marco had closed the outer door and drained the water, so I went around to another door. By that time, a passerby saw Marco unconscious and picked him up, tapping and shaking him to wake him up. We do not know what to do if a human inhale too much water. Marco began to remove the water from his insides and was breathing, but he stayed asleep longer. But as you see, he is here now."

"Yes, he is here now." Jordie agrees. "I will teach you how to clear water from Marco's body if that happens again. We must discuss how to keep Marco safe from Tratrvo. Have you told the authorities about the incident?"

"No, not yet." Jutte answers. "I thought it might not happen again."

"And it might not, but let's tell them about it in case it does happen again. Then we show a history of Tratrvo intending to harm Marco." Jordie is tapping on his tablet. I wonder if it's the same one he had during orientation? Does he have a file on me? I wonder what all it says.

I chime in. "And we can tell them how he yelled at me and tried to grab me that first day at the market." I turn to Jordie. "He started yelling something like "no pets allowed" and grabbed my arm, yanking me from behind Jutte. I bit him, hard." I smile and nod.

Jordie turns to me. "I am glad you were not harmed, but you must not bite the Mari."

"But he grabbed me and started dragging me away." I interrupt.

"Yes, I understand. But Tratrvo may say you are aggressive, and biting him will prove his point. Jutte will protect you. Please, do not bite him or any other Mari."

"So, I'm just supposed to let him kidnap me?" I can't believe Jordie is actually saying this. I will always defend myself. Maybe I'll bite that alien every time I see him, just because I can. I'm not letting some freaky alien hurt me. What if Jutte isn't around, I'm just supposed to let this alien yank me around? Maybe try to kill me again?

"Marco, please sit down." Jordie catches my attention. I didn't realize I was pacing. I'm still stomping around. "Marco, listen to me." I stop and glare at Jordie, daring him to tell me again not to bite. "On Earth, what happens to aggressive dogs who bite humans?"

I stop.

"They're put down." I whisper. "Do you think they would actually put me down?"

"We don't know. Humans are still an exotic pet on Oonala, but you *are* a pet. Do not forget that."

Leave it to Jordie to bring me down.

I look at Jutte. I've started to think of him as a friend, not as his pet. To me, pet is just a word. But I guess Jutte sees me as beneath him. Maybe like a cute little being. Crud, just when I start to feel confident.

"So now what?" I ask, looking back and forth between them.

"Well, there is not much to do." Jordie says. "Jutte will always protect you. He will talk with the authorities, but mainly, you will go about your life with little change. Just be aware of your surroundings. If you see Tratrvo, notify Jutte, but stay away from him."

Jutte bends down to me. "Don't' worry, I will take care of you. Tratrvo is angry, but he would never get himself into trouble. But be careful, he will be mad at you."

"All right." Jordie gets my attention. "Let's talk about what you need."

What does he mean 'what I need'? I need to go home. I need to not be a pet anymore.

"How is your feeding schedule?" Jordie asks.

I shrug and look at Jutte. "We really don't have a set schedule. I tell him when I'm hungry and he feeds me. I sit on a bench, I kind of miss having a table, or something like a table. Oh, and we were just talking about him finding something small enough so I can have water whenever I want."

"You have a cup."

"Well, yeah, but I have to ask him to fill it all the time. Maybe with access to my own water, I can fill my cup whenever I want during the day.'

Jordie nods and taps away on his electronic pad.

"If you're making a list of things I need, I could also use some sand paper and sealant for my carvings. Here, I'll show you what I mean." I run to my room before Jordie can answer.

I come out with a carving in each hand. "See, I'm pretty well finished with the eagle ray, and am still working on the dolphin." I hold them out to Jordie so he can hold one. He doesn't. "Have you ever seen a dolphin or eagle ray?" I ask Jordie.

"I am aware of all animals on Earth. I don't need to see each one" Jordie says while tapping on his tablet. He finally looks up. "Those are very nice. I understand why you want to finish them."

Jutte has his mouth open wide, obviously enjoying looking at my carvings as I show them to Jordie.

"Yeah well, Jutte said the wood from the square trees are similar to this. Is that true, can I whittle that wood? If not, can you bring me wood from the gumbo limbo tree? And maybe another knife. I'll go get mine so you can take a picture of it and get me the right kind." I run back to my room, set the carvings down and grab my knife. "Here, I could use another of these." I hold it out for Jordie, assuming his tablet can take pictures.

"All right. A knife, sand paper, sealant, and a jug for water. Is there anything else you need?"

Oh, is this a never-ending question? There are a ton of things that would be cool to have. Of course, none come to mind at the moment.

"Not that I can think of." Crud, why can't I think of anything? I probably will as soon as he leaves.

"Well then, this was a productive visit. It is good to see you settling in, Marco." Jordie stands to leave.

"Wait!" I jump up. "How is everything? How are my parents? And Arturo? And Earth?" I ask while looking at my bare feet.

Jordie sits down again. "They are all good. They miss you, but they are doing well and are healthy. I do not keep up with them, just know that everything is fine."

I nod without looking up.

"I know this is hard for you, but this is your life now. You do understand that?" Jordie waits for my answer.

I finally respond. "Yes, I understand."

I look at Jutte. "You are really great, and I like it here okay, I just miss home."

Jutte simply nods and gives my chest a tap.

"All right then." Jordie stands. "I must be leaving. I will check on you from time to time. If you need anything, let Jutte know and he will help you."

Both Jutte and I nod as we walk Jordie to the door. I see the spaceship outside and momentarily debate whether I could steal it.

Jordie must sense my thoughts, because he steps in my line of sight. "No need to run away. This is your home now."

Jutte says his goodbyes. We watch as Jordie's ship silently takes off and disappears into the sky.

Jutte turns towards the house. I follow and push the door to close it behind me.

CHAPTER 27

"Can I try selling the bags to the store?" I ask Jutte as we are walking through the market. He glances at me sideways. "No really, I think I can do it. I know how much money we should receive for each bag, and I'm good with math, so I can figure the total. Please let me try?"

"Okay." He finally concedes. "You can help me sell the bags today. But I am going inside with you so the shop keepers know they are allowed to work with you."

Sweet, I can deal with that. I walk through the market ahead of Jutte, sidestepping the other Mari people, I haven't been stepped on yet, and I don't plan on starting today.

We come to the corner and I point left, looking at Jutte. He nods. Ha, I'm learning my way around the market with no problem. The Mari people still point and open their mouths wide as I walk by, but they don't crowd me and try to touch me, so I'm okay with this. It's cool, but also a bother being a unique animal on a planet of aliens.

We arrive at the first shop, the one with the lady. I turn to Jutte. "Okay, I'll talk with her, explain that I'm helping you by learning how to make and sell the bags."

Jutte nods and taps my chest. "You go in, I will be behind you." He hands me four large bags and four small ones. So, we get three marigees for each large bag and one marigee for each small bag. I do the math in my head. "She should pay us sixteen marigees."

"Very good. You learn fast." He says as I'm getting the bags in order. I want to tell him I'm not a complete idiot, but hold my tongue. Maybe Jordie told him that we are a smart species, but I guess you never really know until you deal with one of us.

The lady of the shop is standing with her back to me. "Hello." I begin. "I hope the water is good to you today."

With this she spins around with her mouth open. "Hello again, I wish you the same. Hello Jutte." She greets him.

I talk to get her attention back on me. "I am learning to help him. I try to make the bags, but he is still better. I am here to sell the bags today. I have four large bags and four small bags. Jutte said that is how many you need."

"He is a very wise Mari and always makes sure that I don't run out. Let me look at the bags, please."

I hold the large bags on one outstretched arm and the small ones on the other. I'm doing just fine with two arms and don't need four right now.

She bends down and takes them from me, laying them on the counter to inspect. "Did you make any of these?" she asks while looking closely at each one.

"No, I'm still learning. These are all Jutte's."

She stops inspecting each so closely. "All right then, four of each; do you know how much I should pay you?"

I know she is testing me so I don't hesitate with my answer. "Yes, it would be a total of sixteen marigees."

She stands up tall, smiling, and clearly impressed. "Very good; wait one moment please while I get the marigees."

While she is gone, I wander around the shop. There's a couple of items I see but have no idea what they are. I heft up a stone that reminds me of obsidian, a type of volcanic glass. It's larger than I can carry comfortably, but about the size of a laptop computer. Even if I wanted it, it wouldn't fit inside my bag. Plus, it would so totally drag me to the bottom of the ocean.

"That's called trahallah. It is believed to be an ancient stone." I jump and almost drop the rock. Crud, how do I not hear her with feet that big coming up behind me?

I set the stone back on the shelf and calmly turn; no reason to let her know she scared the bejesus out of me. "It's very nice."

When she hands me the marigees, I count them to make sure all sixteen are there. When satisfied, I smile. "Thank you very much. I have enjoyed working with you today."

"And I have enjoyed working with you." She turns to Jutte. "Thank you for the bags. As always, they are very well made."

I nod. I know Jutte takes pride in his work. It is how I felt when I saw tourists happily eating the fish I caught that morning.

Walking out of the store, I hold up the sixteen marigees for him. "Very well." He tells me. "She worked well with you." He puts the marigees in his bag. Why wouldn't she be all right working with me? I'm a good business man.

We are walking to the next store when I notice a Mari child. That must be the first one I've ever seen. I guess they have to be kids at some point, but I never thought about it. Can they automatically hold their breath a long time or do they have to practice? I don't realize I have stopped to stare until the kid notices me and stops too. He is taller than me, but not as big as Jutte.

"Ama, look! What is that?" He's yells and points at me. I assume it's his mom who picks him up and explains that I'm a human pet. Then quietly mutters that I should be on a leash.

Bite me.

I catch up with Jutte, who notices only now that I stopped walking. *Wow, I feel protected; he's not even watching me.*

I try control my anger at that stupid kid. Breathe in, two, three, four. Out, two, three, four. *Let it go*, I tell myself. I keep up with my deep breathing and start to feel better.

Jutte stops in front of the next store. "Do you want to talk with this shop owner as well?" he asks as he pulls more bags out of his carrying bag.

"Yes, please." Jutte hands me three large bags and two small ones. "Eleven marigees." I quickly tell him.

"Yes, eleven marigees. You are very smart."

I stand up tall, straighten my clothes, and head into the store with Jutte right behind me.

"Hello, I hope the water is good to you today." I say to the guy who runs this store. He looks at me, and then looks at Jutte.

I walk up to him and hold my hand out for a fist-bump. He grudgingly returns the gesture.

I speak in my professional voice. "Jutte has allowed me to work with you today. If you do not mind, I have five bags for you." I hold up the bags on my arms like I did in the other shop.

"How odd it is to deal with a pet." He asks without taking the bags.

I keep my voice calm. "I am helping him by learning to make the bags and sell them. Jutte made all of these bags." I hold my arms up a bit higher.

"Very well, let me see them." He brusquely takes the bags from me and inspects each one. He sets them on the counter. "Wait here." He mutters as he walks away. Yeah, like I'm leaving here without the marigees.

He comes back, holding out his hand. I take the marigees and quickly count them. Yep, eleven.

"Did you think I would not pay correctly" He scowls as he asks me.

Again, I choose to stay professional. "I would not want to give the wrong amount to Jutte. I want to do this properly." I tell him with a smile. I like a challenge.

The guy's shoulders relax a little. "Fine," he says more to Jutte than to me

"And thank you." I say as we fist-bump. I think I won that battle

I strut out of the store and hand the marigees to Jutte. "All eleven, I counted." I tell him. He recounts and puts them in his bag.

"You have done very well today. I am happy with you." Jutte stands over me with a smile.

Alien or not, it feels good to have someone proud of me.

All in all, I think today is a productive day.

CHAPTER 28

Sitting on the floor of the living room, I hold up my bag. "Done!" I say to Jutte, who is busy working on his own bags.

"You have completed a bag, very good." He takes the bag from my hands to inspect. "Very nice, the weaving is tight without folding over. You have sealed it as well. It is a bit heavy, but let's take it outside and see if it leaks."

This is it, the test. It took me about a week to completely weave and seal the bag, but I did it all on my own.

We walk to the shore's edge and Jutte pushes the closed bag underwater. I hold my breath. He swishes it back and forth and brings it up. He first inspects the outside, finding it suitable, then unwraps it and looks inside. He reaches a small hand into the bag, feeling around for water.

"It seems very good. I do not feel any water." He smiles at me, holding the bag down for me to inspect. I double check the bag, inside and out. Dry as a desert, no water in sight. I let my breath out with a woosh, happy it passed the test.

Heck yeah!

We walk back to the house and I'm excited to start on another bag, but Jutte surprises me. "Let's go see if the square tree wood will work for you."

With Jordie visiting and me selling bags, I almost forgot about finding wood for my carvings. I start to drop the bag in the entry when I notice Jutte watching me. Fine. I go into the main room and place the bag in its correct spot with the others. I walk past him and out of the room, raising my eyebrows and cocking my head as I pass him. See, I'm not a complete slob.

Jutte disappears into a back room and comes out with a

weapon of sorts in his hands. Holy Neptune! What is that? We go around the back of the house and past the line of trees where he collects the sap, or sealant. Note to self: try the sealant on some of the square wood and see how it dries.

I follow him further into the woods, finally finding a square tree. It's a tree shaped like a square. I mean, that's just not right.

I reach out and touch the wood, feeling the bark and the strength of the branch. I pull, tug, and try to break a smaller branch with no luck; so, I step back and watch Jutte.

The weapon in his hand reminds me of a cross between a machete and an ax. It's thick like an ax, but long like a machete. Jutte swings one time and cleanly cuts away a large branch. I have got to get me one of those.

I heft the branch to eye level, it's heavier than I imagined. No wonder it didn't break. Once I strip off the bark, I see the reddish hue, reminding me of cedar. I smell it, nothing. Okay, it's not cedar.

I'm wishing I would have brought my knife with me. "Can you cut this smaller so I can bring it back to the house with us?"

Jutte takes it from me. I step back as he raises the machete-axe. It takes work for him to slice through it, so it's not soft, but maybe not too hard for me to carve.

He cuts me a piece about the size of my arm. Perfect. I prop it on my shoulder as we walk back to the house. I still don't think of the house as home yet, just a place where I stay.

With my knife, I clean away the remaining bark from the limb, hold it up, looking for what it could be. I twist it around until I can make out the outline of a lizard. When I was young, Grandfather and I would find animals in clouds, before he taught me how to find them in wood.

I get to work, cutting away layers in just the right spots until a distinct shape appears. Sometimes I know what I want to make, but usually the shape of the branch determines what I see.

Jutte walks into my room and I hold up the beginning of my carving. "This is working great; I think you're right that I can use this. Thanks."

"I am glad." Jutte says. "But you are making a mess; maybe you should work outside."

I hate to admit it, but he's right, I am making a mess. I stand up and brush my clothes clean, but now I'm not sure how to clean up what's on the floor. I look to Jutte.

"You go outside, I will clean this." He tells me as he walks out of my room. Sweet! He'll clean up after me. He doesn't have to tell me twice. I grab my work and make my way to the front door that Jutte propped open and keep walking all the way to the beach.

On the beach, I decide I don't want to sit in the hot sun, or rather both suns. I walk behind the house and sit down under a tall tree. I'm right, it's cooler and more comfortable here.

Turning the stick over in my hand, I think about carving a lizard, but other ideas are taking shape as well. Maybe I should carve a fish from this planet. I suppose it's hard to appreciate the carving of the eagle ray without having seen one. There is the eel fish, or maybe the eye fish; yes, that's the one, the eye fish, that's what I'll carve.

Sitting in the sand with my back against a tree almost feels familiar; like back home.

Almost.

Lost in my work, I almost don't hear Jutte calling me. "I'm back here." I holler back. Jutte comes around the house and finds me among the trees.

"You were gone. I was worried." Jutte tells me, his lips pressed closed.

I'm totally floored. "I was here the whole time. See, I've been working on this." I hold up the beginning of carvings to show him. "I didn't run away." I bitterly add.

"No, thankfully you didn't run away and Tratrvo didn't take you." He sighs.

Oh, yeah, I can see how both would be possible. My shoulders fall; "Yeah, okay. I should have told you I came back here. The suns are hot, so I came to sit in the shade."

Jutte looks up at the suns. "This is hot for you?" He slightly tilts his head.

"Yes, I can get too hot, and my skin will turn darker, even pink when it burns. I don't burn often, but it hurts when it happens." I grew up in the Caribbean sun and know when to cover myself, but I bet I would burn quicker with two suns shining on me.

With a quick intake of his breath, Jutte's eyes open wide, "You change colors?"

I guess Jordie never told him about that. "Yes, I get darker the longer I'm in the sun, and my skin will turn a little pink if I'm in the sun too long."

He stares at me and nods his head. I wonder if this will change things between us.

Jutte thinks about this a bit more and slowly opens his mouth, smiling. "My human changes color!" He exclaims and claps all four hands together.

Oh great, what have I done? I hope he doesn't think I can do it on command, like a chameleon or party trick. I set him straight. "I can't control it; it just happens sometimes. You probably won't ever notice it since you always have sunshine." This disappoints him for a moment, but then snaps right back to happy. "My human changes color!"

Fine, whatever.

Time to change the subject. I hold up the carving again. "I'm going to make the fish that looks like an eye. An eye fish. What do you think?"

Jutte takes the stick from me. "A crabacrabamoshoo? Interesting."

"Crabacrabamoshoo? That's what it's called? Then I guess that's what I'm making." I take the stick back and turn it over a couple of times. While Jutte inspects his sap pails, I whittle and eventually forget Jutte is around.

I decide I'm done when my butt is asleep and sore. I stand and stretch. I don't see Jutte anywhere, so I walk back to the house to find the door still propped open for me. I go in and close the door behind me. As soon as I hear it click, I wonder if I should have checked to see if he is inside. I didn't lock him out, but what if he is not here and I can't leave. I guess I can't leave without him opening the door for me anyways, so that should be okay. *Don't panic, just go look for him.* I find him in the main room, watching water flow on the wall, like an aquarium. When did we get an aquarium? And one that is this big? What the heck? Jutte looks to me and points to the aquarium. "Do you like it? I thought you could get more ideas of fish to make."

Oh, so it's like a movie or video. Wow, that was nice of him. I sit on the floor and watch the fish. So many strange looking creatures! Some look like fish and some look like monsters out of my nightmares. "Please wait." I tell him. I want him to pause the pictures. I need to draw some of these so I don't forget.

Once I have my pad and pencil, I sketch some of the interesting creatures, and some pretty normal looking ones. This is great research.

If I can't be in the water, it's cool to be here looking under it. It's relaxing and entertaining at the same time, if that makes sense.

CHAPTER 29

Jutte is letting me sell bags again. We walk through the market, but spend more time just looking around. Normally we sell our bags and go home, but today we get to linger. I like people-watching, or is it alien-watching? Are these aliens' buying materials for hobbies?

Do I have a boring Mari? I wonder what it would be like if Jutte took me traveling, and we could have adventures like alien skydiving or something. Do they have transportation pods that take you somewhere, or can you be zapped and wham, you're there?

All these ideas run through my mind as I stand beside one of the market isles, just watching life go by. I feel someone walk up behind me, and step aside to let them by, but they stop. Crap, probably someone wants to pet the human; ugh, I hope not.

I turn around to see Travtro.

I turn to run. But he is fast and grabs me before I even make it two steps.

I manage a squeak before he covers my mouth and picks me up and runs down the back aisle where he came from. I crane my head around to see Jutte running after us.

Oh, thank goodness.

I try to bite Travtro's hand. Let them try to say I'm vicious, he is kidnapping me! Again!

I kick, I bite, I punch. I'm not going down easy.

Travtro is at a full run. He's holding me with his big arm and has his small hand over my mouth. My biting and kicking aren't working. I'm amazed at how fast we are going; I thought their flipper feet would slow them down.

We turn a corner into the backside of the market, with trash scattered among the boxes and debris. It's as if we're in the bad part of town.

We go around another corner, and I see Jutte still chasing us, jumping and running, and pissed off as can be. Thankfully, he is closer than he was a moment ago.

I don't know if Tratrvo tripped or tackled Jutte, but we go down. I curl into a ball and wait for impact, hoping this guy doesn't land on top of me. We hit the ground and he still has a hold of me. Jutte stands above us and lets out a roar like I've never heard. I freeze, and even Travtro hesitates; and that's all it takes for Jutte to make his move.

I see one of Jutte's legs flash out and kick Travtro in the stomach. Travtro loses his grip, and I manage to scuttle out of his arm and away from the both of them.

Travtro jumps up and squares off with Jutte.

Holy crap, this is bad!

I frantically scan left and right, hoping someone will come break this up; but we are behind the market, with no one in sight. I huddle behind some rubble and watch in horror as the fight unfolds.

I've never seen such violence.

Travtro doesn't back down or run away, but Jutte isn't letting him go. Teeth flash, guttural roars come from one or both of them, hands and feet fly and make contact.

This is bad. Really, really bad.

I want to run and find help; I want to jump in and help. I need to do something. This is not like breaking up a dog fight, which can hurt if you get between two dogs, this is much worse. It's trying to break up a fight between two monsters that are twice the size of me.

They are brutal with kicks and all four arms are punching.

How long can they keep this up?

Jutte hits Travtro so hard that he is stunned and staggers. Without waiting, Jutte lunges, pinning Travtro to the ground, his large hands are around Travtro's throat as the small ones pummel his body. Travtro blocks the blows and rolls sideways, knocking Jutte away from him.

Travtro jumps up a moment before Jutte, and uses that extra second to kick Jutte's legs out from under him.

Travtro doesn't stop. He follows Jutte down, landing his elbow into Jutte's neck.

Jutte rolls to his side, getting up on his knees, coughing and gasping.

Jutte doesn't fight back.

Travtro doesn't stop. He twirls around, a foot making contact with the side of Jutte's head, knocking him over.

Jutte doesn't move.

Travtro doesn't stop.

Screaming, I run out from my hiding place. I jump between the two of them, standing over Jutte's head.

"Stop!" I'm yelling in Mari and English. "Stop! Stop! Stop!"

Travtro finally stops. Breathing heavily, he glares at me. I'll stand over Jutte and fight until my last breath. Now it's the both of us against Travtro.

Except Jutte isn't moving.

Fine, I'll take on Travtro if I have to. "Come on!" I yell.

He looks at Jutte, at me, and at Jutte again, then turns and runs away.

I collapse next to my friend. Finally admitting to myself that I do think of him as a friend.

"Jutte, Jutte. It's over, he's gone. Wake up Jutte, you can wake up now. Please." I'm shaking and can barely speak.

I try gently touching his face. "Come on, wake up. He's gone, he ran away like a coward. Wake up, Jutte."

He still doesn't move.

"Help!" I scream. "Help! Somebody, help!"

I call out for so long that I'm hoarse and losing my voice, when someone finally hears me. A Mari woman cautiously walks up to us, looking from me to Jutte.

"Please help him; he's hurt."

I stand up and point, hoping she believes me. "There was a

fight, and Travtro hit and kicked him. They fought bad, then Jutte didn't get up. Please help."

She rushes to Jutte. I stay close, protecting him from any more hurt. The lady lays her one hand on his chest and one on his head. "Stay." She orders me as she gets up and chases Travtro down the alley.

"It's okay now, I think she went to get help. It's okay now Jutte; you'll be okay. I promise. Just hold on, okay? You can open your eyes, I'm here. It's okay" I'm repeat babbling, nose running, and tears falling on Jutte.

Finally, finally, I hear people running towards us. I can barely make out how many Mari have arrived; I don't care as long as they help him.

They try to pull me away from him. I wrench myself loose and crouch over Jutte again, I don't want to leave him. Two Maris touch and talk to him. A third man pulls me away again.

"No! Let me with him. I must stay with him!" Why don't they understand this? I need to be there when he wakes up. He needs to see I'm okay since it's my fault he is hurt.

They begin to inflate a bubble around Jutte. I try to fight loose, but a big Mari guy has all four arms wrapped around me. I look up at him, pleading. "Please, let me go with him. Please."

The Mari man is startled, and looks wide-eyed at me. "You can talk?"

"Yes, I can talk. Please let me go with him."

The Mari doesn't loosen his grip, but he talks softly to me. "I will take you with us, but you are in the way. Stay with me and we will follow."

I take a breath, and nod. As long as they don't take me away from Jutte, and as long as they are helping him.

They pick up the bubble that is holding Jutte and carry him down the nearest aisle. They are all talking and giving orders. I walk next to the guy who said he would help me. They bring Jutte to a release door. The interior door is opened and I step inside with the group. The one in charge of me taps my head. "Can you swim?"

I nod. "Yes, I can hold my breath a pretty long time. I hope I can keep up with all of you, I don't swim fast."

The room begins to fill with water; I now understand the reason for the bubble, to prevent Jutte from drowning. When the outer door opens, the guy grabs my hand and pulls me out with him. I don't have my flippers or mask on, but I don't need them. I just have to keep up.

I'm swimming and the Mari man pulls me along next to him. This is not the normal door that Jutte and I use, but I suppose they are taking him somewhere else. I keep swimming.

This can't be real. This can't be happening. How can everything change so fast? One moment I'm hanging out with Jutte, watching aliens go by, and the next I'm following him as he is taken to get help. Why would Travtro do this?

When we break the surface, I wipe my eyes and look around. Land is in front of us with a spaceship on the beach. We hurry to the ship and the Maris deflate the bubble and lift Jutte inside. I slip in and position myself next to his head. The Mari barely glance at me while they place an arch over Jutte. It begins to slide above his body, from head to foot, and back up again. Is the arch healing him? I stay back to avoid interfering but close enough to see what's going on.

Before, all the talking was simply background noise, nothing was louder than the rushing in my head. But now that we are stopped, I begin to listen. They murmur to each other. "I wonder what happened? Who did this? How did he get hurt?"

I speak up. "I know what happened."

They all notice me for the first time.

"It was Travtro. He kidnapped me and Jutte came to save me. Then they fought. Travtro kicked him in the head, then hit him with his elbow on his throat." I mime what happened, in case I'm not saying something right.

One of the Mari ladies looks up at the arch, then back at me. "Yes, he does have injuries that could have been caused by what the human said. I didn't know you could talk."

What? The main concern, is that I can talk?

"Will he be okay?" I ask. As I look around, everyone looks away. No one will make eye contact with me. "What? Please tell me you can help him. Make him okay." My voice trembles and my nose is running. I don't care, I just need Jutte to wake up.

The man who helped me swim leans down to be face to face with me.

"I'm sorry, little human; your owner is dead."

CHAPTER 30

The words don't make sense. I must have heard wrong or misunderstood what he said. Jutte can't be dead. He's right here, about to wake up. He's going to be okay and we will make bags together again. This cannot happen.

I don't accept it.

"No!" I scream at everyone; they all look down so as to avoid eye contact with me. "No, he can't be gone. Keep trying; keep working on him! Please, you have to." My words are softer, but the pain is louder. I frantically pull at the hands of the guy who helped me. "Come on, you have to do something." I keep pulling at all of their hands, willing them to fix Jutte.

One man grips my shoulders and leans his face into mine. "We can't do more; he is gone." The Mari man is wrong, I know he is.

Turn to the lady in charge, I plead. "Please, make him better. I understand he must heal, but eventually he will be okay. Make him be okay." She nervously looks away.

I beg to the next Mari person, and the next. None will help.

I flop across his body, sobbing. Why did this happen? They try pulling me off him again but I won't let go; I hold on tight. They finally leave me alone with Jutte.

He is all I have in this weird world.

"His pet is so sad; I didn't know human pets had emotions." I hear this over the jumble in my head. What? Bite me, Jutte's gone and they did nothing. I don't care what they say or what they think; they don't matter. Of course, humans have emotions.

Jutte's gone.

The man looking after me taps me on the back. I ignore him.

He taps again, "We are about to land. You must let go of him. I will make sure you stay close to him."

I look out a window and see that we really are about to land somewhere. I sit up, wipe my eyes and nose on my sleeve, and breathe. In, two, three, four. Out, two, three, four.

After the door opens, commotion begins again. They pick up Jutte and hand him to others waiting outside. I jump out the door and run after them, never taking my eyes from Jutte.

The Mari surround him, and all I can see is his hand, hanging limp towards the ground.

Jutte's gone.

The waves of anguish almost knock me over and drown me.

I jog after them.

I trip and fall, but the Mari guy helps me stand. "You okay?" He asks. No. No, I'm not okay. How can I possibly be okay? I wipe my hands on my pants and jog after Jutte again.

The fight happened so fast, and now time has become too slow. My head hurts, my eyes hurt, my heart hurts. I'm lost.

They take Jutte into a room where I'm set against a wall. I'll sit wherever I need to, as long as I can see him. They work over him, talk about him, and keep glancing at me.

When they take him away, I jump up to follow but a Mari lady stops me, holding me back.

"No! Let me go with him. I have to be with him. Let me go." I kick, yell, and pull, but she holds me tight. I fight until my legs quit working and I collapse onto the cold floor. I'm done, I can't move, I don't care.

The one helpful Mari guy finds me and picks me up under the arms, and stands me on my feet. "I didn't get to say goodbye." I tell him.

He nods, but doesn't respond. He starts walking and turns back to me. "I will bring you to another room." He begins walking again. I don't know what else to do, so I follow him. At least he doesn't try to carry me.

We walk down a long hallway with a ceiling that must be at least three stories high and walls that are at least thirty feet apart. Why is this hallway so big? How many Mari people need to use it at once? What an odd thing to focus on, but it's what I notice and wonder about even now.

We turn into a comfortable, living-room style space where Mari people sit with soft flooring and subtle lighting. Oh, I get it, this is like a family waiting room at a hospital. Wait, I don't like this; this is when the doctor comes in with bad news.

I turn around and leave the room. I want no part of this.

I head further down the hallway, checking all open doors. I need to find Jutte and make sure he is not alone. I check doors on the left and the right.

One door isn't closed tight and I push it open. That was a mistake. There is a Mari person laid out on a skinny, long table with five other Mari people around him, all wearing gear that completely covers them, leaving only their eyes visible. They all stop and stare in wonder at me. We assess each other for a moment before I mumble a "sorry" and back out of the room. OK, no more opening doors.

I continue searching for Jutte but that same Mari guy steps in front of me. "No." He tells me. Surprised, I stop in my tracks. Did he just tell me no? As if to scold me like a dog? I step around him. He steps in front of me again. "Stop. Come this way, I will bring you to your owner." That's all I wanted: to see Jutte. I follow him back the way we came. It seems I was going the wrong way anyway - good thing he caught me.

When we pass by the family waiting room, I glance inside to see a different set of Mari people, looking worried and despondent. I understand how they feel. I trot to catch up to the guy. I suppose I should ask his name, but I don't care; Jutte is my only concern right now.

He takes me to a sterile room. It's large, cold, and impersonal. Jutte is on a table too high for me to reach. I look around for a chair to climb on. The Mari guy sees my intentions and helps bring a chair next to the table. He uses his smaller hands to lift me onto the chair.

I reach out and gently touch Jutte. He's cold and

unresponsive.

He's dead.

I see that now. The pain is too much. I break down crying again. I totally don't care who sees me like this. "I'm so sorry, I'm sorry." I quietly repeat over and over. I know it's my fault Jutte is gone, he died trying to protect me. I want to go back in time and stop the fight between him and Travtro.

If only I had gotten away from him.

If only Jutte and I were in a shop instead of people-watching.

If only I had helped fight instead of hiding.

If only I ran to get help sooner.

If only everything was different.

If only...

I cry until I'm out of tears. Looking at Jutte, I gently take one of his small hands; it's still quite large compared to mine. It's heavier than I remember, and cold. "Good bye." I tell him, my voice hoarse and raw. I set his hand down and jump off the chair.

I nod to the guy watching me and he leads the way out. But to where? Will he take me home with him? Will I be taken to the pound? Is there such a thing?

My head hurts and I want to go to sleep. Wanting this day over, I follow the Mari outside. What happens to me now?

CHAPTER 31

I think I've been in this room at the hospital for a couple of days, but who knows how long it's actually been. I can't see the outside and various Mari have come and gone. Thankfully they brought me food and water. My room is a perfectly square cell block: grey-blue walls, no windows. My twin-size cot is against the wall and a table with one chair occupies the center. For a planet with such vibrant colors, I'm surprised by these drabby surroundings. I must be in prison.

"Hello little human." It's the guy who originally helped me. I jump up. My butt was getting sore on the hard ground anyways.

"Hello. Thank you for being here." I want to shake his hand, but that means nothing here. "I want to go home, or at least back to Jutte's house here on Oonala." Then I pause and add, "Please." The big guy nods but doesn't say anything right away, so I keep talking, hoping he can help. "I mean, have people been to the house for this food and water? Is that how it's here, and if so, can't I just go there myself?"

"What is your name?" he says instead of answering me.

I take a calming breath. "My name is Marco. I never did ask your name." I'm hoping politeness will work to my advantage. I hold out my fist moving it back and forth a bit, encouraging him to do the same. He extends his fist and I gently bump it. "On Earth, that is kind of how we greet each other."

He opens his mouth and holds out a fist on his small hand for me to bump again. I do so, smiling back at him. "My name is Bakao., I'm surprised at how well you speak our language." This guy isn't so bad after all. Actually, he was never bad. He had helped Jutte.

"Yeah well, thanks for helping me the other day." I quietly tell him. I still miss Jutte - a lot. I had not realized how much I liked him. Even when he was going on about cleaning my room or putting my bag away, he really was an awesome alien. "Do you know what's going to happen to me?" I look up at him, hoping he has answers - good answers. I totally understand what a dog must feel like when living in isolation. If I were in a pound it would have more humans around. But I don't' even know how many humans are on this planet. I haven't seen any other humans.

Bakao pulls me away from my rambling thoughts and back to the here and now. "We went to your owner's house and found food and water for you. But we are not sure what to do with you just yet. How did Jutte buy you?"

I bounce a bit on my toes. "From Jordie; can you get in touch with Jordie? He can help me." In all the hoopla I forgot to ask about Jordie. Now things might be okay. Jordie can bring me back to Earth! "Jordie will come and help, he can take me home. Can you call him?" Do the Mari people 'call' each other?

"We will go back to your owner's house and look for information regarding Jordie." Bakao confirmed. Okay, we are on to something. I hate that Jutte is gone, but I'm happy about going back to Earth. Imagine the party they'll have for me.

"Can I go back to the house with you? I can stay there. I know where the food and water is. All my stuff is there. Please, can I go back to the house instead of being locked up here?" I want to go back to the house. I'm in prison here.

Bakao pauses. "Hmm, I am not sure about that; let me ask the others." He is taking my request seriously. That's a good sign.

"I'm an independent pet, and Jutte has taught me well. I promise I won't run away if you bring me to his house. I can't run anyways, I tried once. The island is small and has nothing else on it anyways. So, you see, it would be okay to bring me there." I'm giving my best arguments. That would be pretty cool to live there alone for a while. The run of the house.

"I'll come back" Bakao says as he heads for the door. "Do you need anything special?"

"My wood and knife." I always want to be carving, sitting here doing nothing is killing me.

He stops and tilts his head. "What is your wood and knife?"

Oh crud, I have to try to explain it. I don't even have a pencil and paper to draw it for him. "The wood is a piece from the square tree that's found not far from the house. And my knife is about this long," I hold my fingers about twelve inches apart, "and is metal and shiny. I may have left it in the big general room, next to Jutte's bags that he makes." I bite my lip, trying to remember what we were doing before this all happened. Wow, one moment I was carving, then wham! I'm here in this prison.

I may not get to go to that home again. But then again, one moment I was fishing on Earth and wham! I ended up a pet on the planet Oonala. You'd think I'd get used to this.

Bakao is looking at me with a scrunched-up face. "Why do you have wood and shiny metal?"

I sigh and try to figure out how to explain a carving to an alien who has never seen statues or pictures. "Look in my room where I have other carvings of fish from my planet. I want to make a fish from this planet."

I can tell he doesn't get it, but he shrugs anyways. "Okay, I will look for those. I'll come back as soon as I can." The click of the door closing behind him reminds me that I'm just a pet locked up and waiting for someone to decide my fate.

I pace twenty-two steps one way and twenty-two steps back to the door. How long do I have to stay here? Can I go back to Jutte's house? Will Jordie come and fix things? Will he take me back to Earth? How long have I been gone?

That question stops me. I don't know how long I've been gone. How the heck can I cope with all of this? Too many things to figure out! I lay on the cot, my finger and thumb tapping. If I could have my wood and knife, at least I could carve.

It's no wonder cats and dogs at home on Earth either sleep all day or destroy things, what else is there to do? I'm bored and tired but can't sleep. I want to go home.

I get up again. Twenty-two paces across the room, twenty-two paces back.

That's it. I'm getting out of here.

I go to the door just to double check that it locked after Bakao left. I slide the chair to the door and climb on it to reach the handle.

The door opens.

I'm so surprised I lose my balance. My arms flail in circles until I find my footing.

Holy Neptune, the door is open. I could have escaped earlier.

I don't bother pushing the chair back. Holding my breath, I peek into the hallway, see no one around, no one walking up or down the hall, and hear no noise.

My bare feet don't make a sound as I creep toward the end of the hall. It turns one way only, so that makes my choice of direction easy. At the corner I stop breathing and lower myself to my stomach to peek around the corner. I see a closed door at the end, but a clear hall.

Low and close to the wall, I run to the door. I can't reach the handles, and the only directions to go are out through the door or back toward the room and down the hall the other way. I try pushing on the door, it doesn't give. I tap the wall around the door, hoping for a hidden button or switch. Nothing.

I turn back the other way. I'm just past my room when I hear the door I just left open and someone clomps down the hallway towards me. Crap, crap, crap. I turn around, dive into my room, and shove my chair back to the table. A lady Mari walks in and sets food and water on my table. "Here you go, Little One. I bet you're hungry."

Whatever, I don't bother to answer her. I'm not some little scared animal that needs baby talk. I look at the wall until she sighs and leaves... but the door doesn't close all the way.

I sneak out of the door again and watch as she rounds the corner. I run to the edge of the hallway, peeking around the corner to watch her swing the door open wide and go through. I make my break, run as fast and quietly as I can, and slide feet first through the door before it closes. Any baseball player would be impressed with that move.

Now what?

I back against the door and crouch low, hoping that most tall Maris don't look down at my level. I slip to the corner of the wall, swiveling my head right and left. I'm at the end of a short hallway. Mari people pass by in a larger corridor, none of them looking my way.

I keep moving along the wall towards the large corridor. Now, down on my stomach, I look into a large, bright lobby. Mari people mill around, talking to each other, some purposefully walking somewhere, and others lounging on couches. Above me, I notice a clear dome ceiling, but we're not underwater; instead, I see two suns. Okay, we're on land, that's good. I dart out and run behind a nearby pillar, executing another award-winning slide.

I can do this, I can escape.

No one looks down while walking. Good! They're all too busy having to get somewhere, or talking together. Not one Mari person is simply looking around...except one Mari kid. Crud, I think he's staring right at me. Why is it the kids, human or alien, always seem to notice what adults are too busy to see? Why can't alien kids be oblivious too? Where's his Gameboy?

I freeze. Maybe if I don't move, he'll get bored and look away. I refuse to make eye contact, but I can still see him. He's still staring at me with his mouth open. Crud, he thinks I'm fun to watch.

Look away kid, look away.

He points and makes a noise. I duck back behind the pillar, hoping the adult scolds him and gives him something else to hold his attention. Once he stops the racket he was making, I ease my head out to assess the situation.

He's still there, still watching, mouth wide open, but thankfully quiet. I peek again and this time he waves at me. I wave, hoping to appease him, and hide behind the pillar again.

I need to keep moving. I'll get caught if I stay put.

I glance around to make sure no one is looking, then run to

the next pillar. Safe and no alarm ringing. I can do this; I just need to get to an outside door. A bored guard sits near the door, but I think I can sneak past him.

I run again to hide behind a couch, and see the outside. It's about a football field away and to my right. Crouching, I wait for the perfect moment when someone leaves and I can slip out behind them.

A Mari lady is distracted with something in her hand as she walks towards the door. This is it! this is my chance!

I take a breath and run.

Right into Tratrvo.

CHAPTER 32

Holy Neptune! I try to stop, arms flailing and end up falling onto my backside, staring up at him. This can't be happening; really, *this can't be happening*. What are the actual chances that he would walk in as I'm running out? We stare at each other, eyes wide and breathing stopped. But then our feelings split; I'm terrified, my instincts yell for me to run. I try to oblige, scramble backwards and flip over, trying to get to my feet to take off. His instinct must have been to kidnap me again, because his long arm shoots out and grabs a hold on to my shirt.

I try to pull out of his grasp, but he holds firm and yanks me backwards. I fall over and roll onto my side, hoping he'll lose his grip. He holds strong. I inhale deeply and feel a scream working its way into my throat. Travtro uses three hands to pick me up and his fourth to cover my mouth.

My arms are pinned by my side as he hefts me under his arm. I'm kicking, biting, and squirming. My mind has almost shut down and is works on pure fear and adrenaline. I frantically look for a way out and make eye contact with the same kid that I was hiding from earlier. I try telepathy to cry out for help. I think it works because he suddenly cries and points at me.

Help me kid! Scream and point!

The guard stops Tratrvo "What's going on here?" *He's kidnapping me! He's going to kill me!* I try telling all this with my eyes, my body fighting, and my will. He's got to help me; he's just got to.

"It's okay." Tratrvo gives a slimy smile. "My pet human escaped and I'm taking him home. I'm actually quite surprised he got past you and into this building."

OMG, he is evil. Realizing that he didn't see me come in through the door, the guard shifts from one long leg to the other. "Well, I uh, just got here. He must have snuck in earlier. But I'm glad you found him." The guard says as he ushers us out the door.

No! No! Help! I bite Tratrvo's hand as hard as possible, but he doesn't remove it from my mouth. In fact, he holds on tighter, almost cutting off all air. The sound of the kid's cries is cut off as the door closes behind us. No one intervenes or comes to my rescue. There is no Jutte to help me.

I'm on my own.

We're outside. Wow, I never knew there was this whole town above water. I always stayed near Jutte's house and only went to the domed market. Normally, I would like to look around, but the soul-freezing terror has me totally preoccupied.

Mari people glance our way, but keep walking. They must think I'm an unruly pet being taken home. On Earth, anytime I saw a human dragging a pet around by its collar, I just assumed it was theirs. It never occurred to me that the human might be stealing the dog or cat.

Travtro has loosened his hand over my mouth so I can breathe, but I still can't yell. I'm grunting, as loud as possible, kicking, and trying to work myself free from his hold. I don't know where he's taking me, but I know it won't end well.

We walk past buildings and into the water. Holy Neptune, he's going to drown me, again. He removes his hand and I take one last deep breath before he pulls me under. Travtro has a hold of my arm and is dragging me next to him as he swims downward. I'm so busy trying to get away that I don't see the domes until we are almost on top of them. At least a hundred small domes sit all clumped so close that they're almost touching, all the same size, many have a soft glow inside. I can see the glow, but not actually into the domes. I stop flailing and wonder what these are.

We are about a hundred yards above the domes when Travtro stops, and I mean completely stops moving. If we were on land he would be standing still, we're no longer descending, we are simply feet down, standing in the water. I look where he is looking. Things are blurry without my goggles, but I see a humongous shape of a fish swimming towards us.

Anything that scares Travtro terrifies me.

The fish grows larger as it nears us. It moves like a snake, or an eel...

Or a dragon.

It's Shamo Loonolo, the dragon fish! Hoooollllyyy Neptune. I'm frozen in place next to Travtro. My mind is trying to make sense of something so huge coming straight for us.

I break the spell first, and notice that in Tratrvo's surprise, his grip on my arm has loosened. The water dragon's eyes are locked on Tratrvo, keeping him locked in a trance. Its mouth opens and will easily gobble both of us. The razor-sharp teeth are each as big as my forearm.

There is no way in heck I'm going to be eaten by a dragon. At the last moment I plant my feet against Tratrvro's chest and push off backwards, dodging out of the way.

I barely miss being eaten. Unfortunately, kicking off from Tratrvo pushed him out of harm's way as well.

The Old One roars at the emptiness of it jaws. Its huge size means it can't turn quickly, and this gives me the chance to shoot upwards.

I break the surface, gasping for air. Further from shore than I had realized, I paddle furiously in that direction.

Now I have Tratrvo and a water dragon after me.

How did this happen? I was kidnapped from my fishing boat, turned into a pet, made into an orphaned pet by a psycho who is trying to kill me, and now I have a water dragon wanting to eat me. What the actual heck?

Travtro surfaces behind me and easily catches up. "Not so fast you wretched little human." He growls as he grabs me by the arm again. I manage a deep breath before he pulls me under again.

Why are we swimming back down? Did he already forget about almost being killed?

I see the water dragon in the distance. It seems to be taking its time to turn back for us, but it is definitely turning around.

Travtro swims fast and hard, dragging me along. We make it to the domes when I glance back and see Shamo Loonol heading our way. We are dodging between domes, staying low enough to be out of biting range.

We weave between the domes and stop at one on the edge of the cluster. He pushes a button, allowing a door to rise. It's like the doors into the market. He shoves me through and presses the inside button. As the water drains, Travtro lets go of me and I swim to the top of the room, breathing while the water drains. I swim back under the water and try to escape, but the door is closed tight and the receding water carries me to the floor

He grabs me again and drags me through the next door and into a home. I'm in his home. I can't think of any worse place to be than in the lair of the enemy. He has now officially kidnapped me. I twist and kick until he finally releases me, shoving me to the ground.

"What are you doing? Let me go." I demand; Grandfather taught me to never show my fear, even when it threatens to overtake me. But my trembling gives me away.

"Shut up. I'm not going to hurt you." He says as he walks into a second room. *Yeah right. You just took me for no reason.* I make my break and run back to the door we came in, I don't care if I flood his entire house, I'm getting out of here. I spot the button to open the door way high and out of my reach. I try my best not to freak-out. Instead, I look for something to climb on.

I run around the room, pushing every possible object towards the door. I soon have a nice heap. Scrambling as fast as possible to the top, I reach for the button.

The door opens!

I crawl under the door before it even fully opens and spot the button for the outer door. I jump but I need a couple of more inches to reach it. My fingers graze the bottom of the button. I back up and take a running jump and try my best to climb the wall.

The momentum works because I slap the button and water

floods in.

I'm knocked off my feet and pushed against the back wall near the inner door. Holding onto the wall, I push myself to the door opening. I take a big breath and use all my might to pull myself out and around the side of the door.

I did it, I'm outside!

The water is trying to pull me back in. I kick off and swim parallel to the house. I know that when in a rip tide, you swim parallel to the shore instead of fighting the current. That works I'm far enough away from the pull that I can then head towards the surface.

I'm almost to the top when I feel something fall over me.

A net is pulling me down.

I can't breathe. Water is everywhere, and I fight to figure out which way is up. I look for light; I try to spot bubbles rising. My lungs are ready to burst, but the net will not release its death grip on me. I fling the net around, looking for an end, a hole, anything that will allow me to swim to the surface. Blackness is creeping in from the sides, and my vision fades. This is it; this is how I die, caught in a fishing net.

CHAPTER 33

"Good morning, Marco." Comes a voice from the distance. Is there morning in Heaven? Is God telling me good morning? I expected to see an angel, not the Big Man himself.

"Can you open your eyes?" He says. Well, that explains why I don't actually see God.

My eyes not following orders to open, seem to have decided to stay shut. I try again, willing them to open at least a little bit. They finally flutter open to a blurry scene.

I blink a couple of times, trying to bring the world into focus. Ha, wouldn't that be nice? My world has been turmoil since I was brought to this planet. Before that, I lived a quiet and simple life. I want peace back. I want my world back in focus.

"Hi there." I turn my head and see Bakao, the guy who helped me when Jutte died, sitting in a large chair next to me.

"You rescued me again." This isn't a question I need answering, simply a statement. He opens his mouth and pats my hand.

"Yes, I went to the room and found you gone. I went outside and saw people gathered around the water, pointing and talking about a house that had been destroyed. They thought you had been the one to flood the house, so they captured you. What happened?"

I close my eyes. What did happen? I try to remember when it went wrong. I could say it all began the day Jordie took me, but I don't think that's what Bakao is asking.

Speaking of Jordie, "Were you able to call Jordie?" I ask.

"Yes, he should be here soon." Thank goodness. Maybe now I can go home and this whole nightmare will be over.

I bolt upright. "Where is Tratrvo?" Holy Neptune, what if they let him at me again? What if he comes in here and kills me right here? I feel a trickle of sweat on my back.

"It's okay." Bakao says, gently pushing me back down. "They found his body. They know he is the one who killed Jutte. But he is dead now and so they are satisfied."

"I killed him?" I whisper. I don't like him but I didn't mean to kill him.

The next thought stuns me more. What will happen to me? Will they think I'm aggressive and put me down? My entire body shakes.

"It's okay. You are safe." Bakao is trying to calm me down. It's not working. I need to talk to Jordie, to tell him everything that happened. Why isn't he here for me?

I want to run.

Wait. Running got me into trouble, it's how Tratrvo got me. I will my muscles to relax and stay put. I will my mind to relax and stay put.

Breathe in, two, three four. Out, two, three, four.

I'm finally able to open my eyes and look at Bakao, I'm okay now.

He opens his mouth to smile at me. He's a good guy and at least for the moment, I feel safe. The weight of losing Jutte is still there, but I feel safe now.

I finally look around to see I'm in a different room, this one has a larger bed and a window, I must be special. The room is large by human standards, it's at least fifty feet wide and long. The door is across the room, and the window beside my bed lets in daylight. Not that it tells me what day it is, but hey, it's light outside.

I see a table near the door and spot my bag. I jump out of bed, and am immediately dizzy. Bakao catches me as I slump to the floor.

"Whoa, slow down Little Human Marco. You have been asleep for quite some time. You need to move slow." Yeah, I agree. I sit back onto the bed, my feet on the floor and my hands grasping the bed. Wait, this bed is my size. That's pretty cool. Where did they get it?

"May I have some water?" I'm hoping they have some here. Bakao leans over the bed to a nightstand I didn't realize was there. He hands me a container of cold water. Oh my, water has never tasted so good.

I take a couple of sips, and sit up a bit straighter. My head is sore and my thoughts are fuzzy, but I can deal with that. I take another sip of water and savor the way it soothes my mouth and throat. It's like the time I woke up after the night Arturo and I had a yelling contest. I smile at that memory.

The door opens and Jordie stands in the doorway, assessing me. "Good, you're awake."

Well, hello to you too.

"Barely." I croak back at him.

Bakao stands up and greets Jordie. "Hello, you must be Jordie, Marco's handler. I am Bakao."

My what?!

Jordie puts his hand up to stop me from coming unglued.

"Hello Bakao. It is nice to meet you. Thank you for calling me."

Whatever.

Jordie stands in front of me. "How are you, Marco?" Such a loaded question that I don't know how to answer. I'm not doing so well, but I'm alive. How do I explain that I'm somewhere between fine and not dead?

So, I shrug.

"I hear a lot has happened in the last sun cycle." He says. "Are you hungry?"

It's only been one sun cycle since Jutte and I were standing in the market place watching people go by? It seems forever ago.

"I can't even begin to tell you how hungry I am." I reply.

I don't know how Jordie does it, but the door opens and a Mari lady walks in with a tray. She sets it on the table and leaves again, closing the door behind her.

I look at Bakao whose eyes are wide and mouth open. Good,

I'm not the only one surprised.

"Bakao gave me some water. It was good." I smile at Bakao, I want Jordie to know he has taken care of me.

Bakao stands a little straighter and opens his mouth in a smile. I can't help but smile back.

"Can you stand?" Jordie asks. I test my legs. This time they seem to hold me, but Bakao is right there in case I fall again.

I shuffle to the table and sink into the chair. That bit of walking exhausts me. Good thing I don't want to run.

Bakao sets water in front of me while Jordie takes the lids off the food plates. I close my eyes and imagine chicken, juicy and warm from the grill. I picture rice and beans on the side, and a coleslaw to top it all off. My stomach rumbles loud.

I place the bowl in front of me and dig in. Thankfully, Jordie doesn't try talking to me yet. I stop eating only to take a sip of water, then I'm back to eating.

I slow down when I'm halfway through the bowl. I stop and sit up straight, looking sideways at Jordie and Bakao. I've embarrassed myself and Jordie probably thinks I've completely lost all manners.

"I didn't realize how hungry I was." Hoping he understands, I manage to finish the food like a normal human being and not an animal.

I sigh deeply and sit back. For as hungry as I was, I sure am full now. A nap sounds wonderful.

"Are you ready to tell us what happened?" Jordie asks as Bakao pulls his chair closer to us. Jordie's face is void of feelings, as usual. Bakao is looking expectantly back at me.

I nod, and tell them everything. "Jutte and I were at the market, just hanging out and watching aliens go by…" I tell them how Tratrvo grabbed me from behind, how he and Jutte fought, and how Tratrvo killed Jutte. I tell them how Bakao was there for me. Then I was left in a room for a long time, so I escaped. I tell them everything. I explain how Tratrvo grabbed me again. When I tell them about almost being eaten by the water dragon, Bakao gasps. Jordie is confused but doesn't interrupt. I tell them about escaping from Tratvro's house and then a net being thrown over me. "And I woke up here." I finish with my head down.

"I didn't mean to kill Tratrvo; I just wanted to get away." I raise my eyes to Jordie, pleading with him to believe me. "Are they going to put me down?" I ask.

Bakao tilts his head and looks at Jordie. He doesn't understand what I'm asking. I don't want to say it out loud, so I don't explain it to him.

"I don't know what's going to happen. I just arrived on Oonala, but I will talk with the Deciders and explain your story to them." Jordie answers. At least he's honest. "Stay here and rest. I see Bakao brought your bag, it will give you something to do."

Remembering my bag, I grab it. "Thank you for this, Bakao." I start happily digging through it. He brought my knife and the wood I was working on. I also find my notepad and pencil. All the great things.

"Hey Jordie, can I get a toothbrush and a regular brush? And a shower?" My skin feels like I haven't showered in days, and my mouth feels like it's been longer.

Jordie gives me a small nod. "Yes, I will have more things brought to you. I am going to speak with the Deciders and I'll be back later. But please rest, I need you alert."

No problem. A nap, a shower, and a toothbrush will have me feeling whole again.

"I must go too." Bakao says as he stands. "I will be back to check on you." He says with a small open mouth smile.

"Thank you, Bakao. Thank you for everything."

He nods and gives me a fist-bump.

When he and Jordie leave together, I don't hear the door lock behind them. That's ok, I'm not going anywhere. I need to stay and face whatever will happen next.

So, I guess I'll either be put to death, or sent back to Earth.

CHAPTER 34

I never knew how hard it would be to pass time when confined to one room. I can lose myself in my carvings, but only for so long. Sleep, pace, carve, eat, and repeat.

A knock on the door has me sitting upright and at attention. Bakao comes in. "Hello Little Human Marco. How are you?"

Little Human Marco, I wonder if that's his nickname for me. I guess it could be worse. I mean, I've had nicknames for people; there was Big Head Mary (in my defense, her head was way too big for her body), Crazy Jaco (he really was a strange kid), and Floppy Fred (the guy didn't walk or sit normal, he was tall and lanky and flopped his arms and body whenever he moved). So, all in all, I can live with the nickname Little Human Marco, maybe he can drop the 'Little' part.

"What are you doing?" He asks as he stands in front of me. I'm sitting on the bed, working on the eye fish carving that I started at Jutte's home.

I hold up the carving. "Making an eye fish. At least that's what I call it, I'm not sure what your name for it is." I shrug, holding up my work-in-process.

I hear a sharp intake of breath and look up to see his huge eyes staring at me. Oh crud, I forgot Mari people don't have artistic representations of anything.

I decide to have some fun. "Here, watch." I take out my pencil and pad of paper and begin drawing Jordie. I let him watch as the graphite glides across the paper. To him, I'm making magic.

I glance at his wide eyes and mouth open in a surprise rather than a smile. I look back at the page and keep drawing. It's a rough sketch so I finish quickly. "It's Jordie." I smile and hold the picture for him to see.

"What is this? How did you make Jordie?" he breathlessly asks as he takes the notepad from me.

As if on cue, there's a knock and the door and Jordie walks in. "Oh good, you're both here."

Bakao drops the picture, walking backwards until he bumps into the wall. "You summonsed him."

I can't help but laugh at that.

"Marco, what are you doing?" Somehow, Jordie can make a simple question sound like an accusation.

"Nothing. I showed him my carving of an eye fish, and then I sketched a picture of you, and here you are." I couldn't stop my laughter if I tried.

Jordie sighs and shakes his head but I see him trying not to smile. "I have news about your situation." That stops my laughter. I set my notepad down and stand up. This is it, another life changing moment. I take a deep breath.

I'm ready.

"The Deciders want to talk to you. They want to hear from you what exactly happened."

Good. Someone else gets to hear my side of the story. I didn't mean to destroy his house and I didn't mean to kill him. Maybe they'll believe me, understand the whole thing was a mistake, and send me home.

"Great, when can I talk to them?" I'm not sure how long I need to prepare my speech, but not too long.

"Now." Jordie replies.

Oh, heck. Now. Okay.

I take a deep breath and square my shoulders. I am Marco. I can do this.

Jordie leads the way to another room. Five Mari's total, three women and two men are gathered around a table, waiting for me. Seeing no open seats, I look to Jordie, wondering what to do. He points me to the head of the table.

I stand in front of the Deciders, tapping my finger and thumb together behind my back. I get that this is important. Once again, I'm in a fight for my life.

One of the Mari ladies stands and speaks. "Human Marco, do you understand what I am saying?"

I take a deep breath, stand up tall, and answer loud enough for everyone to hear. "Yes. I understand your language and speak it as well."

Not one of them seems impressed by me. They watch me with mouths closed. "Good." She replies. "Do you understand why you are here?"

I don't want to bluntly say it's because I killed Tratrvo, so instead I tell them, "To explain the events that lead me here. To tell you what happened."

She nods. "You may begin."

Where do I begin? I doubt they want to hear that one day I was fishing and got taken by Jordie. Or how we flew in a spaceship to meet Jutte. So, I start where this story begins. "I had been on your planet a very short time, less than the passing of one sun, when Jutte, my owner, first took me to the market place. We had just arrived and I was looking around, trying to take it all in. Then some guy came up and started yelling and pointing at me. I didn't understand much of your language yet, but he was upset. It was Tratrvo. He was mad at me from the first time he saw me."

I tell them about each incident. Of how Tratrvo kidnapped me off the beach and how I think I died for a little while. Then I begin to tell them about his fight with Jutte. I angrily wipe my tears away when I describe how he killed Jutte. It explains how I ended up in this building.

I regain my composure and tell how I escaped from my room. I'm not going to lie about that. And how just as I was almost out the door Tratrvo came walking in.

I pause. I never thought about why Tratrvo was coming into the building. Was he planning to steal and kill me again?

I shake away the scary thought and tell them the rest of the story. I expected some reaction, especially when we were almost eaten by the sea dragon. But none of the Deciders gasp or even flinch. They watch me finish my story. At least they're not interrupting with a million questions.

"That's all of it." I end my story. "That's what happened and why I'm here."

The lady in charge stands again. "Thank you, Human Marco. You have shown us that humans are more than we knew. You are intelligent beings that have care, compassion, and poise. You have changed how we will treat humans in the future. Now, please return to your holding area while we discuss your situation."

Jordie leads me out of the room. I speak up right away. "That Mari lady in charged talked like a robot, are they real Mari people?"

Jordie looks at me like I've officially lost it, but doesn't break his stride. "The Deciders are real Mari people. They have no emotional stake in your situation. This is new, human pets are fairly new. And never before has a human pet killed a Mari."

I start to object, but Jordie holds his hand up to stop me. "I know, even if it was self-defense. The decision they make will set the standard for all future decisions regarding pets. This is important."

Well, I didn't set out to be important.

I start pacing as soon as we enter the holding room. "I wonder how long I have to wait before they decide my fate." I ask out loud, but mainly to myself.

Bakao is still here. That was nice of him to wait.

"Marco." Jordie distracts me from my worrying. I stop pacing. He continues. "I'll be back as soon as the Deciders have ruled on your situation." And with that he unceremoniously walks out the door, leaving me and Bakao to stare at each other.

"Well." Bakao says loud enough to make me jump. "Okay then." This time the volume is a little more normal.

I flop onto the bed and stare at the ceiling. Bakao quietly leaves while I lie still.

About half an hour later, the door opens again. Jordie and Bakao come in and stand at the table. Neither speak, but I jump up, looking back and forth between them, hoping to get a reading. "Have the Deciders made a decision?"

My head keeps swiveling between them. Bakao has his mouth closed and Jordie isn't staring at his tablet.

This can't be good.

Jordie speaks. "The Deciders understand the Tratrvo killed Jutte and took you against your will; and in trying to get away you accidently killed him. They do not hold you responsible."

I let out my breath in a woosh and sink onto the bed. They are not going to put me down. Right?

"So, I won't be killed?"

Bakao steps up. "Why do you think they would have killed you?"

"Well, on Earth, if a pet is aggressive enough to kill a human, the pet has to be put down, or killed. That way it can't harm another human."

"Oh, I didn't realize how brutal humans are." He steps back again.

"Wait, no. We aren't brutal. In fact, many humans believe their pets are their family and actually treat them better than expected. It's just what I assumed would happen to me." I don't want Bakao afraid of me.

His mouth opens wide. "Humans have pets? I bet that is great to see!" I get it, a pet has a pet, ha ha. I let the remark go without a snide response, at least not out loud, and turn back to Jordie.

"So, I can go back to Earth now?" I figure that if I'm not being killed, then I can go home.

"Why would you think that? Do you not remember in orientation when I told you that you cannot go back to Earth? That is still true. Circumstances don't necessarily change the policies."

I thought I had two options only. I blink rapidly at Jordie, my mouth hanging open, afraid to ask. "Then what happens to me?"

"I'm not sure yet, this is an unusual situation." He seems to be thinking out loud. Does he not understand that this is my life hanging here, blowing in the breeze, left hung out to dry; all those clichés. The poster of the little cat hanging from a limb - that's my life right now.

"Can I at least go back to Jutte's house and live there until we know what's going to happen to me? My room and all my things are there. I'm comfortable there. And now with Tratrvo gone, I'm safe there. I promise I won't run away; I've learned that bad things happen when I try to run." I refuse to beg, but I really want to go there. It's my only home, now that Earth is off the table. I don't want to be stuck in a hospital room for however long it takes for Jordie to figure this all out.

He stares at me for a moment, considering my request. "That may be permissible." He drawls, as if considering my request.

"It would be the best option." I try to control my excitement. "That way you'll know where I am and what I'm doing. You'll need to show me how to prepare my food and make sure I have enough water. I can carve and hang out until this is worked out. I promise to be good." By this time, I'm pacing in front of Jordie and Bakao, who has silently watched this whole interaction.

Bakao offers, "I live close by and can check on him."

I smile warmly at Bakao, giving him a quick nod in thanks.

Jordie still isn't totally convinced, so I keep trying. "I mean really, what is the difference if I'm here or there - especially with Bakao stopping by? At least there I'll have my clothes, my carving material, and all my own things. I'll even make my bed and clean the house. I'll be okay. And I'll be happier there." I'm laying it on thick, but this is important.

He's actually thinking about this, so I shut up. That's a trick I learned with Grandfather: to state my point and then let him be. If I pestered too much, he would get agitated and tell me "no". It's hard, but I wait patiently, glancing at Bakao, who is also watching Jordie for his response. My finger and thumb are rapidly tapping together.

"I suppose we can accommodate that." Jordie finally decides.

"Yes!" I jump up, whooping and offering a high five to Bakao, who simply stares open mouthed at me, not knowing what a high five is. So, I fist-bump him in celebration. "I promise to behave. You won't have to worry about me at all." I'm talking as I pack up the meager contents of my bag.

I'm ready in like five seconds.

"All right, settle down. Let me go take care of things first. Then we will bring you back to Jutte's house." Jordie smiles and almost pats me on the back.

I sit on the edge of my bed with my bag at my feet, as Jordie leaves the room. I turn to Bakao. "Thank you for helping me, once again. Why do you keep helping me? Don't get me wrong, I'm happy for it, just not sure why you do it."

"You are a small pet new to this planet, your owner died, and you needed help. I'm happy to do so." He nods in my direction.

I decide not to be offended by the pet remark. Whether I feel like a pet or not, they think I'm one. I wonder if dogs and cats ever realize they are pets, or do they consider themselves a member of the pack or the family? On Earth, dogs usually understand who's in charge, but I'm not so sure about cats. And what about other pets such as birds, turtles, hamsters? Does a hamster even know that there's a world outside the glass cage?

Never mind, I'm fine with him thinking of me as a pet; I know who and what I am.

I get to live in Jutte's house, back on the beach. I don't know for how long, but do any of us really know how long we have in our current situation?

We just have to make the best of right now.

CHAPTER 35

We arrive at Jutte's place, my place for now, by flying in Bakao's spaceship. Actually, they don't call them spaceships, but simply refer to them as transportation. So, we take Bakao's transportation due to the fact that while Jordie's ship's perfect for us, Bakao is too big to fit. So, by default, here we are.

It's weird coming back to the house without Jutte being here. Last time I left we went to market for a day of selling bags, and then my world turned upside down, shaken, and set down sideways.

I stop outside the door as Bakao lets us in. Jordie notices my hesitation. "It's all right to come inside," he quietly tells me. I know I can go in, I'm just not sure I want to. Is there a waiting period before you go into a dead alien's home?

Taking a deep breath, I step over the threshold.

It's quiet in here, too quiet. To make some noise, I talk and show Jordie and Bakao around. "See, here are the bags we were working on. Jutte taught me how to make these bags that we sell at the market. He sold to two shops and he even let me make the sale last time. I know the currency is *marigees* and I know the smaller bags get one marigees each and the larger bags get three marigees." I can't seem to stop babbling. "I don't make them as well as Jutte did, but I'm getting better. Look, Jutte made this one for me. See, it fits me and keeps anything I need dry."

I'm finally silent as I caress the gift Jutte made for me. It's kind of freaky to realize I'll actually be alone here.

I shake the thought off and go into my room. The bed is still made and my room is actually quite clean. It looks good. I set my bag on the table and go back to the main room. Jordie is busy on his tablet and Bakao is awkwardly standing in the middle of the room. "It's ok, please sit down." I have company and forgot my manners.

"So Jordie, do you want to show me where the food is and how to prepare it?"

"Good idea. Bakao, perhaps you can help?" Jordie puts away his tablet and Bakao seems happy to have something to do. He rummages through the shelves.

"Here it is, human food. It looks quite bland if you ask me." He peers into the bag, not realizing he's being funny.

"I know, right? But the cool thing is that I can think about what I want to eat, and it tastes exactly like that. So, the flavor is great and satisfies any craving I have. So how do we make it?" I want to climb up on something so I can look at the bag with Bakao. Not that it matters since I can't read Mari. Thankfully he can.

"It simply states to heat the food, that's it. Well, that's pretty easy." He says, looking at me.

I look back and forth between Bakao and Jordie, hoping one of them will show me how to heat the food. Do they have microwaves or something similar? Jordie stares at me, so I look at Bakao. "How do I heat it?"

It may seem simple to him, but it's a total puzzle to me. Bakao doesn't hesitate to teach me. "Here, you put some food in a container. Let's find a container..." He rummages through the shelves again. "Here we go, you put just this much in there, see?" I nod. "Then you put it in the warmer here." He opens an appliance, but the problem is that it's too tall for me to reach.

We all three look around for something for me to stand on.

Bakao spots a box-like thing and positions it under the warmer. "Can you climb this?" I easily hop up and inspect the heater... microwave... oven...

"What is this called?" I point at the appliance.

"It's called a lankaii." Bakao says

"Lankaii" I repeat after him. Got it. "Okay, so how do I heat up food?"

Bakao continues his demonstration. "You put this much in the bowl, and then open the door here. Be sure to close the door, it won't work otherwise." Looking sternly at me as he imparts this wisdom. I don't want to be a jerk and tell him how obvious that step is, so I nod.

Smugly, I look at Jordie and raise my eyebrows. See, I can play nice.

"Then you push this button here." Bakao points to the only button on the machine. Seems easy enough.

"I don't have to set a timer?" I ask.

"No, it senses when it's done." Very cool, I push the button. I'm hungry and figure since the food is out and in the bowl; eating would be good about now. I pop the container in the lankaii and push the start button. Jordie and Bakao look at me like I'm crazy.

"What? I haven't eaten for hours, I'm hungry."

With a sigh, Jordie walks away.

"Can you help me with the water?" I ask Bakao, since he is kind enough to stay with me. I point to the water on the shelf I can reach, but I remember a larger jug somewhere.

We look around and find a huge vat of water in a closet. No way will I be able to pick that up and fill my jug. I look around, trying to figure a solution. I don't want to depend on Bakao for water; what if I run out and he's not around?

"Hey Jordie?" I call, hoping he's not far. I find him in the main room on his tablet. "Hey, Jordie, when Jutte buys water, can we buy it in smaller containers? And do I buy it from you? I didn't see any at the market. And how do I buy food, is that from you too? What if I need something else, like a knife? So basically, how can I contact you when I need something?"

We have a lot more logistics to work out than I initially thought about.

Jordie sets down his tablet and hands me a device. It's smaller than a television remote and has a screen that comes about half of its surface. "I found Jutte's receiver. It's already programmed to alert me. Push this button and talk into it, tell me what you need and I will bring it personally if I'm in this galaxy."

So, this is a remote that sends my message to Jordie. Got it.

I zone out for a moment but come back and give him a slight nod, hopefully convincing him that I've been listening the entire time. "I'll bring you smaller containers of water and food so you can handle them on your own."

"Great. Well, we seem to have that all worked out." I clap my hands together and turn to get my food.

Jordie stops me. "There is one more item to discuss. You must decide how to pay for your food, water, and other items. These are not provided for free." I stop mid-stride. I never thought about Jutte having to pay for the things I asked for. Then I remember the marigees in the bag in the kitchen. I hold up a finger, telling Jordie to wait a moment.

I run into the food area, sliding to a stop in front of the closet with the bag of marigees. I snort a laugh, remembering when I thought these were bells. I grab the bag and run back to Jordie. I proudly hold up my prize. "Will this get us started?" I hand the bag to him, trying to be cool about it all.

He looks in the bag and counts the money. I count along with him; there are a total of twenty-three marigees. Whew, that's a lot of bags Jutte made to save this much. Jordie takes four and hands the bag back to me. "Yes, this will do for now."

Cool, I have food and water coming. I'm set. I grab my bowl of food and close my eyes. I think of a seafood omelet and fry jacks on the side. I take the first bite and can almost taste the saltiness of the fish; with my second bite I imagine the warm fry jacks. It's all perfect.

I can't believe I get to live here. I give a happy nod to Bakao as he watches me eat. I stop and remember my manners. "Do you want some?" I offer, holding my bowl out to him.

"Eww, no. I have no desire to eat pet food." He doesn't make a face, but his tone once again reminds me that he thinks of me as a pet. I never wanted to eat dog food, so I can't say I blame him. But still, he didn't have to be rude about it.

Whatever, I shrug and keep eating.

Oh wait; there is another thing I need. I hurriedly set down my bowl of food, change my mind, take one more bite, and then set it down again.

I try to swallow quickly and talk at the same time. "Bakao? Can you show me how to get in and out of the front door? Is there another door that I never knew of?" With this I scan the room; there's no telling what I may have missed.

"Why would a house need more than one door?" Bakao tilts his head, looking at me like I'm crazy. I'm not even going to get into the idea of several doors with him. "But yes, come and I'll show you."

Jordie and I follow him to the front (and only) door. Bakao begins his tutorial. "Here is the button to leave the house." He shows us a small button located quite high up, and beside the door. Hmm, I'm going to have to drag something tall over here. Bakao is thinking the same because he looks from the button to me and back again. "I will find something for you to stand on so you can reach." He pushes the button, the door slips open, and we all step outside. Bakao continues. "To open or close the door from here, you must push this button." Again, these buttons are placed for tall Mari people, not us short human pets. He nods, "We will find a way for you to reach here as well. It is that easy, just push the buttons."

Okay, that is easy. I can push buttons to get in and out.

I run and grab my eating bench and sit it under the button inside the door. I climb up and easily reach the button. Problem solved.

We go inside to the main room. I think of one more thing to ask of Jordie. "Hey Jordie, when you come back with food and water can you bring me flippers and a face mask? I lost mine in all the commotion."

If Jordie had emotions, it would be suspicion that crosses his face. "Why do you need those?"

"Well, if I have to buy my own food and water, I need to make and sell Jutte's waterproof bags. And before you protest, I told you that the two shops know me and have worked with me. I bet they will still buy from me." Actually, I'm not sure about the shop with the male Mari owner, he seemed to only buy from Jutte because they were friends. But I don't tell Jordie that.

He is looking at me through squinty eyes.

"I promise, I'm not going to escape. Why would I need to? I have my own place here with a business to take care of." I look at the floor with the next sentence. "Besides, I've learned how bad running away can be around here."

Jordie sighs. "Fine, since you are living here anyways, I will get you the items you need to swim. Is there anything else?"

I debate for a moment. I have a new knife, enough clothes, paper and pencil, food and water coming. "No, I think I'm all set." I say as I nod, still wondering if I need anything.

"In that case, Bakao, if you are ready, can you drop me back off at my transportation?" Jordie asks.

Bakao nods as he walks in from the kitchen. They both start towards the door with me following behind.

"Please, allow me." I properly ask as I climb on the bench near the door. I push the button and the door swings open, showing that it's still daylight outside, but then again, it's usually daylight out there.

Bakao and Jordie walk out the door and turn to me. Jordie speaks first, "Remember, if you need anything use your device for requests. I'll bring more food and water soon."

Bakao pipes up. "And I'll be by soon to check on you."

With that, they close the door, leaving me alone.

Now what do I do? It's eerily quiet. I'll have to ask Jordie for some music. I grab the remote thingy and tell it music.

Now what? I sit on the floor and contemplate how to live on my own for the first time in my life.

CHAPTER 36

Okay, I have two large bags that Jutte had already made, three small bags that still need sealing, and one small bag about half way woven. I need to tap the tree for sap to seal the bags. I'm a little nervous to go outside by myself just yet, even though I know Tratrvo isn't around to kidnap me. Instead, I bide my time taking inventory and rearranging the house so it works best for me.

I have enough food and water to last until Jordie returns; which could mean days or a weeks; maybe I need to plan on making my supplies last for several weeks, just in case.

I decide I can't keep hiding. I climb onto the bench at the front door to push the button. I'm calling it the front door. Yes, I know there's only one door, but I can't help it. I take a deep breath and push the button.

Success! I open and close the door several times. Now I need to find a crate or box to keep outside so I can close the door when I'm gone. In the hall closet I find a box. I slap it a couple of times to see if it will open – nope. Okay, whatever, it does seem about the right size. I work up a sweat dragging it outside. How can this be so heavy if it doesn't open and nothing's inside of it? After some finagling, I finally have it outside and under the button. I actually debate on going for a swim to cool off, but I think I'll wait on that.

I forgot to ask Bakao how to wash my bowl and spoon, so for today I'll use a small amount of water. Or duh, I have an entire ocean out my front door; I can wash them in the ocean and rinse with a little bit of drinking water. Yeah, that sounds better. Actually, going back inside sounds pretty good. I get my bowl and spoon while trying not to overthink it all. I gather my inner strength, straighten my back, hold up my head, stride to the front door, and walk out without peeping around me.

I am Marco. I got this.

I walk to the ocean shore and do a quick check for scary fish close by that might snap at me. After making sure that the water is clear and nothing waits to grab me, I bend down and clean my dishes. I stand up and take in my surroundings. It's a beautiful day, two suns shining, and I'm a free human, not merely a pet. If this is what it feels like to be an adult, then I'm all for it.

I calmly walk back into the house, no longer afraid, and find a new, lower shelf for my dishes. I look around to see what else to do.

My room is already clean, so I don't have to worry about that. Not that I have anyone to admit it to, but it is nice to come home to a clean house and room. I look up and give a quick nod to Jutte; *now I get what you were trying to teach me.*

I take my carvings out to the main room. They consist of a completed eagle ray and a dolphin. There is also the beginnings of an eye fish. I have some rough wood perfect for a sea dragon. Man, it still seems unreal with all that has happened. I shake away these bad thoughts.

I line up the bags on the floor with the carvings next to them. Okay, that's in order. I feel good. Organizing my things gives me a sense of purpose, something to make things better. Grandfather would be proud of me for stepping up and handling things like this. I refuse to be sent to a pound for pets (I wonder what other creatures might be there hoping some Mari person will adopt them). I will live this life on my terms; at least until Jordie decides where I must live. I wonder if I can refuse. What if a dog never wanted to go somewhere new and live with a new owner? Huh, this could be why some dogs seem mean - maybe they were just ticked off about not having a say in their situation.

I decide to work on the eye fish carving. Cross-legged, I sit on the floor and turn the wood over in my hands, getting the feel of it again, finding the fish within the wood. I can see it trying to show itself to me, trying to come out; I pick up my knife and help it make itself known.

I get lost in my work. By the time I come back to Earth (or Oonala), my butt is asleep and my legs are locked in place. I lay on my back to stretch. Trying to stand up, I roll over on my stomach and stretch more. I eventually work my way onto my feet. I'm happy with how the eye fish and sea dragon are coming along.

I walk around for a bit, kind of lost, before I realize how tired I am. So much has happened today and I'm ready for a full night's sleep. I tap my bed open and crawl into the weightlessness of it. Before I can replay the events of the day, or make plans for tomorrow, I fall asleep.

~~~

I wake up in my bed on Oonala, and all seems right in this world. Until I remember that Jutte is gone, I remember that I'm alone. Yet, I'm actually dealing with it better than I thought I would.

The house is dark, so I decide to open the door. I've never seen bugs flying around, so why not let in some fresh air? How does this species live without windows or art work? Even the walls are painted like an underwater cave. They love beauty and color, but fail to bring it into their lives. I don't get it. If I manage to stay here, I just might cut a couple of holes in the house and use them as windows.

I ponder that thought as I prepare my food. When it's done, I close my eyes and imagine a large plate of spaghetti and meatballs. Not a common dinner back home, but it sounds good right about now. I imagine the garlicky tang of the sauce when I take my first bite. It's perfect. Too bad we don't have this type of food on Earth; full of nutrients and tasting like whatever the person wants.

I finish eating and take my dishes out to the water to clean them. Juja is the dominant sun in the sky. I need to start learning to tell time. Not that it really matters, but I kind of want to know for myself.

When back inside, I stand over the bags and carvings, debating what to work on today. I decide the bags since I'll eventually need money. I find the tapper and decide to tap some trees for the sap to seal the bags. Plus, the sap will act as a sealant for my carvings; killing two birds with one stone. Look at me, acting all grown-up and stuff.

I look around as I'm walking: look there's a square tree, the suns are high; the water is beautiful... nope, I'm not watching for predators, just taking in the area. It's what I tell myself anyways. You know what, why should I pretend? I was attacked and almost killed, yeah, I'm on the lookout and not so trusting.

The heck with it all. I'm not scared, but I'm never going to be a victim again either. I do a full circle to check out the area. All is clear and quiet. I pick up the bucket and go on to tap the tree. I watched Jutte do it the one time only, and he wasn't this messy. I manage to spill quite a bit of sap. I'm not worried, it's not like I have anyone to scold me for making a mess; plus, it's outside. Does it count as a mess if it's outside? I don't think so.

I bring the sap-filled bucket to the ocean and clean off the outside of it. Suddenly I'm surrounded by small fish that are biting my feet and jumping out of the water to get more of me. What's going on?!

I scurry back onto shore, almost spilling the sap. The small fish are in a frenzy and I'm a bit freaked out. One minute the ocean is calm and the next I'm attacked by alien piranhas.

Will this planet ever stop trying to kill me?

I set the bucket down and wade into the water, but far enough away from the little killers that they completely ignore me and are still in a school of frenzy. I splash my hands around a bit, but they don't come after me. Weird, so why did they attack me twenty seconds ago but not now?

The sap.

I bet it was the sap they were after. To test my theory, I dip my finger into the bucket and flick a small amount of sap into the water.

Yep, feeding frenzy.

Okay, good to know; fish on this planet will kill for sap.

I take the sap back into the house and seal the three small bags. There, now they just have to dry and I can sell them. I need to prove that I am a responsible human and can provide for myself. I wonder how long until Jordie comes back with my mask and flippers.

It takes a while for the bags to dry completely. If I was on Earth, I would estimate two days for them to be ready. I go outside and look at the two suns, Juja and what I think is Troxi, but I'm not positive.

I kick the sand with my toes; I'm not good at simply sitting and waiting. I go inside and begin work on the next batch of bags. I need to practice weaving the palm fronds anyways.

Is this what it's like to be an adult, doing what you must to pass time? I hope there is more to adulthood than the drudgery of this.

CHAPTER 37

I don't know why I was bummed out about earlier being an adult. I mean, I'm alive and I'm free. How great is that? And, most importantly, I'm not a pet; I am a free citizen of Oonala and king of this house. I still think of it as Jutte's house, but one day it might be mine.

I'm outside cleaning up the mess I made with the sap, since you never know what other creature on this planet may kill for it, when Bakao's spaceship lands near the beach. I stomp on the area where I buried the sap and jog to the ship.

"Hello." I wave as he gets out.

"Hello, Little Human Marco." Bakao has all four arms loaded down with various items that I can't figure out.

"Here, let me help you carry something." I hold out my hands to take something from him. He bends down and hands me a bag that almost pulls me over backwards as I try to sling it over my shoulder.

"Wow, this is heavy. What do you have in here?" I try to pretend that I'm not having trouble carrying the bag, but I really just want to set it down and drag it.

Bakao chuckles and walks ahead of me into the house, leaving me to wrestle with the bag. "I brought you a few items I thought you might want." He places the bags on the floor in the main room. I can't think of what more I need, but that was nice of him to bring me stuff.

"Thank you for thinking of me." I really mean it; that was nice of him. It almost feels like Christmas as I open the bags to see what loot I just acquired. I pull out an empty container about the size of a small television. I open it up, hold it upside down, look inside. I'm trying to be polite and thankful, but I look to Bakao for answers on this one.

"Oh, that is a smaller container to put your food in, so you don't have to pour from the big container each day." He says in passing while walking through the house. "There's another for water."

"Hey, thanks!" It is hard to get a small amount of food out of that big bag. I set it aside and dig into the bag again. This time I pull out a flimsy object about the size of a pen - it bends in my hand.

Bakao comes closer. "I thought you might like that. Watch me." He says as he takes the bendy pen thing and picks up a raw piece of wood from behind my carvings. "Is this important?" he holds it up. I shake my head no. I watch in amazement as a laser beam shoots out and slices the wood. It shears through it like butter left on the table.

"Oh my God! That bendy nothing of a pen just cut that driftwood?" Bakao opens his mouth wide as he hands it back to me. "Why didn't Jutte have one of these?" I wonder out loud, but to myself.

"You assume he didn't." Bakao shrugs and picks up the bag to see what else in is there. He's totally right, I figured that if Jutte had one of these, he would have shown me. I point it at a piece of the cut wood and try it out for myself. Sure enough, zap, it easily cuts through it.

"How big of a piece of wood can this cut?" I'm thinking how much easier it will be to get pieces to carve with.

"Big." Is the only reply I get. Cool. He reaches into the bag with both small hands and uses his big hands to push the bag down around a ball. Great, he brought me a concrete ball. I smile, wishing he understood my jokes the way Arturo did. Bakao picks it up, sets it in the middle of the room, steps back all smiling and proud, and looks to me for approval. I look at him, confused.

"What is it?" I walk around the ball, waiting for it to do something. When I poke it with my finger, nothing happens. I nudge it with my foot; nothing happens. I give up and look to

Bakao who is watching me with his mouth wide open. Well, if he's is excited about it, then I'm really intrigued.

Bakao walks up to the concrete ball and taps three times on the top. A small door opens and a rectangle piece slides up. From there a small ball unfurls, casting streams of light around the entire room. I look up and around in awe, now it *really* feels like we are underwater. The light reflects waves on the wall, and even an occasional fish. Bakao lightly punches my shoulder. "So, you like?" He looks expectantly at me with his mouth open.

I nod, but let me get this straight. The small, flimsy pen can do something amazing like laser-cut wood. And this huge concrete ball is not much different from a disco ball. Am I in an opposite world?

It is interesting, so I can't take that away from Bakao. He watches for my reaction, so I give him a good one. "This is sooo cool!" I exaggerate a little. he buys it and punches me on my shoulder.

"I thought you might like it."

It is great; I'm just not sure why it has to be so heavy. Oh, I bet it would be neat to lie in my bed with this around me; like sleeping in my boat on Earth with the stars surrounding me. "Can we put it in my room?" I ask.

Bakao seems happy with the request. He slaps the side of it three times and after it all folds itself back inside, he picks it up with his large arms and carries it into my room, placing it smack dab in the center. Oh, Jutte would not like that. But hey, I'm not disrespecting Jutte at all by having it, so I'm happy.

"Thank you for all this, I mean it." I tell Bakao.

"I'm glad you like it all." He waves away my gratefulness. "But I cannot stay long. I'll be back when I can." He makes his way to the front door. "Your door is open." He tells me.

"Yeah, I like it open." I reply without really thinking about it, instead I'm gathering the food and water containers to put away.

Bakao stops mid stride and stares at me. "Why would you keep your door open?" He looks at me, truly baffled.

"I like letting in the sunlight and the fresh breeze. On Earth

I would sleep outside sometimes during the day, sometimes during the night. I like being outside. This way I bring a little bit of outside inside."

He looks at me like I've grown a second and third head. "Why would you sleep outside?"

True understanding hits me like a flash. I get it. The Mari people are comfortable under water and in caves. They are accustomed to walls and dim lighting. That's why he thinks the light he got me is so wonderful; it's as if we were in an underwater cave. How do I explain that I like the openness – it's almost has hard as explaining art.

"I like feeling the warmth of the suns, I like breathing the air around the ocean, the saltiness of it. I like the wide open outside." Yep, according to his reaction, I just grew the fourth head.

"You're a funny little human." Bakao mutters as he walks out the door.

Whatever, they're just big weird aliens. But he's still my friend, so we're okay.

I walk beside him towards his spaceship. "Thank you for the things you brought and for coming by to check on me. I'm glad we are neighbors and friends." I pause. "Hey, Bakao, one day will you help me swim to the market so I can sell some bags?"

He doesn't hesitate. "Sure, we go to market soon."

"Thank you, thank you so much." I'm already thinking of what I need to get ready.

Bakao fist-bumps me. "See you soon."

"See you soon." I step back and watch his ship rise and fly away. I'm getting used to seeing flying vehicles, but it still doesn't get old. I can't wait until I can fly one. Once I steal one, then I'll worry about where to go with it.

My life on Earth has prepared me for my life here on this empty island. I miss having other people around, but I definitely don't want the big cities and large crowds. I contemplate this as I walk back inside, leaving the door open. I actually have a pretty good life here.

After he leaves, I double check which bags are ready, and which are still in progress. I only have two large bags ready, but I don't want to wait too long and let the store owners find other people to provide bags for them. I need to let them know I'm still making them with Jutte's same quality. Grandfather has taught me to keep your buyer happy.

Since the door is still open, I grab my carving of the eye fish and bring it outside. I prop myself under a tree and begin to whittle.

I lose track of time and soon my eyes are crossing and I'm having trouble seeing. I stand up, brush myself off, and head back into the house, setting the eye fish next to the other carvings.

I figure it's dinner-time, so I prepare some porridge stuff. I pour a portion into the new container which I use to pour it into my bowl. Yep, much easier. I climb onto my bench and put the bowl in the lankaii and heat it up. I close my eyes and think of a large steak, with a lobster tail on the side, picturing the butter melting on both and I feel my mouth start to water. I dig in.

After dinner I wash the dishes in the ocean, and close the door behind me. I'm not too sure about leaving the door open while sleeping. I decide it's a lot like home: open when I'm awake and alert but closed when I'm sleeping.

I put away the dishes, stretch, and decide what the heck, I can go to sleep now and wake up whenever I want.

In my room I tap the concrete ball three times, and sure enough a small door opens and a rectangle piece comes out. The lights start swirling around my room. I really do feel like I'm underwater.

I open my bed and float in the weightlessness of it. Couple that with the lights and I'm soon sleeping like a baby.

CHAPTER 38

I wonder if I can weave a hammock with these palm fronds. I don't have rope and I don't see vines hanging from the trees, so maybe I can weave one. It would take a lot of fronds to make an entire hammock, but if I have enough time, I bet I can do it. I miss napping in my hammock. I find the perfect place with two trees spaced apart just enough for what I need. Well, it's something to think about. I hate to take away from making bags...hmmm...again, something to think about.

I split a thin blade from a frond and use it to tie my hair back into a pony tail at the base of my neck. Huh, I didn't realize my hair had grown this long. That means it's probably time for Jordie to take me back to the Orientation place and have my hair cut and teeth cleaned - or groomed as he so nicely put it.

Whatever. I check on the bags. The three small bags are still damp with sap, so I leave those to dry, and pack the two large bags into my own sack, making sure to have everything ready when Bakao arrives.

Let's see, what do I want for breakfast? Let's have a breakfast burrito just like Luna used to make. I close my eyes, but can't quite conjure it up. I try again; Okay, I got it this time, scrambled eggs, black beans, and her fresh salsa. Yes, that's exactly what I want this morning. I try not to over-think the fact that I almost forgot a staple in my life on Earth. I avoid thinking about how long it's been since I left and about how my friends and family are doing. I don't want to forget them or my life on Earth.

I eat without tasting the burrito. *Shake it off Marco, it is what it is.* Grandfather tried to teach me that it's foolish to worry about matters that we have no control over. Instead, think about what we can change, what we can make better – then it's not worry, it's taking control.

While washing my bowl and spoon, I look deep into the water and see an eye fish, and other small fish. Amazing, life will find its form on any planet.

I decide to go for a quick swim, like I used to on Earth. A swim before starting the day; and I think it's a good idea to do that each morning here. I don't plan on going far, or deep; just enough to stretch my arms and legs. To relax my mind and body and get me right for the day. I set down my bowl and wade in. The small fish scatter and regroup around me. I dive under and swim parallel along the shore, keeping an eye on where I am and where I'm going.

I'll like this better when Jordie brings me a new mask, but for now, this feels fabulous. I miss swimming for fun. Do adult Mari know how to have fun? I remember Jutte telling me about when he and Tratrvo had fun as kids, although I never saw Jutte have a hobby.

Bakao brought me the underwater disco ball, and he seems to enjoy that a lot. Maybe just being underwater is fun for them.

When I swim back, my mind is clear and I'm ready for the day. I try to shake off as much water as I can before walking to my bathroom for a towel. I bring it outside and leave it hanging on a low tree limb. There, now I'll have a towel ready for morning swims.

I check again on the small bags. They're all drying well, a little tacky to touch, but almost done. I debate on bringing them with us today to the market. No, I need to be responsible about this and make sure I present only the best to the shop keepers. I can sell only one to each, but mainly my trip will be to let them know I'm still in business.

Wait. When did I start being responsible? I'm only eleven; I shouldn't need to be all grown up. By the way, what day is today? On Earth, my birthday is on August 5th – maybe I'm twelve years old already.

Whatever, I'm still me whether I'm eleven or twelve; On

Oonala or Earth; a pet or not; I am Marco.

"I am Marco!" I shout to the universe. "That's right, hear me now! I am Marco!" No one should have any questions after that.

I bring the eye fish carving, sit near the water, and use the sand to smooth the wood. Sandpaper works better, but this will have to do for now. I'm busy sanding and rinsing when Bakao arrives. I'm glad he came early rather than me sitting around all day. I meet him at his ship.

"Hi Bakao. How are you?" I greet him as he jumps to the ground.

"Hello Little Human Marco. I'm doing well, how are you doing today? Did you use the magic ball to sleep?" He really is excited about that ball.

"I actually did, it helped me fall asleep fast." I tell him. He beams at me, mouth open and eyes dancing. He is an odd guy. Happy; but odd.

He looks at the eye fish in my hand. It's not finished, but it's a pretty good representation. I hold it up for him to see. "I'm carving an eye fish. I don't know what they're actually called, but since they have the one big eye, I just named them *eye fish*. Do you know what these are called?"

Bakao takes a step back, eyes wide and mouth closed tight. I forget pictures and statues freak him out. I bring the carving down in front of me, so it's not pushed up to him. "It's okay, it's not a real eye fish. It's just pretend. Like your light isn't really underwater, just pretend." I try explaining to him. He's not buying it. He is still looking at it like it's going to come to life and bite him. "It's an eye, if it tries to harm you, you can poke it. Get it? Poke it in the eye!"

Again, I wish Arturo were here to get my jokes. I'm laughing and poking it. I'm not looking at Bakao when I hear a great roar. I whip my head upwards to see what is causing the noise. Bakao has his mouth open wider than I've ever seen, and roars again. He pushes me so hard on the shoulder that he knocks me down. I admit it, I'm a bit afraid of him and the roaring.

Wait a minute, he's laughing! He got my joke!

I stand up now, laughing with him. I laugh until my stomach hurts and my cheeks are sore. "You are very funny Little Human Marco." Bakao wipes his mouth and I wipe my eyes. "Please, let me see?" He asks as he holds his small hand down to me.

I hand him my carving, waiting for his opinion. Any artist will tell you that it's absolutely nerve-wracking to have someone study your creation while you watch. He runs his fingers over the edges, and flips the fish a couple of times in his hands; still not saying anything. I shift from one foot to the other, "It's not done. It will be smoother when it's finished. I'm waiting for Jordie to bring sandpaper. Then I can touch it up a little more." I ramble on as he inspects it.

"This is very interesting. Do all humans make representations of things around them?" Bakao asks as he hands it back to me.

I let out my breath, relieved that he likes it. "No, not exactly like this. My grandfather taught me how to make carvings from wood." I brush my hand over it to try to smooth it out more. "I like to do this. It keeps me busy and happy." I explain.

"I see." He says, and then he pushes my shoulder. "I see!" he says louder and begins laughing and poking me again. I groan, oh, that was bad, but I can't help laughing too.

"You're a funny Mari man." I tell him between snorting laughs.

We finally calm down, and Bakao turns toward the house. "Do you still want to go to market today?" he questions while walking. He stops when he sees the door open. But to his credit, he doesn't say anything, simply shakes his head and walks in. I smile; for some reason I'm proud to be different.

"Yes, I have my bag ready, just let me get a couple things and we can go." I grab my bag and check on the two larger bags inside of it. That's it until I get more bags ready, and until Jordie brings me flippers and a mask.

I strap my bag onto the front of my body. "Okay, I'm ready. I may need some help getting down, I don't have my flippers for my feet to help me swim faster." I'm explaining this as we go outside. I climb the box and push the button to shut the door behind us.

"You shut the door." Bakao is looking at me.

"Um, yeah. I leave it open when I'm home and awake. I close it when I sleep, and I guess when I leave." Bakao mutters something under his breath and starts walking to the shore. It doesn't bother me if he doesn't understand, it's my house and it's what I like. Plus, he's not making a big deal out of it. I mean, we're friends who accept each other's oddities. I think we are friends, and I guess that's what friends do.

He stops just before entering the water. "How do you want to do this?" He's looking me up and down like he wants to pick me up and hold me under his arm like a football. No way.

"Let me try by myself first, and if I'm not moving fast enough, maybe you can grab my hand and pull me along?" I'm totally making this up as I go, I don't know how to go about this either.

"All right then, let's go." Without hesitating, he strides into the ocean. I shrug and follow. I guess we're ready them.

I wade out and swim on top of the water. I try to get closer to the underwater domes so I don't have as far to swim. I look to Bakao who is watching me. I take a deep breath and dive under. I can see shapes, but without my mask, nothing is clear. That is until Bakao swims below and in front of me, I can definitely see something that big.

Before long, I see a blurry building; I'm getting better with direction and finding where I need to swim. I follow Bakao as he swims deeper, heading for the door. He constantly checks on me, but I'm doing pretty good. He swims ahead and pushes the outer doors button. I'm just about to swim inside when Bakao grabs me by the hand and drags me the last few feet inside. He closes the outer door as I swim up, sucking in a deep breath when I break the surface.

Yeah, I'll need my mask and flippers. That was a lot harder than normal.

When the water finally reaches the ground, I sit for a couple of minutes, catching my breath. "Are you okay?" Bakao has stooped down and has his face right in mine.

I lean back and nod. "I'm okay. Just need a moment." I'm still trying to breath. Thankfully, he moves away and stands up to open the inner door.

"We need to go inside in case someone else arrives." He says as he is pointing into the market. Crap, I never thought that the door wouldn't automatically open when we are outside. If someone is inside, we would have to wait for the water to refill. Just the thought of waiting that long has me out of breath again.

I stand, remove the bag from my chest, and walk into the market. It seems long ago that I was here with Jutte, and yet it seems like just yesterday. I'm not ready for the flood of emotions that crash into me. I sit down, leaning my back against a wall. Once again, Bakao's face appears smack dab in front of mine. "You okay Little Human Marco?" His voice is quiet.

How do I explain feelings when I'm not sure what they are? My chest constricts, my throat closes completely, and my heart is pounding its way out of my chest. When I don't answer Bakao, he lightly taps me on the shoulder. "Little Human Marco?" he quietly asks.

I look up, right into his eyes. I never noticed that they're the color of the ocean: various blues and moving, like with waves or current. I look away. "I haven't been here since that day with Jutte." I croak.

I hear Bakao exhale as he stands. He reaches down and pats me on the back. "It's okay Little Human Marco, I will wait."

After some time, the rushing noise in my ears lessens, and eventually I'm able to look up and around again. Things come into focus: the shops, the Mari people walking around, the clear domed ceiling. I take a deep breath and stand up. "I'm okay now. Thanks for waiting."

Bakao simply nods and we walk towards the shops. We come to the shop that is run by the guy. He's not my favorite, but I need to let him know I'm still in business. We walk in and the owner soon appears.

"Well, look who's here, it's the human. Where is Jutte?" He's not smiling, but he doesn't seem angry either.

I stand up straight and answer before Bakao can. "Hello, I hope the water is good to you today." I start with the greeting to let him know that I noticed he neglected such niceties. That's fine, Grandfather taught me to be polite, even when others are not. "Jutte has passed away, but I wanted to let you know that I will be continuing to make both large and small bags for you. As you know, Jutte taught me how to make them waterproof and the quality will remain the same." I take one bag out and hold it out to him. I would rather sell these bags to the next store with the lady, but I need him to know that they will be as good as Jutte's bags.

The guy eyes me for several long seconds before he looks at Bakao, then at the bag I'm holding out for him to inspect. "I heard there was trouble; I didn't realize it involved Jutte." He says flatly. He takes the bag from my hands and begins to inspect it. He opens it and holds it up to the light; I'm sure looking for holes. I know he won't find any, so I stand my ground.

I get straight down to business. "I keep the quality the same as Jutte's. He taught me well and out of respect for him and myself, I keep the quality very well too." I say this with no emotion, he doesn't miss Jutte, and probably didn't want his bags here in the first place. But I need to show that I can do this, I can keep supplying him with bags. I don't want his pity; I want his respect; I can get money elsewhere.

Finally, the store owner sighs and hands the bag back to me. "No, I don't need any bags. I purchased them from Jutte out of obligation, but now that he is gone, I don't need them. They take up room that I could keep something more expensive." He gives me a bored shrug.

What a jerk.

"People need these bags and buy them; you really should keep selling them." I'm franticly trying to think of a better reason other than I need the money. He looks at me, then past me. He wants me to leave; which means I need to stay. "My bags are high quality; you know it and I know it." I'm not walking out of here without a fight.

He leans in close, "No, Jutte's bags were high quality, you're just a pet. There is no way a pet can be reliable and talented enough to do anything worthwhile. In case you forgot, you are only a human, not a Mari. Now, why don't you go do whatever humans do." With this he turns and walks away.

¡Dios Mio! did he really just say that to me? He really views me as a lowly pet, nothing special. I don't think dogs are below humans. Wait, do I? I mean, a dog could never support me, but it could live on the streets alone. I would never let a dog take care of me... huh. This completely changes how I think of the Mari. I forgot I'm a pet, or I never fully accepted it.

Bakao nudges my shoulder, so we turn and leave.

Once we are clear of that shop, I look up at Bakao. He's looking up, around, and everywhere but at me. "It's fine, I don't care what he thinks." I say with as much conviction as I can manage. I walk determinedly towards the next store. Bakao nudges me and falls in step.

Near the next shop, I stop and take a deep breath. Just because the one guy won't buy my bags doesn't mean this lady will turn me away too. I need to impress her. I take a moment to sort my thoughts before continuing on.

We enter the store and the shop lady greets me. "Marco, I hope the water is good to you today." I'm touched that she remembered my name.

"Hello, I hope the water is good to you today as well." I reply. "This is my friend Bakao." I make the introduction without mentioning Jutte's absence, I'm not sure if she knows about him or not. I kind of figured everyone would know that he was killed just out back, but maybe gossip doesn't spread as fast here as it does in Earth.

The shop lady nods to Bakao and looks back at me, her eyes filled with sadness, her mouth closed tight. Yep, she knows. I don't want to hear her pity, so I start talking. "I wanted to let you know that I will still be making the bags just like Jutte taught me.

And, I'll still be bringing them here for sale." I hand her the bag for inspection.

She is still looking at me with such hurt, but I have enough pain of my own that I don't need to take on someone else's too. I am thankful for her feelings, but I really need to move on. She stares at me a few more seconds, maybe wanting to hug me. Do the Mari people hug each other? Do they hug their pets? Jutte and I would fist-bump, and he tried to rub my hair that time in the beginning, but he never tried to hug me.

She finally sighs and looks at the bag. "Did you make this?" She asks, back to business.

"I did. I followed Jutte's exact process. I actually have two large bags." I say as I take the other bag out of mine. "I only have these two right now, but I have more in progress. I wanted to come by and let you know that I am still here and still making the bags for you to sell." Grandfather taught me to avoid ending with a question that would allow the customer to say no.

She carefully inspects both bags, holding them up to see if any light shines through. I smile as she does this, knowing the other guy did the same thing. It's hard to stay quiet - it's human nature to fill stretches of silence - but I hold my tongue, giving her time to inspect each bag.

When done, she nods and sets the bags on the counter. "If these bags are for sale, I would like to take both of these. I will need more before long."

Sweet! I didn't expect to sell both, but I'm ecstatic that she wants them. I may actually be able to support myself by selling bags. "Yes, you may take those today. And I will bring you more when they are ready. Of course, the prices are still the same, three marigees for the large bag and one marigee for the small one."

My business sense seems to please her because she smiles wide and holds a small hand up to me. "One moment, I will get you the marigees." I hop up and down a bit as she walks away, wanting to give Bakao a high five. He stands there, staring after her. Whatever, I'm happy.

I pull it together and act cool when she comes back, holding the marigees out in her small hand. "I am very glad you are safe, human, and happy to see you have continued to make and sell Jutte's bags." She does a quick pause before continuing, "Will you be all right? What will happen to you now?"

I gently remove the bell/balls from her hand and put them into my bag, taking a moment to decide how much to tell her. I might as well be honest. "Thank you. I'm really not sure what will happen now. I am trying to convince Jordie, he is the one that sold me to Jutte, I'm trying to convince him to let me live by myself in Jutte's house. Selling the bags will show him I can pay for my own food and necessities. Bakao has become a friend and checks on me daily. He made sure I got here safe today." There it is, laid out on the table for her. It's scary and exhilarating to tell the whole truth.

"Wow, I've never heard of a pet human living alone. Do you live alone where you come from?" she asks as she clasps all four hands and leans down to me.

"Back on Earth, my planet, I lived with my family, but once humans get older, it is perfectly normal for them to leave their family to live on their own. So, yeah, this isn't that different for me. Except, of course, that I'm on a whole different planet." I shrug my answer.

She laughs a nice full laugh. I hear Bakao quietly gasp. Startled, I look up to see what's wrong. He is staring at the shop lady with his mouth partially open, eyes unblinking. I look at her, and back at him, trying to figure out what's happening. The shop lady doesn't notice anything and continues to talk. "Well, if any human can make it on his own, you seem to be one that can do it."

I stand taller. "Thank you very much. I am happy that you will still be a customer and I won't let you down. On Earth, once a happy deal is made, we shake hands like this." I hold my hand for her. She holds out a smaller hand, keeping it several inches away from mine. I smile and take her hand, giving it two quick pumps and releasing it. "We call that shaking hands."

She smiles big and nods her head. "Shaking hands. I like that."

"Show her the fist-bump!" Bakao practically shouts, making me jump. He is nudging me and smiling too big. He holds his fist out to me.

What?

I'm sure I'm blushing a bit as I explain to the shop lady. "Often times, male friends will fist-bump each other in greeting and when leaving." I fist-bump Bakao to show her.

"Little Human Marco and I are friends." Bakao tells her. Strange, he's barely able to hide his excitement.

The shop lady laughs. "Maybe one day we will be friends too." She says to me, but looks at Bakao.

Things are getting weird and I'm ready to go.

"He also makes animals." Bakao babbles. I have no idea what he's talking about. I scrunch my face as I look at him. How do I make animals?

The shop lady has the same expression I do. We both look at Bakao like he's crazy. "He makes animals?" She politely asks.

"Yes, he takes wood and cuts it until it becomes an animal. About this big." He is holding his large hands about twelve inches apart.

Oh, my carvings.

I try to explain his weird ramblings to her. "On Earth, we make representations of things we see. I use wood to carve pictures of fish or animals that I remember from my planet." She is still confused, and I don't blame her a bit. "I'll bring one next time to show you what Bakao is talking about." I try to dismiss the whole subject.

She kind of nods and looks back and forth between me and Bakao. "Well, thank you very much. We will be back when more bags are ready." I say, inching my way to the door. Bakao isn't moving, so I poke his leg to get his attention.

"What? Oh, yes. We must be going, I guess." He stammers and backs away.

She laughs and gives us a small wave.

As soon as we are around the corner, I stop and glare at Bakao. "What is wrong with you?"

Unaware of my agitation, he stares back at the store. "She is beautiful." He swoons.

OMG, is he serious? He was acting so weird because he likes her? "Dude, was that your version of trying to talk to her?" I laugh because he was so not cool.

"She's beautiful." Is all he can say.

I poke him in the leg until he finally snaps out of it and looks down at me. "What?" He asks as if he just came out of a trance.

"Oh man, you got it bad." I'm laughing and start walking back to the outside door. I can't believe that he was trying to flirt with her!

"What? What do I have bad?" Bakao asks as he strides to catch up with me.

"You like her. It's fine. I've never seen a Mari man like a Mari woman. It's interesting to watch, that's all." I try not to embarrass him too much.

"But what do I have?" He persists.

"It's a saying we have on Earth. It means you like her a lot; you have it bad for her."

Bakao snorts. "That doesn't even make sense. To have something bad when it is really good. You humans are strange. No wonder you're pets."

I stop walking, glaring at him. When Bakao realizes I have stopped, he comes back to me. "What?" He asks, truly baffled.

"That was a mean comment. I'm a human. I'm not stupid and I'm not below other species. Just because we are smaller makes you think we should automatically be your pet. You have no idea what humans are like and you have no business talking about me like that." I keep talking. "How can you talk down to me after watching me strike a business deal? The Mari aren't better than humans. Different doesn't mean better." I turn and kick the wall.

Bakao rushes down to me. "Little Human Marco, I did not mean to offend you. I am sorry with my comment. You are smart and I am happy to watch you make that business deal. I am sorry

Little Human Marco. Please do not be mad at me." He pleads as he taps my shoulder.

As he was talking, I realized that on Earth, we humans think we are above all other species. We think every animal should be a pet or need us to take care of them. From saving the turtles to keeping tigers in the back yard; we think we rule the planet. I see the irony in what I'm saying, but there is no way I'm admitting that to Bakao. I know he didn't mean to offend me, and I easily accept his apology.

"It's okay." I shrug. "I apologize for being so gruff with you." Bakao smiles and holds his fist out. I bump it as he pushes the button for the door. And just like that, everything is back to good again.

Well, I now officially have a friend, and am on my way to success as a businessman. I can't wait to let Jordie know that at least one shopkeeper will continue to buy from me. I hope he hasn't found another owner for me and will let me live on my own.

Because I can so do this.

CHAPTER 39

My mission is to make bags. I mean, like the best bags the Mari people have ever seen. Bags that even Jutte would be proud of. This isn't something I can rush. Besides waiting for the sealant to dry, I still weave fairly slowly. But now I have a mission. I spent the morning weaving bags, and now I need to move around. I grab some water and sunglasses, shut the house door, and make my way to the beach. I need to clear my mind and refocus my eyes.

Does it ever rain on Oonala? Once again, the sky is clear, the air is hot, although only one sun is in the sky. Another perfect day at the beach. There aren't any shells to pick up. That's odd. So, I have two questions to ask Jordie: does it rain on Oonala and why no shells?

I think back to that first day when I ran away. I came down this same beach. I didn't know where I was going or what I would find, but I ran. How was I to know the island was a circle and I would end up back at Jutte's house? It's funny now when I look back on it. And now here I am living in this house by myself.

Careful, I tell myself, *every time I think that I'm free, something else crazy happens.*

I have an open beach in front of me and decide to run. Maybe I should start a routine of running each morning, like I did on Earth. Granted, I have nowhere to run to, but maybe I can make a lap around the island. There is something calming about finding your stride and just running. No worries right now, nothing chasing me, just stretching my legs and lungs. Then a swim afterwards, especially since there's little else on my busy schedule.

I catch a movement out of the corner of my eye, something glinting out in the water. I stop and squint, trying to figure out what could be there.

There it is again, a fish fin cutting the top of the water and going back down. I've seen many dolphins surface, but this isn't blowing air, this is just a fin breaking the water and going down. I wade in up to my hips.

The fish turns and comes towards me.

I scramble backwards to shore. Since every animal wants to kill me, I'm not taking chances.

The fin cuts the surface again, this time closer, but still too deep for me to see. My heart races with fear and excitement of the unknown. Whatever it is, it's big. So many strange fish live on this planet that it could be absolutely anything.

My body tenses and I fight an urge to move closer. Instead, I stay ankle-deep in the water, watching for it to resurface. It does, but not it's fin. The head of the sea dragon slips from the water and stops swimming. The unblinking eyes stare at me.

I freeze, stop breathing. I'm mesmerized by the sight of those historic eyes watching me. We regard each other with fascination. Well, I regard him with fascination, who knows what he is thinking. He could be analyzing me as a new species, or as food, or remembering my fight with Travtro... there's no telling.

His head is probably eight feet across, and his eyes set forward on each side, gives him full view of every creature in front and around him. His mouth stays closed, but I clearly remember the size of his teeth, I don't need to see them again.

Caught in a spell, we observe each other for seconds or minutes, time has stopped. When he blinks, I shake my head back to reality and find that I have walked forward and am waist deep in the water again. Did he call to me or do I simply want to get closer? I know I'm not a threat, but I won't move closer to him. The last thing I want to do is make him angry.

The beast snorts and calmly sinks into the water, leaving me amazed and confused. I didn't know I was interesting enough to stop and look at.

On shore, I turn back to the house; I'm ready to go home instead of loop around the island. That was crazy, and Bakao probably won't believe me when I tell him what just happened. In fact, I may just keep that tidbit of information to myself.

I need to carve this beast. I need to capture the essence of this magnificent creature.

On my way home I look for large limbs to use. I look over the square trees, wondering how far Bakao's laser works. I spot several good candidates and hurry home.

I now have two missions: make amazing bags and carve the sea dragon. That should keep me busy for a while.

At home I grab the laser cutter thingy. Trekking back out I find the limbs that seem long and thick enough to carve. I easily cut three different ones. Yep, I really like this bendy laser. I grab ends and drag two limbs back to the house and around the side. With the third one, I make a nice, neat pile safely away from the door. Bakao's feet are big and might get caught up in them. See, I'm nice and thinking of others. Plus, it would be my luck that Jordie would arrive and think I left a mess out front.

Speak of the devil. Just as I wonder what Jordie would think, he arrives. Maybe I am able to summons him. I stand back and watch his transportation land on the clearing near the beach. I'm hoping he brought me the mask, fins, and other items, but I'm terrified that he didn't. If he's empty handed, it might mean that he is taking me to a new owner.

I wait and watch. I can't look, but I can't look away either.

As he steps out of the transportation, he reaches back in and grabs a bag.

My breath whooshes out of me.

"Hello Marco. Why are you outside?" Jordie asks.

Well, that's a nice greeting. "Hey Jordie. I was gathering some large branches to carve. Am I not supposed to be outside?" I challenge him. I plan to spend a lot of my time out here.

"It's fine. Just making sure you are all right." He waves a hand dismissively at me. "How are you?" He stops when we are about to walk into the house. "Why is your door open?"

Why does that confuse everyone? "I like how it feels outside. I leave the door open so I can feel it inside too. Plus, the handle is so high up, it's easier to open and close it once a day." I bet that logic wins points with him, but who knows since he just keeps walking without saying anything.

Inside, he sets down the bag. "I brought you some things."

Score! I scoot closer. He begins pulling items out. "Here is a new mask and fins for you, I know you use them often. Also, I brought food and water. Do you have money to pay for your items?"

"Well, don't worry about pleasantries." I scoff. "I've been doing well, thank you for asking. Bakao stopped by and took me to the market." I continue without waiting for him to answer. This time it's my turn to sigh. "Yes, I have marigees for you, how much do you need?"

I think he got the point. Jordie stops what he's doing and looks at me. "You are right, my apologies. I should have spoken with you first. How are things going for you? What did you do at the market?"

Can you hold a grudge against someone just because they don't know any better? I start telling him about our time at the market. "Well, it was weird at first. That was the first time back since Jutte's fight. But once I got myself together, I went to the two shops where Jutte sold his bags. The first guy doesn't want to keep buying from me, but he was a jerk anyways. But the other lady was impressed with my bags and she wants to keep buying them. So, I'll be able to keep earning money." I stand up tall as I tell him this. What other pet of his has ever been able to earn their keep?

"Well, let me see these special bags of yours." Jordie actually smiles as he says this. Yep, I knew he was impressed.

I show him the ones that are almost ready. "These just need to finish drying. I made them tight and waterproof like Jutte taught me. I need to pull more fronds and make more."

We wander back into the kitchen area where I pick up my

mask and fins. "Thanks for these, they make it much easier to get to the market. I did it with Bakao the other day, but it was pretty hard." I'm flipping the mask over in my hands and putting it up to my face, testing out the fit. "These are good." I tell him, nodding and checking the fit of the flippers.

"I just keep buying the same ones since they seem to work." Jordie says while looking at his tablet.

So much for being sentimental.

"I plan on doing more around here. I want to build some steps for the door button so I don't have to climb on the bench. I also want to make a hammock, unless you can bring me one? I still have Jutte's money, maybe I can buy one from you? I have to make more bags and I want to finish some of my carvings." I'm telling him as I'm pointing at my things. "Oh yeah, Jordie. Does it ever rain here? I've been here a while and never seen it rain. I've been watching for some amazing storms over the water. And why haven't I found any seashells?"

Jordie stares at me for a moment. "Well, those are interesting questions. No, it never rains here, the humidity keeps it damp enough that rain is not necessary. You haven't found any seashells because the land is a volcanic sediment that comes from deep in the oceans." He answered my questions and offered no more; not that I really expected more anyway.

He looks up from his tablet. "That reminds me, I brought you some sand paper as well. I know you mentioned that would help with your carvings."

"That's great! Thanks, Jordie!" I grab the sand paper he is holding out. Man, this is going to make smoothing the wood so much easier. Food, water, swim gear, and sand paper... what more could a guy ask for?

I can survive here on my own with no problem. "So, since I've shown you that I can support myself, I guess that means I'll be your first pet to live on his own. That's gotta be something to tell people." Grandfather always told me I was independent, now I've proven it.

Jordie's head snaps up. "Why do you think you can live here

by yourself? Marco, you're a pet, that hasn't changed. I'm not sure how long you can live here, I am still working on finding another owner for you."

My mind and body freeze, then spiral.

"But I thought if I showed you that I can support myself that you would let me stay here. I have Bakao to check on me, and I'm selling bags to earn money. I can do this Jordie, I can live on my own." I know I can, now I just have to make Jordie see that. "I know it's out of your way to bring me food and water, but maybe we can do it sparingly, so you don't have to come by too often. Jordie, I want to stay here."

Jordie levels his gaze at me. "Marco, you are a pet. As a human you have been taught that you can do anything and be anything; but that's on your world. Here, you are bought and sold as needed. Don't get confused at what you are. You are to be taken in and become a pet for another Mari."

I blink rapidly. Wow, don't hold back.

"I'm sorry if this has come as a surprise to you. I didn't realize you thought otherwise. I'm not sure how long it will take me to find the right home for you. As you know, I put my customers through a rigorous interview process, so it will take some time to re-home you. But in the meantime, please continue to make bags and earn money for your food and water."

So, he's basically telling me I must earn my keep until I get resold. I would hate for him to lose money on me.

Jerk.

"You are upset. Please understand that even in your world, a pet is not allowed to live alone and earn keep as a member of the community." There are stray animals everywhere, but I guess we don't let them work and earn their independence. But still, I'm a human, not a dog or cat. I don't know what to say to him, so I fiddle with my mask.

"How long do I have here?" I quietly ask.

"It may be a while, I did not have another Mari client, so I'm looking at other planets as well to match you with the best owner possible."

"Wait! I might be sent to another planet? But I'm finally beginning to understand this planet, its language and the people! Why would you send me somewhere else?" So now not only will I have a different owner, but it might be a whole different alien species on another planet?

I sag to the floor.

"Marco." Jordie touches my shoulder until I look up at him. "You still think of yourself as a human on the planet where you believed that you are above all. Please realize that you are a pet now. Nothing more."

This sucks.

My thoughts are bouncing around against each other until one idea stands out. One light to cling to.

"So, I may be here a while and should still continue to sell my bags?" I double check with him to make sure I'm right.

"Yes, go ahead and continue your daily life." He confirms.

The idea takes hold and makes it hard for me to speak. This means I have time to change his mind. I'm Marco, and I can live on this island by myself. I can earn enough money to buy my own food and water. I can stock up so Jordie doesn't have to come here often. I can do this.

I just have to convince Jordie.

CHAPTER 40

Building steps is definitely not an easy task. For such a basic item, you'd think they would be easy to slap together. But no, this is turning out harder than I imagined. I know the flat step part of the steps is pretty easy, and having the laser that Bakao gave me makes cutting branches a cinch, but the sides give me trouble. I cut them the same size, but the edges are hard to make the same angles. These steps don't need to be perfect, just enough to hold me while I open and close the house door.

I place each of the sides on the ground again, lining them up as well as I can. I think this will work. Since I don't have hammer and nails, I use the sap to glue the steps to the side. Hopefully it will hold long enough for Bakao to offer advice. I lay down a side and glue the steps to it, placing the other side on top. I slowly move my hands away, hoping it will balance.

Steady.... Steady... okay, it stayed. I wipe the sweat from my brow and back away.

It falls apart.

Forget it. I give up. I kick the pile of fallen wood.

I thought this would be easier than climbing up and down from the bench every time I wanted to open and close the door.

I quit. I need a dip in the water to cool off. Since I wear my board shorts like regular clothing, I don't go inside to change. I like this life, having my own beach and my own house. I'm a real-life castaway, but with friends, food, and the market place. I like thinking of myself as a castaway.

Floating in the salty ocean, I contemplate my life. What would Grandfather think if he could see me on this planet? I wonder how my parents are, and who is Arturo hanging around with now. It's hard to let go of a life that you never wanted to leave.

I flip over and open my eyes under water, watching small fish dart around but, thankfully, not biting me. Finally, something that's not trying to kill me. I dive down, swim along the shore line and resurface. If I have to be on another planet, I'm thankful I'm on one with an ocean. I can't imagine living without the open water.

I swim, float, and swim until my fingers turn prune-ish. I walk out and flop down on my towel. *Yep, I could live here forever* is my last thought before drifting off to sleep.

I've fallen into an easy routine of doing what I absolutely have to, and then relaxing between these chores.

After my quick nap, I stretch and decide it's time to get back to work again. The three small bags are dry and ready for sale. I bring the basket of palm fronds outside and find my favorite shady spot and begin to make some large bags. I hear Jutte's voice guiding my fingers as they weave each line.

I've made an assembly line of sorts. I spend one day cutting enough fronds for several bags, trimming them and getting them ready. Then I'll spend the next several weeks weaving several bags. It's slow and tedious, but knowing that I'm supporting myself keeps me going.

This is where I am when Bakao's ship lands. It's the perfect time for a break anyways. "Hello Little Human Marco. It is good to see you today." He greets me.

"Hey Bakao. How are you?" He's a good friend and I'm glad he stops to check on me. I don't need it, but it's nice that he does.

He notices my attempt at building steps. "What is this?" He has pieces of wood in all four hands, flipping them over and looking at them.

I sigh. "I was trying to build some steps, but I don't know what to use to keep them together."

He looks at me blankly

"You know." I continue. "Steps. So, I can step on them and reach the door button without having to climb on things."

He still stares unknowingly at me.

"Here, let me show you." I hold my hands out for the two side planks. I hold them step width apart. "See, now those pieces that you have goes between these here." I'm motioning him. "Then I can climb them to push the button. Steps."

How can a race that believes they are superior to humans not know what steps are?

"Well," he contemplates. "I suppose that would work, but why don't you just use a galator?"

"What's a galator?" Something else cool that I don't know about?

Bakao shrugs. "It lifts you up. I didn't know you needed one."

Something that can lift me up? How can he not know how much easier life would be with a convenience like that? Does he not see how high everything is to me?

Getting information out of him is like pulling teeth. "How big is a galator? Where can I get one? How much does it cost?" I have so many questions.

He looks at me, surprised. "It is such a normal thing? Jutte may have one. Have you looked?"

Have I looked? How would I know if I found one? I close my eyes and take a deep breath before I continue. "I don't know what one looks like. Can you help me look?"

He perks up at this. "Sure! Let's go find Jutte's galator." He heads into the house, open mouthed and almost bouncing. "Your door is open." He observes.

I shake my head and follow him inside. You gotta love him.

"Most Mari keep their galators put away, but easy to reach. You never know when you might need it." He looks knowingly at me. "So, let's start with the closet."

Um, okay. He opens the door in the hallway on the way to my room. "See, it's right here!" He smiles and holds up the flat disc.

"Okay, so that's a galator, how does it work?" I'm excited now, imagining all that I can reach. Even fixing food will be much easier.

He hands me the disc; I hold it with both hands and balance it against my chest. It's the size of a shield and just as heavy. "Okay, you can set it anywhere to start." Then why did he hand it to me? Why couldn't he set it down? I trudge into the main room and set it down gently. Knowing my luck, I'll break it before I get to use it.

He uses his foot to tap the edge and lights around the disc begin to blink. I get down on my hands and knees to see what he pushed. Nothing, no button, no indention to push. "What did you do?" I ask.

"I just touch here." He did it again and the lights go out. I stand up and try to tap the same area; nothing happens.

"No, he says, you have to move your foot as you touch it." I watch again as he taps the side, but then slightly drags his toe across the edge. The lights blink on again. I try, and sure enough, the lights go out. I look up at him, smiling, and try again. Dragging my toe along the edge causes the lights to flash on once again. Okay, this is pretty cool.

"Now what?" I ask

He's looking at me like I'm clueless, and I am. How am I supposed to know what to do? He talks to me slowly, like I'm dumb or something. "You. Step. On. It." He steps on the disc. One moment of hesitation, and then bam! He's levitating.

Whoa! I fall as I jump back. He's just floating – in the air – feet down floating! Bakao floats back to the ground, steps off the disc, and looks to me. "Do you want to try?"

Heck yea; I want to try! I step onto the disc and sure enough, I feel a tingling on the bottom of my feet, and I'm pushed upwards. It's as if I'm still standing on a platform, it just happens to be rising; and rising; and rising. "How do I stop this?" I begin to panic, holding my hands above me to protect my head from crashing into the ceiling. I'm level with Bakao when he speaks.

"Lean forward a little." He quickly tells me. I lean forward and drop, hit the ground hard, and roll off the disc. It happens so fast that Bakao and I stare at each other. "You leaned too far forward." He states matter-of-factly.

I stand up, brush myself off, and step back onto the disc.

The tingling starts and I levitate. I barely lean forward and the upward motion slows. Pretty soon I'm hovering eye to eye with Bakao. He smiles and fist-bumps me. "Now lean forward more to go down." He tells me.

I know better this time, and shift my weight... ever so slightly. Sure enough, I float down. I stand up straight, then lean forward; floating up and down until I get the hang of it.

"This is so cool! How come you never told me about this?" I ask, floating up and down.

"You never asked."

He's right, I didn't.

"Is there more than one, or do I just move this where I need it?" I imagine it gets heavy hauling around. "And does it run on batteries?"

I step off the disc and inspect it more. I'm looking for a battery door, or some sort of power source. Bakao watches me. "We have to look around to see if Jutte has more. Mari don't need it very often. But what are batteries?" He moves his face next to mine, inspecting the bottom of the disc with me.

"Batteries, the power source. How does it run and what happens if it runs out?"

"Runs out of what?" I really need to be more specific.

"What if it stops working?"

"Why would it stop working?" He is clearly confused about why I don't understand something so simple. I guess if it stops working, I'll just ask him then.

"Nothing. Never mind. This is so great. Let's go look for another one." I could use like five of these. One inside the front door, one outside, one by the food, and who knows where else I can use the others.

We search the house, but don't find more galators. That's fine, at least I have this one; and much to everyone's dismay, I often leave the front door open. Now I can easily close it when I need to.

"Wow, I'm sure glad you stopped by today." I tell him as we sit in the main room. For some reason, he prefers to hang out inside rather than outside. Probably the whole underwater thing.

"I actually came for a reason." He tells me. I'm surprised, then feel bad that I haven't asked him why he's here and if he needs something. I just assumed he was here to check on me.

"Okay, did you need something from me?" Because again, it's all about me.

"Well, not really, but a little." He stammers. Oh crud, what doesn't he want to tell me? Before I can worry too much, he blurts out, "I want to see the shop lady again. Do you have more bags for her?"

I stare blankly at him, then quickly recover, "Sure, I have a couple small bags ready. I was going to wait to bring her more, but we can go sooner if you like."

He breaks into a wide grin. "All right! Let's go then." He pushes me on the shoulder and heads for the door.

"Wait, you mean now? Um, okay, hold on a moment. I'm not ready." I'm not prepared for this. I quickly gather my things. I roll the three bags and work them into my carry bag. Bakao spots me grabbing my mask and flippers.

"Was Jordie here? I didn't see him. Did he say anything about your new home?"

Even Bakao doubts that I can manage here by myself. I'll show him and Jordie and everyone else. "Yeah, he was here." I mumble, unwilling to rehash it all. "He is still looking for a suitable owner for me. For now, I stay here." I leave out the part that I have no intention of going anywhere else. "But he did bring me some items, like a new mask and fins. He also brought me sandpaper to make my carvings smooth." I say this fast to keep him from mentioning more about my leaving.

"We need to bring a carving. Remember, I told her I would show her. That means I must do so. Remember?" Bakao is admiring and touching my carvings. I protectively grab the dolphin away from him.

"Be careful, they can break." I gently set it back down. He fails to notice and picks up both the eye fish and the spotted eagle ray.

"Maybe we should bring her something she recognizes," he

says more to himself than to me. He sets down the eagle ray and keeps ahold of the eye fish, making his final decision. "We can bring this one." He states, as if it's his choice.

I get nervous showing people my art. I don't do it for their approval, so I really don't care; but it still makes me uncomfortable. "Are you sure she wants to see it? I mean, it's just an eye fish." I try to reach up to take it from his hand.

He pulls it out of my reach. "Yes, Little Human Marco. We must take it to her as I told her I would." He looks at me like he can't believe I would let him go against his word. The bro code exists even on Oonala, so I can't let him fall short of his promise to a girl.

I sigh. "Okay, if you think that one is good enough, we can bring that." He nods and hands it to me. I pack it carefully, making sure it won't break.

I haul the galator to the button spot just outside the door. Bakao watches me, smiling and happy. Once outside, I levitate and press the button to close the door. When I'm back on the ground, I nod to Bakao. He pushes my shoulder "See, much easier. Maybe now you will keep the door closed." I give up trying to explain that I like the door open.

We set off; me to prove my independence to Bakao and Jordie, and Bakao to lose his independence to a woman.

CHAPTER 41

"Hello human, I hope the water is good to you today." The shopkeeper smiles as Bakao and I enter her store.

"And to you as well." I say "I'm sorry, I never asked your name."

She reaches down to give me a fist-bump like Bakao showed her. "I am Mar'keeria." I suppose it was about time to learn her name, seeing as how we will be working together. Bakao nudges me so hard that I almost fall over.

I step back and hold my arm out to Bakao. "And this is Bakao; Bakao, this is Mar'keeria." I make the formal introductions, being a good wingman to my friend.

Bakao steps forward, shuffles, looks down, and then back up at her. "Hello Mar'keeria." Even I can see the hearts in his eyes from way down here.

Mar'keeria blushes a little, "Hello Bakao, it is nice to see you again." Wait, is she shy too? This will either be a disaster or turn out great.

They stand there, wordlessly gawking at each other. I interrupt before it gets awkward. "I brought three small bags to sell." I glance over at the wall to assess how many she currently has on hand. I count three already there, but three more won't hurt.

She regains her composure and looks at me. "Wonderful, I will put them with the rest. One moment and I'll bring you the marigees." She turns to leave, giving one more look at Bakao before she walks away.

I nudge his leg. "Look at you, she likes you." I'm smiling so big I feel like my mouth is wide open. Bakao straightens himself up, and stands tall.

I reach into my bag and remove the three bags for sale. I barely catch the eye fish as it falls out of its wrapping. Oh, that was close; another reason why I don't like taking my carvings anywhere. Bakao grabs the figure from my hands and holds it poised, watching the direction from which Mar'keeria should be returning.

Before she can hand me my money, Bakao thrusts the eye fish towards her. "See this is how Little Human Marco makes animals. See, it's a fish."

Whether she jumps back from Bakao's almost yelling at her or at the surprise of seeing a replica of a fish may never be known, but she almost loses her balance. Bakao catches her, carefully standing her upright.

"Weird, isn't it." He clearly assumes her shock is due to never seeing art before. He knows the confusion it causes. "Look, he carved a piece of a tree to make it look like a fish. Isn't it interesting what humans do?"

I want to explain that many humans make different art, but I keep my mouth closed and let these two have their moment.

"What does it do?" she asks, still afraid to touch it.

Bakao shrugs. "I don't know, what does it do Little Human Marco?"

They both look expectantly at me. "It doesn't actually do anything. It's made for people to look at, and enjoy." Explaining art is difficult.

"It doesn't swim? But you said it was a fish" She works up the nerve to tentatively touch the carving.

"No, it doesn't swim. You set it on your shelf, or desk, or wherever you want. Then when you look at it, it makes you happy." Even to me that sounds silly.

"You can have this." Bakao offers, holding it out to her.

Wait, what?

"Here take it, then when you look at it you will remember me and Little Human Marco." He holds it closer to her. "And me." He adds again.

Well crud, he just gave away one of my carvings.

Mar'keeria gently takes it from Bakao. "Thank you. I will set it over here, I guess." She turns and places it on the table behind her.

Now how am I going to get that back. And she could thank me instead of Bakao; I'm the one who made it.

"Would you like to swim together one day?" Bakao blurts out.

Mar'keeria blinks several times before giving him a small smile. "Yes, I would like to swim with you."

I don't know if 'to swim' means to actually swim or more, and I really don't want to know. I leave the store and let the two of them work out the details.

Outside the store, I keep my back to the wall and watch Mari walk by. Some see me and point and smile, others are in too much of a hurry to notice me. The children always spot me and want to come running over. Thankfully, their parents stop them. I wonder if they are warning them not to touch me, I might bite. One younger kid walks by and I smile and chomp my teeth together, just to mess with her.

A couple of minutes pass before Bakao comes looking for me. "Little Human Marco, where did you go? I was afraid you were lost." I know he means taken, but I'm glad he didn't say it.

"I'm sorry, I didn't mean to frighten you. I was giving you alone time with Mar'keeria."

"Why do you think we need alone time?" He cocks his head, looking at me like I'm crazy.

"Well." I begin. "You don't need me in the way when you're setting a time to go swimming with her."

Again, he is baffled. "You are not my pet, but you are only a human, a pet. I'm not afraid to say anything in front of you."

I instantly bristle at the 'only' part of that sentence. But I stop before saying anything hurtful. He's right. I wouldn't have censored my conversation with anyone in front of a dog or cat; so why should he feel like he needs privacy around me. I'm only a pet to them.

I hate being reminded about that.

"I felt like hanging out here. You ready?" I change the subject.

We're walking towards the exit when I hear a collective gasp and see Mari people looking up and pointing. I try moving to an open spot where I can see around people, but it isn't necessary. The sea dragon glides overhead, looking down at us.

It spots me and I swear it looks me right in the eye.

Others must think so too, because they all take a collective away from me and Bakao. I can't look away, wondering if the beast remembers trying to kill me - or maybe it saved me... who knows? But does it recognize me? Bakao must think so because I hear him whisper, "It's looking right at you Little Human Marco."

So, I'm not imagining it.

The dragon stares at me a moment longer, and then glides away into the blue ocean. Bakao's eyes are huge as he looks at me. He nudges me and smiles, "That was cool. Maybe it's never seen a human before"

He's always good at lightening the mood.

"Whatever." I smile and lightly punch his leg, letting the freakiness of the moment leave with the dragon. "So," I broach the subject. "Did you ask the shopkeeper on a date? To spend time with you?"

Bakao stands up straighter. "Yes, I did. We are going to meet with each other in a half rotation." He stops and looks at me. "I might not be able to visit you then." He worriedly adds.

"That's okay. You go have fun. I'll be fine on my own for a short time." If I plan to live alone, one day will hardly kill me. I can handle the lack of supervision. In fact, I like the idea of having an entire day to myself, with no surprise visits to the market.

We laugh and chat as we get ready to leave. Bakao gives me extra time to put on my mask and flippers. Happy to have these again, I give him a nod when I'm ready, and he opens the outer door, allowing the water to fill the room. When the door is fully open, we swim out and head for home.

Without warning, my neck tingles and I get the creepy feeling of being watched. I catch a movement out of the corner of my eye, spin to my right, and see the sea dragon swimming straight at me.

I can't scream or even inhale since I'm underwater; instead, I try to move out of its way. Bakao sees the creature coming at me and rushes to my side, grabbing my arm and pulling me out of the way. But the sea dragon, undeterred, turns and beelines for me.

And then it stops.

Smack dab in front of me, it stops and studies me. I look into its eyes, feeling a connection with this animal. It could have eaten me, but instead it stares at me.

I reach out and tentatively touch its snout, and it allows me to do so.

Bakao must not feel the connection, because he grabs my arm and yanks me away and towards the surface. I gasp as soon as we get to the top, immediately take a deep breath, and put my head underwater to look down. I want to see it again; I want to see if it's still there and waiting for me, but it's gone.

I search in all directions, hoping to catch sight of the sea dragon. I want to dive down, but Bakao has a hold of me. "Little Human Marco! You were almost killed again!" Gasping, he holds my arm so tight I'm sure I'll have a bruise to show for it.

"I'm okay." I reassure him. "Did you see that? It looked me right in the eyes and let me touch it. Did you see that? Has it done that before?" I can't keep up with all the thoughts banging around in my head.

"Hurry, let's get you home. That monster was following you." He drags me toward shore. His pulling causes me to get dunked and pulled sideways.

I shake him loose. "I can swim. Besides, it won't hurt me. Didn't you see? It had the chance and it just studied me."

"Says the human before he is eaten," mumbles Bakao.

Regardless of what he thinks, I'm sure the sea dragon won't hurt me. I swim towards shore with my face in the water, hoping to catch a glimpse of it.

On the beach, with one look back, I walk away from the

water.

Once in the house, Bakao paces back and forth. He's wringing all four hands and talking to himself. "I cannot leave you; the beast is after you. Should I stay here or take you to my house?"

"Bakao! Bakao!" I have to say his name twice to get his attention. "Really, I'm fine. You don't need to stay or take me to your house. If it will make you feel better, I'll stay out of the water when you're not here. But I really don't think the dragon will hurt me. It had the perfect chance to eat me, and it didn't. I'm fine." I wave my hands in front of me, hoping to calm him down.

He stops pacing and leans down into my face. "You promise you will stay away from the water?" Crud, why do I have to promise? I actually have every intention of looking for the creature again.

I cross my fingers behind my back. "I promise."

He lets out his breath. "Okay, then you will be safe. This is why you need an owner - to protect you."

Well, this really upsets me. I can take care of myself. I'll prove to him and to Jordie that I can live on my own, earn a living, and make friends with a dragon.

Bakao eventually calms down and I walk him to his ship, reassuring him the entire way. It's nice to have someone worry about me, but it's also a pain when I don't need their worry.

Once he's gone, the quietness hits me, and the adrenaline has definitely worn off, leaving me exhausted. I open my bed, slap the disco ball that Bakao gave me, and slip into a weightless slumber.

Everything on this planet has tried to kill me except the huge monster that terrifies everyone else. Instead, it seems to like me.

Go figure.

CHAPTER 42

I'm actually awake when it's night here. Since there are three suns, darkness happens so rarely. But I love it. It's like a warm summer's night, and so many stars out. Of course, all the constellations are different, and there isn't a moon, but it's still beautiful.

I make up my own constellations, like finding pictures in clouds. I see a tree shape, and there are five stars in a straight line – I decide it's Neptune's trident. If I had a hammock, I could start sleeping out here. I am a bit tired, so I lay back on my towel and look at the stars until I fall asleep.

I have no idea if it's morning or how long the night even lasts, but I feel refreshed and walk down to the water.

I would never admit it, but I watch for the dragon every time I'm near the water. It saw me on the shore once, so maybe it will remember and come back. In the mornings I wade out and splash around, maybe I'll get its attention. If anyone sees me, they'll think I make a mess while cleaning my food bowl, but secretly I'm on the lookout for the creature.

I think of it less as a beast now, and more as a creature that lives in the sea - a huge creature that could eat me, but hardly scary.

I mean, I'm not obsessed with it, just on the watch for it. Maybe it feels the same as I do. That we are both alone and stuck on this planet.

I'm into my own routine of sleeping when I'm tired, eating when I'm hungry, and carrying water with me at all times. I keep the house picked up, dishes clean, and even make the bed. Jutte would be proud of me for how well I'm keeping his house. Plus,

I like it clean. The door is open when I'm awake so the fresh air adds to the good, clean feeling of the house.

Bakao visits fairly often. Since I can't tell time, I never know when he'll be here; yet it's not like I have anywhere to go. It's been fairly recent since our last visit to the market, so I have no need to go again just yet. Plus, I'm not quite ready to go by myself. I suppose I will have to do so sooner or later. If I'm going to be independent, I have to learn to independently go to market.

I pick up the large cut branch and turn it over in my hands, noticing the shape of a sea dragon starting to show itself to me. This wood doesn't have any bark, so that saves me an entire step. I start by cutting away the extra branches and wood, allowing the shape to begin to form.

Back on Earth I would use a marker to draw on the wood as a guide for carving. But this time the shape is so prominent that I can skip that step too. Plus, I don't have a marker.

I hear Bakao's ship arrive, but I'm at an important part of my carving that I don't want to stop. I wait a bit and call out to him, telling him I'm on the side of the house. He comes around and finds me busily carving.

"Hello Little Human Marco. What are you doing? And why are you outside? Your door is open." He squats down and is still tall above me.

"Hey there. I'm working on my next carving." I decide to leave the door issue alone. Instead, I shave a little more of the wood. "Oh wait, I almost forgot to ask. Did you go swimming with the store lady?" I nearly drop my wood and knife, embarrassed that I almost forgot about his date.

Bakao fully sits down. "Yes. Ma'keeria and I went swimming. I really like her." He begins to confide in me. His feelings, his ideas. I try to pay attention and listen, but I can't help thinking that this is what a dog must feel when humans tell them their hopes, dreams, and problems. It feels nice to have someone speak so openly to me. On Earth, we tell our pets everything, knowing they won't use it against us. Maybe Bakao feels the same about me: he trusts me. We figure our pets can't understand us, but I understand Bakao and he still shares with me.

I patiently listen until he's done. "I'm happy for you. I hope you two do really well. Do the Mari people get married?"

Bakao cocks his head sideways and scrunches his eyes. "You have words I don't understand. What is married?"

I hope I'm not being too forward. I may be a pet, but I think of us as friends. "It's when you decide to live together and not go swimming with anyone else. You still have friends, but are committed to each other." I fumble through, hoping he gets the point I'm trying to make.

"We have something similar to that as well. I didn't know humans made commitments to each other. I guess I never thought about it. You mean you choose to be with another human, like for life?"

Oh boy, how do I say yes, but then talk of divorce? I figure I'll just keep it simple. "Yep, for life. Sometimes we find each other when we are young, sometimes when we are older. But if we're lucky, we find that one special person. Like you found Ma'keeria." There, I'll be the ambassador of the good side of humans. And it makes me a bit lonely. I'll have to live out my life without the companionship of friends. But I doubt another human will simply swim up to this beach one day and say hello.

I decide to change the subject before I feel too sorry for myself. "I'm carving the sea dragon." I hold up my stick to show him.

He gasps. "Why? Why would you make something so scary?"

I bring the stick back to my lap to avoid frightening him more and shrug. "It's not scary to me. I actually think it's one of the coolest animals I've seen." I decide that if he can confide in me, I can trust him too.

Bakao shakes his head and stands up. "I like you, but I don't understand you." He tells me. I look up and smile. I like his honesty.

"Thanks, let's go inside." I set down the stick and brush the sand off my clothes. Lacking a broom, I try to keep as much sand outside as I can. "Did you come for a visit, or did you need something?" I try to ask now instead of just assuming he came only to check on me.

"I came to check on you, but also to see when you need to go to market again. How long until you have bags ready?" He asks as we go inside. Thankfully he doesn't comment on my open door, but he does glance at the galator outside, where I keep it as well as a bench for when I need them.

I show him the beginnings of the bags. "I collected more fronds, and started weaving one. But it will be a while before they are ready to sell." I would like to give him a time reference, like two weeks, but I haven't figured out Mari time yet. "Why?" Does he need one? Did Ma'keeria ask for more bags?

"Just checking on you. I don't need anything from the market; Just some idea of when we should go again. I think it's best to wait a while and let the sea dragon leave. It seems to come after you."

Ah, he's afraid for me to go to market. I get it now.

I want to argue that the creature doesn't 'come after' me, but rather seems to check me out. But that's a conversation I choose to avoid. I haven't told him about seeing the dragon from the beach before we went to market last time. He would probably lock me in the house.

I change the subject. "Jordie told me that he is looking for a new owner for me, but I want to stay here. I think I'm doing fine right here." I could use someone on my side. Maybe I can get Bakao to talk to Jordie on my behalf.

"I understand." He nods. "I hate to see you go."

What? That's it?

"But I've shown that I can live here alone. Don't you think I should be able to stay?" He's my friend, he's supposed to have my back.

He looks at me with his head tilted, "Do you not understand that you are a pet? Have you forgotten?" He pats my shoulder. "You are the first human pet I have ever met, and I agree you have surprised me many times. But Marco, you are still a pet; you are not a Mari."

"I know I'm not a Mari. On Earth, humans are the top of all animals. We keep other species as pets. I'm used to being able to live the life I choose and take care of myself; and I think I could do that here. I have a place to live and can sell bags to pay for my food. I don't really need to go anywhere now, but maybe you and Jordie can fly me wherever I might need to go." I take a breath. "I want to stay right here, in this house, and live on this planet on my own. I don't want to have another species decide my fate." I need his help. "Can you talk with Jordie and tell him that you agree that I should live here?"

"But Little Human Marco, you *are* a pet, whether you want to be or not. It is not your decision. It's just what is."

I throw down the bag I was holding. "Fine. Don't talk to Jordie. I thought you were my friend, but obviously I had it wrong all along. We aren't friends; I'm only a pet. I'm just a life form below you without thoughts or feelings. Fine. I don't care and I don't need you." I yell at him. I storm out of the house, wishing I could slam the door.

Forget him, I don't need him. Jordie is the one I need to convince. I don't need Bakao's help for anything anymore. I can swim to the market place on my own and sell the bags on my own.

By this time, I'm stomping along the beach.

Oh, he better not tell Ma'keeria not to buy my bags. I don't think he would do it out of spite; but then again, I thought he was my friend. I guess I was wrong.

I grab some pieces of wood and start throwing them into the water.

I don't need him. I don't need anyone. I took care of Grandfather, not the other way around. I can take care of myself.

Bakao is coming down the beach. I turn my back to him.

"I'm sorry. I did not mean to upset you."

I ignore him.

"Please, do not be mad. I do think of us as friends, as much as a Mari and human can be friends. I have learned a lot about

humans and realize you are more than I would have thought."
He touches my shoulder. "Please come back to Jutte's house. We
can talk and even leave the door open if you like."

I snatch my shoulder away from him. Did he really just say
we are friends as much as a Mari and human can be? That proves
that he really does think of me being below him. How can you be
friends with someone who believes they're better, smarter, and
more advanced than you? Friendships are supposed to be equal.

I turn away and walk further down the beach. I need to be
alone.

Bakao doesn't come after me. After some time, I hear his
ship leave. This whole time, being captured and being a pet has
sucked, but I've never felt more alone than I do right now.

I catch a movement in the water and turn to figure out what
it is. The sea dragon's head gently breaks the surface and looks
right at me. It's cool that he knows where I am, but it's also
freaky, like he's tracking me.

Maybe he gets me. I wonder if he is the last sea dragon
existing alone. What if he swims around all day without other
dragon to be with? Is he the last of his kind? *I feel ya man,* I think
as I give him an up-nod. I mean, maybe I'm not the only human
on this entire planet, but it sure feels like it.

I thought I had a friend in Bakao and I might have become
friends with Ma'keeria, and who knows who else. But not
anymore – I'm a pet, not a friend.

You know what? Forget this. I won't feel sorry for myself. I'm
better than this. I can make bags and sustain myself. The Mari
simply don't know any better. I'll show them that I can be a part
of society.

With that, I wave to The Old One and stomp back to the
house.

CHAPTER 43

I can't sleep. My bed has the perfect buoyancy that I should just drift off, but no such luck. The fact that it's hard to toss and turn in this bed makes me mad. I roll over and almost suffocate. Everything makes me mad right now. I hate that I had a fight with Bakao. I wish I could apologize to him. I feel helpless having to wait here for him, or Jordie, or anyone else.

Do aliens have phones, or some other call system? I know Jordie gave me this thing when I need to reach him, but I'd like to know if there's a way to call Bakao. I'll ask Jordie next time he comes.

I give up and pace the house, I actually clean a bit, at least pick up. Wow, I must really be out of whack if I'm willing to clean without a reason. I check on my bags and put them in order of doneness. I straighten my bowl and spoon (that was quick), then I climb up to open the door. I always feel better outside.

I grab the laser cutter and find more good branches, even ones that don't have the potential to be something. I cut thick branches, thin branches, long ones, and short ones. I'm a one-man cutting machine. then start to remove the small pieces from each branch, making them easier to work with. It's hard work dragging some of these huge branches to the side of the house. I stack those first and go back for the small branches, dropping them by the armload on top of the pile.

I've worked up a good sweat and am in a better mood. Grandfather always told me that manual labor is a good way to work off stress. I guess he was right.

The water looks too inviting to resist. I grab my mask and fins and swim out before I can overthink what I'm doing. I swim out, and then start down. This will be my first trip to the market on my own.

I ignore that worried little voice in my head that tells me to turn back.

I make it to the outer door in record time. No problem. I push the button, swim inside and push the other button to close the doors. I swim up as the water drains out. I could have held my breath longer, but I'm always happy when I can breathe again.

Once all the water is gone, I jump and slap the next button for the market doors to open. Peeking through the doors, I'm unsure what to do now. I don't need to buy anything and I don't have bags to sell.

Standing tall, I stride into the mall. Looking busy and important worked for me before, so I try it again. I walk out with my head high, mask and flippers under my arm.

Yep, everyone is staring at me. They point while talking to each other. I catch bits and pieces of what they say. They're pointing at me wondering where my owner is.

Nope, no owner here. Get used to it, because this is how it's going to be. I'll be walking through the mall alone to sell my bags. I want to smile and wave, but I decide to look professional and give them all a polite nod instead.

The newness wears off and I find myself looking around again. Shoot, I forgot to bring any marigees. I could have bought some fun stuff, like that eye mask that moves. Oh well, I can window-shop today.

I pass by shops that I'm familiar with, staying on the path I know. I'm a bit worried that I'll get lost and forget my way back to the right door. What if I swim out the wrong door and swim to some other land? Before I get myself worked up, I figure if I get lost, I'll just walk until I find my way back. At worst, I can ask other shop owners if they know Ma'keeria. See, no problem.

I walk past the store where I sell to the guy shopkeeper. I don't bother to go in since I don't have bags to sell. I don't like him anyway. I watch a couple of Mari kids goofing around in another store. I wonder if that's a toy store, or if they are just having fun while their parents shop. I step out of people traffic and watch them. You can learn a lot by watching kids. They are grabbing merchandise off the shelf and throwing it back and forth, while running around the shelves. One kid snaps another with something that looks like a towel, but it floats to the new kid, and suddenly wraps itself around him, trapping him in place. The others laugh and push him down. The towel releases him and they all run to the back of the store.

I don't know what that towel thing is, but I want one!

Now that I'm here I'm ready go home, so I head for my door. What if Jordie stops by and I'm not there. He'll think I ran away again. Then my argument about living on my own will be completely shot down.

I feel proud of myself for coming on my own. I've just proved that I can do it, even if I can't tell anyone.

I find the correct door without a problem. I put on my mask, jump up to hit the button, and put on my flippers while the room fills with water.

With a final breath, I open the outer door. I calmly swim out instead of straight up. I know my way and have no reason to panic. I swim through the water, watching for fish or other Mari. A school of small blue and yellow fish passes by me. See, I got this.

I break the surface and see that I'm easily within range of Jutte's house - my house. I flip onto my back and leisurely make my way back. The suns feel good and I think I could actually sleep now.

I grab my towel from the branch and go inside. Before I get to my room, I hear a ship landing. Whoa, that was close.

Outside, I see Bakao's ship. "Hello Little Human Marco." He half-waves as he is climbing out.

He's being tentative, but I'm not; I rush to him. "Bakao! I'm so glad you're here!" I'd hug him if he weren't so tall.

He opens his mouth wide and meets me at the bottom of the steps. "I'm glad I'm here too." He pushes my shoulder. "You are not mad at me anymore?" I don't blame him; I was pretty harsh.

"No, I'm not mad. I'm sorry, it's still hard for me. I want to stay here in Jutte's house with you and live my life. If I can't be on Earth I want to be right here and not in some stranger's house. I want to have some say in what I do." I usually don't talk about my feelings. On Earth I never had to; Grandfather automatically knew what I was thinking.

Bakao kind of freezes. What? What did I say? Did I say something bad? He blinks a couple of times, then opens his mouth wide. "It's okay Little Human Marco. I'm sorry too that I said things that made you mad." He holds out his fist for me to bump. See, we're still friends.

I decide to wait before I tell him about my trip to the market. It might freak him out and we just got over our fight.

"Did you come here for a reason or just to visit?" I ask him. I still have to work on the whole manners thing, but I think I'm getting better.

"No reason, just to check on you. Do you need food or water? Do you need anything?" He walks into the food area, picking up the water jug to see how much is left.

"I'm doing okay, Jordie will probably bring some next time he is here. I gave him some marigees." It's odd to have Bakao waltz in picking things up, but I let it go. Maybe that's what friends do. I felt comfortable walking around Arturo's room, moving his belongings around.

"Well then!" He says a little too loud. "If you're doing okay than I'm going to go'"

Already? "Um, okay. I'll walk you out."

And just like that Bakao climbs into his transportation and leaves.

Was that weird or was that normal for Mari? I shrug and go back inside. Yawning, I climb back in bed. This time I'm asleep before I can review my day at the market.

CHAPTER 44

I stand at the edge of the water, debating my choices. Mask and flippers in hand and bag strapped to my chest, I remember marigees and wrap them in palm fronds so they won't make noise.

I should go. I've been there once already. I should go. But what if Jordie catches me? What if a fish eats me? I should stay.

I decide to go.

I dive down and swim towards the market. About half way there I see movement out of the corner of my eye. I turn to see The Old One coming towards me. When something surprises me, I instinctively breathe in or let out a scream when something scares me. Thankfully I don't do either. I can't imagine he wants to eat me, but how can I be sure? In two swishes of his tail, he is almost on top of me. I kick out of his way while putting out my hands to push away from him.

By freaky chance, I manage to grab one of the pointy scales on his back. I hold on.

OMG! I'm swimming with a sea dragon!

He swims towards the market area. We have already passed my door, but we're approaching another. And I'm almost out of breath. I let go and swim to the door, hitting the button. Once inside, I look back and watch him swim away. See, he wasn't trying to kill me.

After the water drains away, I sit for a moment to gather my thoughts. What just happened? Did I really just hitch a ride on a sea dragon? And he let me? I wonder if any Maris saw us.

When I open the door, every Mari person in the market is staring at me. Crud, they saw. Of course they saw, all they had to do was look though the clear dome.

No one moves, not me and not them. It's a staring standoff.

I want to turn around and leave, but I'm too far from home to swim it on my own. Instead, I stand up tall and walk into the market. The Mari step aside to let me pass.

I stop in the center of a circle of the Mari. We are all silent.

I smile and let out a whoop. "Yeah! Did you see that? That was so cool!" I do a little dance and try to high-five a couple of them; they simply stare at me. "Woah, that was awesome!" I keep dancing and finally a couple of them open their mouth in a smile. The rest walk away.

Oh yeah, that was amazing. I walk through the market, a huge smile stuck on my face. I want to talk about it, to tell everyone what it was like. I want to relive it again. I realize that I'm near Ma'Keeria's shop when she rushes to me. "Little Human Marco! She kneels down, her small hands grabbing me. "Are you all right? I heard The Old One attacked you!" She twists and turns me all around, lifting my arms, inspecting me. Wow, word travels fast.

It takes a couple of tries, but I finally push away. "I'm perfectly fine, thank you for checking," I say, straightening my clothes. "I wasn't attacked. The dragon swam by and I happened to grab hold of him. It was actually pretty cool." I like talking about it.

She's not as excited as I am. "Little Human Marco, you must be careful. Where is Bakao?" She looks around. "Wait. Are you here by yourself? Does Bakao know you are here?" She grabs me by the shoulders. Uh oh, I'm about to be in trouble. I mean, maybe I am, but I'm still too pumped to care.

"I'm here by myself. I need to show Jordie that I can swim here alone and sell my bags. I want to show Jordie that I can be independent enough to do this. I got here just fine and wasn't attacked. It's all okay." I reassure her, hoping she will calm down. She finally releases me and stands up, scrutinizing me.

Finally, she sighs. "Thank goodness you're not hurt. So, what happened?"

Following her into the store, I start from the beginning, "I decided to come to the market today, I brought marigees in case I want to buy something. I was almost here when Shamo Loonolo came at me. At first, I was afraid he would eat me, so I moved out of his way. But then I grabbed onto one of his spikes and he kept swimming, and I kept holding on. He swam down towards the market and I let go when I saw the door. He didn't turn around and come after me, he just kept going. If he wanted to eat me, he would have turned around. Instead, he brought me straight to the market door." I want her to understand that I never was in danger.

I'm having trouble convincing her. I suppose she's heard all her life that he is a monster and it must be hard to think otherwise. He looked scary to me the first time I saw him, but I never thought of him as a monster.

"Bakao is on his way here to get you." She says, snapping me back to reality.

"Why? I can get home by myself." I tell her, but she isn't buying it.

"And have you attacked again? No. Bakao will be here soon. You can wait over there" She points to the wall.

Crud, now I'm in trouble. That sure killed my good mood. I bet she would get along well with Jordie.

You know what? No! That was cool, no matter what they say, I'm staying excited about this. The heck with them all. I wish Arturo was here, he would have grabbed hold right along with me. He would think it was great. I'm nodding and smiling as Bakao walks into the store. Ma'keeria points him my way.

Bakao rushes over and starts twisting and turning me like Ma'keeria did. "Are you hurt? What happened? Why did Shamo Loonolo attack you? Why were you in the water alone?" Questions pour out of him so fast that I barely understand it all.

"I'm okay. Really, I am. Bakao, it was so cool. I rode the sea dragon. Well, not really *rode* him as much as I just held on and he brought me here." I tell him the story. "He didn't want to hurt me. Shamo Loonolo is not the mean monster that everyone thinks he is." I want him to see the sea dragon like I do, as a cool creature and not a monster.

It might take a while for him to believe me.

He stands up tall and assesses me. I hold still and show him that I'm perfectly fine. "Little Human Marco, you must be careful. Please. This is important, you are important. I do not want to see you hurt again."

I get it. I scared them, but it really is not a bad thing. "I promise, I am fine and wasn't in danger. I didn't mean for this all to happen. He was there and I grabbed on, that's all. I promise I'll always be careful."

Bakao sighs and squats down in front of me. "Okay then, let's get you back home."

I hope he can start to believe and trust me. I try to avoid dangerous situations, but that was some freaky cool accident that I'm really glad happened.

CHAPTER 45

I'm taking a break on the beach when Bakao's spaceship arrives. I jog to the craft and wait for him to emerge. "Bakao! How are you?" I'm truly happy to see him, and want to show him that I'm still fine and haven't gone anywhere. "What brings you..." I stop talking when Jordie follows Bakao out of the ship.

Oh no, this can't be good. I bet Bakao told him I was attacked by the dragon.

"Hello, Jordie." Maybe if I'm polite he won't be mad at me. "I see you're both here. Come in, I was just walking the beach." See, not running away, not being attacked, just walking.

"Hello Little Human Marco, I brought Jordie so we can all visit." Bakao pushes my shoulder as he passes by me. "Your door is open again."

Yep, our normal greeting. I can't hide my smile, Bakao is great.

Maybe Jordie came because he brought me something, I try to remember what I asked for. I'm pretty set on food and water, sand paper, and I'm still okay on clothes. Crud, I can't remember asking for anything.

Jordie talks as soon as we are all in the house. "Marco, Bakao and I would like to speak with you."

When I was in trouble with Grandfather, he always began a talk this same way...*we need to talk*...this must be how all bad conversations start. I take a deep breath and sit down. I'll face this head on, take my punishment for going to market on my own, but I need to explain that I wasn't attacked. I let Jordie talk first – I never confess until I know for sure what I'm in trouble for. I learned that early on.

"Bakao told me that you were on your way to the market by yourself and had an encounter with the creature they call Shamo Loonolo."

"But he's not a creature!" I jump up. Yeah, I can't sit still. "He didn't attack me, really! I was on my way to the market and he happened to swim by, I tried to move out of the way but ended up holding on to him. He didn't turn to bite me or shake me off. He swam down near the market and I let go at the door. He was actually bringing me to the market. Really. You guys have to believe me." I plead with both of them.

Jordie holds up his hand to stop my talking. "I'm very glad you are not hurt, but there are a couple of issues I have with your story. Why were you going to market by yourself?"

Hands behind my back, tapping my finger and thumb together, I look down as I answer, "I wanted to show you that I could sell bags and be independent. I thought if I could show you that I can provide for myself that you would let me live here in Jutte's house."

Jordie sighs. "Marco, you cannot live here by yourself. We have discussed this. It is dangerous for a pet to be alone. Your swimming to the marketplace on your own is not good, Marco. You are not allowed to do that again."

Allowed? Did he just say I'm not allowed?

Before I can protest, he continues talking. "Since we cannot let you be alone, we must find you a new home quickly."

Yeah, this is going about as well as I expected.

"But," he continues. "Bakao and I have been talking. Bakao wants to adopt you. What do you think about living with him?"

What? I snap my head up so hard I almost fall over backwards. Me live with Bakao?

That would be...AWESOME!

"Really? You want me to live with you?" I want to make sure this is his idea and not Jordie pushing me on him.

"Yes, Little Human Marco, I would really like for you to come live with me and Ma'keeria."

"You're living with Ma'keeria? When did that happen? Isn't it a little soon?" This surprising news totally distracts me. "Why didn't you tell me? Way to go man!" I fist-bump Bakao. We're both smiling like it's Christmas morning.

"Why do you think it's too soon? We like each other so we now live together." I guess the Mari move fast in their relationships. More power to them.

But back to me.

"So, you really want me to live with you? And it's okay with Ma'keeria?" This is so much better than living with strangers. Even better than living alone. "Wait, can I still make and sell my bags? I still want to carve wood, will I have my own room, will you put me on a schedule or can I eat when I want?" The questions come out of my mouth as fast as they pass through my brain.

"Marco." Jordie taps me on the shoulder. "Calm down. We will go over the plans with you. So, can I assume that you would be happy to live with Bakao?" I enthusiastically nod my head, offering another fist-bump to Bakao. "All right then, this is unusual for an owner and pet to know each other, but then Marco, you are pretty unusual as well." Jordie actually smiles when he says that.

I've won him over.

I swam with a dragon and I now get to live with Bakao. This is a totally awesome week!

CHAPTER 46

"Okay, so, when do I move in with Bakao? I can be ready in a couple of days. I have to pack my bags, my clothes, my whittling knives and wood. I have wood stacked along the side of the house; can I bring that? Oh, and there's that really big disco ball the Bakao gave me. What about a bed? Will I bring this bed or does Bakao have one? Will I have my own room or will he have to get one ready? I know you said it takes new owners a while to get everything ready. So, I can stay here for a while longer while Bakao gets everything ready, I'm okay with that." Bakao is outside getting something out of his spaceship so it's just Jordie and me talking.

"Bakao is getting his ship ready for your belongings. We will leave now." Jordie drops this bomb on me while busy on his tablet.

"Now? As in today, now? Like, right now, now? But I'm not packed."

"Then you better get started."

That's it? That's all he has to say? I slack-jaw stare at him. When he doesn't look up from his tablet, I realize he's serious. I better pack. I turn and run into my room. I gotta pack!

I throw clothes into my bag...but wait, they can't leave without me. I snort laugh at me rushing around like a crazy person. I take a deep breath, empty the contents of the bag on the floor, and start again. I neatly fold my clothes then collect my bathroom supplies. With those done I carefully stow my carvings among my clothes so they don't break. I add my knife, the laser Bakao gave me, my notebook and pens, and realize that's about all that can fit in my bag.

I look around and realize my only other things are my bed and disco ball. I wonder if we should bring those or if Bakao will buy new ones. Will they make me buy them? Oh, my water bags!

I grab my bag of belongings and stop. This is all I have. I'm a little sad at owning so little, but then again, it's freeing to be able to pick up and leave so quickly. Living on an island taught me that I really don't need a lot of superficial things to be happy.

Back in the living area, Jordie taps on his tablet. "What about my bed and other large items?" I ask him.

Jordie sets his table down and answers me. "Bakao already has a bed for you and it's similar to the one you have here. What other large items do you have?"

"Well, Bakao gave me this disco ball thing that looks like I'm underwater. Never mind, I'll ask him to bring it for me. It's really heavy. How are we going to carry my food and water? Do you have a box or something?" In the food area, I discreetly grab the bag of marigees and slip them into my bag. This is my money and I'm bringing it with me. I heft the water container onto the floor and reach for the food. Finally, I set my bowl, spoon, and cup on top of the pile. I assume Bakao has a lankaii I can cook it in. I set my carry bag of belongings near the water and gather the finished bags and the ones in progress. Once I have it all in a pile, I step back and assess it all.

Bakao sees me. "Okay, Little Human Marco, are you almost ready?" "The transportation is ready for you. What should I carry?" At least he's being productive, unlike Jordie.

I point to the pile in the center of the room. "Most of my things are there. Can you carry the disco ball? And, what about the galator, do you have one or should we bring this one? And what about the lankaii to heat my food, do you have one of those?" Bakao nods his head and smiles. I'm sure he's impressed with how organized I am.

"We have a galator and lankaii, so no need to worry about those. I'll go get the 'disco ball' as you funny call it." With that he pushes my shoulder and leaves me to my pile of belongings. I gather my waterproof bags, follow Bakao through the door, and climb inside his spaceship. He stores my belongings in an area I didn't notice before. But then again, I never did have time to fully explore his ship. I was too busy trying to escape.

I run back into the house for my food and water and rush it to Bakao to store away. I make one last trip to get my clothes and personal items. Once I hand that off to Bakao, I walk back into the house – for the last time. The house looks clean. I wouldn't want Jutte disappointed at how I left his place. I check my room and the kitchen area again, making sure I got everything. Then I go into Jutte's room to say a final goodbye. But here is what I have come to realize: those who go before us are always in our hearts; so, I guess I'm saying goodbye to the house rather than Jutte. He will always be a part of me, and that makes me feel safe.

But I do want to see the dragon one last time. Would it be my last time? Where does Bakao live? Is it near the market? It must be if Ma'keeria still works at her store. Good, I want to continue swimming to the market to sell my bags.

Before they can stop me, I run to the beach, hoping to catch a glimpse of the sea dragon. I wish I could tell him where I'm going, but I don't know where Bakao lives, or how to talk to the sea dragon. I scan the flat surface of the water, looking for him to raise his head. I know that's his way to say hi to me. I know he doesn't want to harm me; he could have done that several times by now. *Come on Old One, where are you?*

I wade into the water, splashing around a bit. Maybe he doesn't know I'm here. I splash, look over my shoulder to make sure Jordie isn't coming to say it's time to go, and splash more. Come on, come on, come say bye. With a sigh, I give up.

I guess I never learned how to summon a dragon.

I go back into the house, pretending I'm coming back for any last belongings. I look around but find nothing left. Bakao and I had loaded it all in about three trips. It's easy when Bakao has four arms, and that I had so little to begin with. "All right Jordie, I guess I'm ready." He sets down his tablet and looks around.

Bakao comes from the back room, "I think we have everything, Little Human Marco, unless you forgot something?"

He scans the main room and eating area.

I do a final check, "I think that's it. If I do forget something, can we come back?" How do I know what I forgot until I realize it? I throw a worried glance at Jordie.

"No, we cannot come back; the new family will be moving in soon. But if you need anything Bakao can get it for you. He understands that is part of the responsibility of having you."

Well, that makes me feel like a burden. "Bakao, are you sure you're okay with me moving in with you?" Does he really want me or just felt bad for me? I tap my thumb and finger together.

"Of course, I want you with me! Ma'keeria and I both do! I know that you can't buy everything yourself, so I'll help. I'm very happy that you are moving in with us." The words sound right, and when I look up, I see his mouth open wide; like, really wide open.

Okay, I'm good again. I shouldn't let Jordie worry me like that. I know Bakao and I are friends. I smile and fist-bump him to seal the deal.

When the three of us walk out the door, we close it this time. No more leaving the front door open. Maybe I can get Bakao and Ma'keeria to start leaving their door open. I wonder what their house looks like, maybe their front door is completely different than this one. I could sit here guessing all day what it could be like, or just wait a couple of minutes and see for myself.

Excitement bubbles inside of me. Something new again; good change is happening.

Bakao climbs into the driver's seat. "Shotgun!" I instinctively yell. They both stop and stare at me. "On Earth, when someone yells "shotgun" it means they get to sit in the front seat." I don't apologize. "Can I sit in the front seat so I can see where we go? I rarely ride in a spaceship. I mean, I would have when Jutte had brought me back to the orientation place, but really, I've only been in one a couple of times." I count on my fingers. "When Jutte was hurt, when you brought me back here, and of course, when you first brought me here...I think that's about it. Please can I ride up front" Yep, total excitement happening here.

I bet if Jordie knew how to roll his eyes, he totally would. But he doesn't even sigh this time. "Sure, you can sit up front."

Score!

The seat holds me in, just like Jordie's did on my first ride here. I wiggle around, get comfortable, and plaster my hands and face against the window as the ship floats straight up. I hope this part never gets old. I look down on Jutte's house for the last time. I remember seeing it the first time and thinking it looked like an ant hill. I peer down at the water, hoping to see The Old One again. I wish I could ask Jordie and Bakao about him, but just keep quiet. No worries, I'll find him again.

I am Marco, after all.

CHAPTER 47

The world of Oonala floats below me. We pass mass amounts of water and fragments of land. I don't see the large city where I was held after Travtro died, but then again, how would I know which direction that is? Before I can relax and get used to the ride, we begin to descend. Under the ship I and spot buildings, each has its own land and trees. It looks like a neighborhood of about ten houses lined up along the beach. All right, I'm still on a beach.

I'll have neighbors? I had gotten used to it being just me. Well, Jutte and me, then just me. Time to live in a community again. I like that thought. I miss my village on Earth, so maybe a community is exactly what I need. I blow my breath on the window and draw a smiley face in it.

We land next to one of the houses without stirring up sand. That makes it convenient to park right next to the house. So, like people park cars in the driveway, aliens park spaceships in the yard. Cool. A quick count tells me we are the third house from the end. Got it. Some Mari lady might freak out if I walked into the wrong house. I do a snort laugh, and cover it with a cough. It's easier than explaining what's so funny.

"Here we are. This is your new home." Bakao is one to state the obvious. I smile, unsure what to say. Jordie gets out first. I grab my personal bag and follow him. I'm so going to totally like it here! The beach is right out the front door (I wonder if these houses have a back door.) The trees are further away than at Jutte's house, but that's okay, it should give me more time outside.

I must look lost as I turn in a circle because Bakao taps my shoulder. "This way Little Human Marco. We live right here." Um, yeah, I kinda figured that out already since we parked close to this house.

I grin at him. "This looks great. There's the beach, trees, and other Mari. Do you know all the other aliens that live close by?"

"Sure, we all know each other." Bakao says. He carries my disco ball inside.

Maybe they think of me as the alien. I turn to Jordie because I know he gets offended when I call him an alien. It's fun to egg Jordie on, but I don't want to offend Bakao on my first day here. "So, what do I call them? I can't say other people, or aliens. What do they call themselves? I never needed to know since I only lived with Jutte." I'm surprised this never came up before. I'm still learning new things about this planet.

"You can just call them Mari. You can ask Bakao to introduce you to the Mari that live close by." He tells me this without a bit of bristle. Good, I want to start out right.

We follow Bakao into his house. Surprisingly, he has left the door open, but I bet he'll close it behind us. I walk in and look around. So, this is my new place; I like it. It's laid similarly to Jutte's with a main room. I turn and look for an eating area. Maybe Bakao will make one for me. I can picture a kitchen layout in my head that has food, water, cups, and a lanakii all within my short reach. That way I won't have to depend on help to set a feeding schedule. I'll wait to make recommendations until after Jordie leaves.

Bakao disappears down a hallway, so I walk that way. I pass the first doorway and keep walking. "Here is your room."

Holy Neptune! I practically jump out of my skin as Bakao taps me on the back. I actually do jump, and Bakao laughs. "Sorry, I didn't mean to frighten you. But that was funny. I didn't know I could scare a human." He pushes my shoulder and keeps laughing.

I have to admit, it is kind of funny. I laugh with him and backtrack into my room. I like it. It has the same style bed as my other one. I slap it on top and sure enough, it opens up. I close it and walk to the other side of the room. It's a large open area with round a piece of furniture off to the side. I push it and it sinks in like the bed. I sit down and it comfortably envelopes me. It's a chair just like the bed!

"I thought you could work on your bags here." Bakao tells me. "I know you need a large area to lay them out to dry. And you can sit here when you carve too." Wow, that's nice of him to design this for me. "Of course, you can do all that in the main room too, but I thought you might want some area to yourself as well."

So, I get to keep making and selling my bags. Score!

"Thank you, I like this area a lot." I look around some more and find my own bathroom. Wow, Jordie and Bakao must have discussed this for a while. I don't normally get emotional, but I now realize this wasn't a quick decision. I stay quiet for a moment and take two deep breaths before I walk back into my room. "This is great, I really think I'll be happy here." I hold up my hand for a high-five. He opens his mouth wide and slaps my hand a bit too hard. Of course he does. It makes me like him even more.

"There is one more thing to show you, Little Human Marco!" Bakao booms at me. He must really be excited to be yelling. We go outside and to the trees.

Am I imagining this? Is this a mirage? Is that a hammock?

"You got me a hammock? How did you know?" I beam up at Bakao.

"I asked Jordie what gift I can get you. He said you mentioned this so you can be outside. Do you like it?" Bakao looks expectantly at me.

"I love it! Thanks!" I climb in and show him how I can sleep in the hammock.

We make our way inside and find Jordie still in the main room. He is actually smiling. It's weird to see him like this and I take a step back. "What do you think?" He asks me.

"I think it's perfect. Thank you." I tell him, and I mean it. It would have sucked to have to go live with another stranger.

"The rules are the same. I understand that you have a more

casual relationship with Bakao, but that does not mean you can be rude to him. He is still your owner. Be polite, do as he says, and no running away." Once again, Jordie can suck the fun out of any situation. I hate to admit it, but he is right. I'm a guest in this house, and until I'm completely a part of this family, I should be (as Grandfather would tell me) a good guest. I nod at Jordie and he continues. "Are you okay if I leave now?"

"I think so, thank you. I feel comfortable here. I've seen a ton of Mari by now and I know Bakao, so it's not all new to me this time." I actually appreciate the effort Jordie went through to let me live with Bakao. "Thank you." I look him in the eyes.

His expression softens. "I'm glad we found this home. I'm glad you are happy. My main goal for humans and owners is for them to be happy together." He gives my hand a final pump and turns to Bakao. "Thank you for letting me leave my transportation here. I will go now."

Bakao, smiling, walks out the door with Jordie. They're probably finalizing paperwork that goes with me. When Bakao comes back, he finds me in the eating area. "Are you hungry? I didn't know it was your time to eat."

"No, I'm not hungry, thanks. I was looking around and thinking how we can arrange this area so you don't have to worry about me so much. Like, if we put a shelf here for the food and my bowl and cup." I point to a corner. "Maybe we can put the water here where I can reach it easily. And maybe –"

Bakao cuts me off. "No worries, we will figure it all out." Do you want to go for a swim?"

"I always want to go for a swim!" I yell, running to my room to grab my mask and fins. I run back out still talking. "Are we close to the market? Are we going to say hi to Ma'keeria?"

He laughs and opens the door for us, and closes it behind us. Do Mari people steal from one another like humans? Does he lock the door? Whatever, let's go swimming.

At the beach, Bakao points to his right. "The market is that way. It's the same market, but we enter through a different door. Are you okay to swim that far?" Well, I was okay, but now I'm wondering how far it is.

I remember Grandfather telling me to show no fear. "Sure, I'm okay, but watch out for me in case it's further than I'm used to. Can we swim on the surface for a little way before we go down?"

"Sure, I'll show you the way. It's easy." And with that we wade into the warm water and paddle to our right. Bakao looks at me; I nod and take a deep breath. We are almost on top of the market as we swim down together, easily getting to the door before I run out of breath. When the water is drained from the room, and we walk into the market, I know right away where we are. We're actually close to the other door. Why did we fly so far if we ended up so close? I don't get it, but I'm not going to worry about it.

I smile up at Bakao, he smiles down at me. This is going to work out great.

CHAPTER 48

This is nice, sitting here in the main room with Bakao. I'm busy carving and have almost finished the sea dragon. I run my hand over its body to feel its smoothness. Finding a rough patch, I use the sand paper a bit more. I think about the eye fish that Bakao gave Ma'Keeria, and wonder what I can see and carve here on Oonala. The Mari don't seem to need statues since they don't have pictures either. I'll try a bowl next. You can always use a bowl to put anything in. I'm still not positive what Bakao is doing, or what he does for a living.

"Hey Bakao." I interrupt the quietness. "What do you do for work? I know Jutte made bags and Ma'Keeria works at the store, but what do you do?" He doesn't leave for a regular 9 to 5 job.

"I'm a scientist. I study distant galaxies. We know much more than humans do, but there is still much more out there. I study what distant planets and stars and determine their composition make up." He tells me as he sets down his tablet.

I stand there with my mouth hanging open, blinking at him. Whoa, so this big, goofy guy is actually a genius. That is so cool!

Well, that's settled. Maybe when I grow up and I explore the distant galaxies with him. But back to today's issues. I change the subject.

"Now that we've been to the market three times, I think I'm ready to go by myself? I have bags to sell and Ma'keeria mentioned the other day that she needs more. I promise to be careful."

I try to act cool and keep him from seeing that I'm scared he'll say no, but I have the bags packed in case he says yes. He squats to my level and studies me. "Are you sure you will be okay? I don't want you getting lost or hurt. I worry." He pokes my chest.

"I understand. You don't need to worry. What if I see Ma'keeria right away so she knows I'm safe, then she can tell you?" I figure checking in is a good idea if it makes him feel better. And I do have bags ready to sell.

"So, you'll go to Ma'keeria's store and right back here?"

"Well, I was hoping to look around and maybe find another store where I can sell my bags. I'll cut you in on half of my earnings."

Bakao laughs, "You don't have to give me your money, we have enough. Okay, you can go, but only because I must stay here today. But be careful, and go straight to Ma'keeria's shop. Then tell her when you're leaving so I can watch for you."

I know he still believes the dragon will eat me, but we haven't seen him since I moved here. Plus, I never worry about that creature anyways. "I promise!" I bounce on the balls of my feet. I'm actually going to swim alone to the market and sell my bags. I still have my independence. See, I'm not some ordinary pet! I run and grab my mask, fins, and water bag.

Bakao laughs at me, or with me. Whatever, either way is fine by me. "All right, you be careful and sell your bags. Don't be gone long." With that he gets up and opens the door. We don't have the galator set up yet to let me out.

I race to the water's edge and turn to wave one more time. I dive down right away. I'm so excited that I'm sure I'll swim fast enough. Just as I dive down, I see him...the sea dragon. I'm so surprised that I almost gasp. I stop and watch as he approaches. He found me!

Closer, he gracefully turns just a little and glides next to me. I know this routine and grab on. It's just like the last time. He swims down and slips along the bottom. I give him a hard tap as I let go near the door. He has brought me right to the door! I wait before I go in, and he turns to give me a look before he swims away.

I am now officially friends with a dragon!

I am here much faster than normal, so it's easy to hold my

breath while the water drains from the holding room. I take off my mask and fins and do a victory dance and wait to open the inner door to the market.

In the market, I look around to see... every single Mari in the place standing around staring at me. Yep, they do that again. They step back as I step forward. I try to act cool. "Yes, Shamo Loonolo gave me a ride here. He's not a monster you know, he's my friend." Then I get a crazy thought. "In fact, on Earth it's normal for humans to ride on dragons. We do it all the time." I say with a shrug. I can't help laughing as I hear a collective intake of breath. I wish Arturo was here to witness this. I want to high five everyone, instead I walk through the path they clear for me, and stroll to Ma'keeria's shop.

This is my life now. I'm on the planet of Oonala. Technically, I'm a pet, but with much more independence than any pet I've ever known. I live with friends, make and sell my bags, spend my evenings carving like Grandfather taught me, and now I'm friends with a sea dragon.

Yeah, I got this. I am Marco.

ACKNOWLEDGEMENT

There are so many people I want to thank for helping me publish this first book.

I owe much to my husband, who fed my dreams of becoming an author and helped make it happen.

I send huge hugs to my parents and sisters for encouraging and believing in me.

Thank you to my friends for not only being supportive but putting up with me constantly (and I mean constantly) talking about my books.

To Lala: I still smile at the shenanigans of our youth. Thank you for loving Jordie before he ever made it to the pages.

I'm eternally grateful to my writer's group for listening to my wild ideas and then making them better. I learned so much from DJ Mays when she insisted on being my alpha reader and offered tremendous insights - and I'm humbly impressed by Dawn Radford and her ninja-like editing skills.

Thanks to my beta readers: Andrea, Ivy, Avery, Auntie M, who all took the time to read through the rough drafts.

And thank you to you, the reader, for choosing this book. I hope you enjoyed it.

ABOUT THE AUTHOR

Tiffany Jo Howell

Since her early days, Tiffany Jo Howell has been telling stories of helping her friends get in trouble and instigating mischief. Maybe she never grew up because children still gravitate to her wherever she goes. Perhaps this is why writing in an easy voice for the younger ones comes naturally to her.

Tiffany originally hails from Minnesota but now lives with her husband and most perfect cat, Sweet Pea, along Florida's Gulf Coast. One of her favorite writing spots is at the local sports bar with music playing and sweet tea flowing.

Made in the USA
Columbia, SC
30 June 2022